# Rope Break

Sam Deland Crime Novel Book Two

Mike Fuller

Published by Rogue Phoenix Press




ISBN: 978-1-62420-199-8

**Credits**

Cover Artist: Designs by Ms G
Editor: Kitty Carlisle

Printed in the United States of America

# Dedication

To Maureen, my Child Bride.

## Chapter One

Any moment now, coming in from the right on an angle, the sound of wings dragging on the ground grew a little clearer and louder. Still no movement in that direction, but he was there; they knew it. Sam willed his eyes to move ever so slowly in that direction and then let his head swivel a bit to center up his vision on the hemlock cluster at the edge of the field. He emptied his hands of the slate and striker and kept them still. To his left he could hear the rustle of his partner's clothing and knew Ken was rising up for a sight picture.

"Putt, putt," almost a whisper, Sam used the mouth call to bring the gobbler out to them.

"Gobble, gobble, gobble!" the roar of the close-in bird startled Sam and he jumped just a bit.

The small trees and low bushes were just sprouting a tad of green and the air was still cold and crisp this first week of May. At this altitude, the morning chill wouldn't leave the woods until later on. Even with the now rising bright spring sun, Sam had to control his breathing to keep the steam of his breath from giving away their position. Just past the evergreens the first bit of blue head peeked around and was followed by the black and brown feathers of the tom. His tail was fanned wide and he scraped his down turned wings in the leaves and grass, stirring them with hollow scratching noises. The gobbler stepped deliberately out in to the meadow, tilting his head side to side, seeking the location of the hen that had been calling him to her for the last forty minutes. His cautious approach had been slow and the wait required all the patience these two humans could muster. Two more steps and the sun broke through a space in his spread tail and glistened off his back.

Click clack. The bird startled at the sound and looked right at Sam.

Click clack, click clack, click clack. With that series of sounds, the gobbler exploded into movement, noise and feathers launching the fat bird into the air and away from the threat. Click clack, click clack, click clack, click clack. Grass and dirt flew up into the air to mark the spot of the shot.

"Absolutely beautiful!" Ken shouted and stumbled to his feet from the tree trunk where he had been sitting just in front and to the left of Sam. Ken reached over and gave his father a slap on the shoulder. He pulled down his camouflaged face mask and grinned a big toothy smile. "Gonna be great pictures. The sunbeam came right through his tail in that little space. Wow!"

"So what's the verdict?" Sam nodded at the camera Ken was holding in his gloved hands. "The extra noise of the SLR worth it?"

"Oh yeah," Ken said, turning the Nikon digital over in his hand. "No question. I never could have gotten the shots of his scramble without it. I'm going to have to get used to all the manual features. I did him on auto. Felt more comfortable with that."

Sam got up and stretched. He put the slate call in his pocket and pulled out a plastic bottle for a long swig of sport drink. They had been sitting still, trying to coax the turkey up out of the little valley, and Sam was cramped from the cold air.

"Here, finish this off." Sam handed the bottle to his eighteen year old and only son. Sam looked out over the field at the beautiful sight of the valley. Woodlots of gray, brown and black spattered with light green sprouts, scattered evergreens and plowed fields spread out in a panorama showing that spring was beginning to take a hold on the middle part of Penn's Woods.

"You ready to buy me breakfast, Dad?" Ken asked. "This is going to be the day. I can see the start of a few cloud streets already." He pointed out to the southeast, and Sam could feel the breeze come into his back from the opposite direction. "Might be the only meal I get until tonight at the Airport Diner."

"Let's go then, genius." Sam gathered up his seat cushion from the ground and untied the blaze orange streamer from the tree trunk above his head. Ken slipped his new Nikon camera inside of his camo jacket and together they started back through the woods to the logging trail that brought them up the mountain from the parking area at the edge of Black Moshannon State Forest.

Sam followed behind Ken and watched him glide through the woods. Sam knew that if he stopped for just a minute, he would lose sight of Ken and his son made so little noise that even hearing him in the leaves and underbrush would be impossible. They picked their way down and crossed several small streams bringing the spring waters down from the tops of the hills toward Bald Eagle Creek. In twenty minutes they hit the dirt jeep trail and made their way out to where Sam's Pathfinder was parked.

"Thanks again for the camera, Dad. It's a great graduation present. I won't get to use it a lot this summer, but by Christmas things will loosen up a bit and I can get some winter mountain shots," Ken said as they crossed the small field to the edge of the parking area. Ken was reporting for his plebe year at the Air Force Academy in Colorado this summer and knew that new cadets didn't get any free time for photography. "I'll try it out on the palm trees and saltwater birds when I get down to Sarasota. Grace is going to take us out on her sailboat to shoot the shoreline lights over the water."

"What time does her flight get in on Tuesday?" Sam asked.

"It's in the afternoon. I have the numbers written down at home," Ken replied. "Eileen's okay with Grace staying with her?"

"Oh, she can't wait to see her. Eileen has a million questions for Grace. Our ears will be burning all during graduation week," Sam laughed. Ken's long distance romance with flight attendant, Grace Echaverria, was about to be tested with their first face to face meeting since New Year's. The black haired twenty two year old beauty was finally getting a break in her schedule and was flying into Philadelphia to attend Ken's graduation at Varnum Military Academy out on the Main Line on Wednesday. Sam arranged for her to stay with Sam's most recent lady friend, Eileen Matthews. The men had plenty of room at their house, but Sam thought it was a better idea to keep some distance, especially at night, between the youngsters.

The meeting last fall of these two had sprouted a telephone and online courtship that somehow lasted over the long winter. This, in spite of their age difference, her new job and his final semester of preparation to go to Colorado Springs. The couple managed a brief visit in Miami over the New Year's holiday and since had planned her visit to Pennsylvania and Ken's trip back with her to meet Grace's mom in Sarasota for a few days before Grace had to go back to work at the airline. Grace was still a rookie and didn't get much say about her own schedule. A few of her fellow stews swapped days and flights to give her the several days off she needed to string together so she could be with Ken.

At the sound of an approaching vehicle, both Sam and Ken looked up and saw a black pick-up truck come around the curve and skid into the parking lot stopping next to Sam's burgundy Pathfinder.

"Heck of a hurry," Sam muttered.

They took the last few yards up the bank, and as they stepped into the lot, a small, fair haired man wearing a denim jacket over a flannel shirt and jeans jumped out of the black pick-up and walked quickly over to them.

"Game commission. Hold it right there," the man ordered. Both Sam and Ken stopped, looked at each other and then back to the other man. "Doin' a little Sunday huntin' are ya'? Let me see your licenses right now." He held out his hand, waiting for them to comply.

Sam smiled and shook his head. "Who put you up to this? Did Jack Conner set this up; very funny." Their host for the weekend was old, but he was notorious for pulling a leg here and there. "Old Jack thinks he's real funny."

"I said the licenses," the man pulled his hand back and slid his jacket aside to show Sam and Ken the .357 Smith and Wesson revolver he had in a holster on his right side.

Sam said, "Whoa, friend. You need to show me some ID. No need for any guns here," Sam held his hands up to show he was unarmed. Ken stood beside his dad and tried to figure if this guy was for real or not.

The man went into his jacket pocket and came out with a black leather case which he opened and showed Sam a badge and identity card that said he was a Deputy Wildlife Conservation Officer. Sam recognized the credentials as genuine.

"Deputy...Souder," Sam said, picking up the name from the ID card. Sam and Ken stood stunned for a moment then first Sam then Ken complied and got out their hunting licenses. Ken kept his eyes on the bulge at the deputy's belt and handed his to Sam. Sam handed the two licenses to the deputy.

"Look, Souder. We're not shooting any birds, just out with a camera taking pictures," Sam said. Ken held up his graduation present to show the officer.

"Yeah, right. Give me your car keys and stay here. I'm going to search your vehicle and check the woods over there for your shotguns and any poached turkeys you've taken," Souder held out his hand again for the keys.

Sam thought a minute and said, "No, I don't think that you're going to do any of that. We haven't been hunting with anything but a camera. Far as I know, that's still legal here in Pennsylvania, even on a Sunday. You have no probable cause to search anything. You can look in the woods all you want, you're not going to find anything."

"Now listen here, pal! You shut the fuck up and give me those keys. Else I'll smash a window if I have to and haul you two off to the magistrate for resisting!" the deputy shouted and turned into a defensive stance.

Sam replied in a calm voice, "You don't get it, do you? You're out of line here. I don't think you want to pick this fight. I think you'd better cool down and try to listen to what I'm telling you."

The deputy looked at Sam and then at Ken as if deciding if he was going to take the next step. "You going to give me those keys?" he asked, a little less loud this time.

Sam slowly reached into his hip pocket and came out with his own black leather case and handed it to the deputy. "My ID, deputy. Take a look. We can go as far with this as you want. Right down to Elmerton Avenue in Harrisburg if need be. My son and I are not going to be pushed around by some rabbit cop." State Police Headquarters was just down the road from the Game Commission's.

After he opened the case Sam handed him, the deputy said. "Shit. Look, you know I'm just trying to do my job..." Souder didn't get to finish.

"Your job? It's Sunday, deputy. You're not even on duty now are you?" Sam flashed a little anger.

"Well, I, I..." Souder stuttered.

Sam snatched back the case from the man's hand and pulled out a business card. He handed the card to Souder and took back the hunting licenses. "You find anything in the woods, come look me up down in Lehigh County at the Straus Valley State Police Barracks."

The deputy said, "I'm sorry, Corporal Deland. We work with the state police all the time. I didn't mean anything by this. I saw the truck parked here and assumed it might be poachers..."

"Then you know you should have called in and had a full time game protector come out or you should have called the state police to handle this. Off duty and out of uniform is the wrong time to start acting like some cowboy out here. If we had been poachers, you'd have been outnumbered and outgunned. Think about it. You don't get paid enough for that," Sam lectured. "Any further business here or can I take my son to breakfast now? He's mighty hungry."

The deputy just shook his head, walked back to his truck and left.

"Man, I thought he was going to go nuts on us," Ken said, almost out of breath.

"Part time volunteer cop wanna be's. Thought he would roust us and buff up his ego. Makes me sick. These deputies have a bad enough reputation. The few really good ones have to suffer for all the jokers like him. Come on, I'm not letting Barney Fife spoil the day," Sam tossed the keys to Ken. "Drive us to Mabel's, genius."

In twenty minutes they were laughing and drinking hot chocolate at the small family restaurant next to the gliderport on Route 220.

The room smelled like stale cigarettes and cat piss. His arm was around her shoulder and her hair was frizzled and dirty. She didn't move in the bed when he rolled over to sit up and let his head settle down. He was pretty sure her name was Kathy or Kate or something that started with a K or a C. It was hard to remember. Two big black flies waddled one after the other on the torn screen at the bedroom window and buzzed as they flew up and over him to the other window on the opposite side of the small, desperately dirty and cluttered room.

Toby needed to piss and get another hit of crank going to start the day. He fumbled at his dirty jeans on the floor at the side of the bed and found the bag in the side pocket. He held it up and cringed at the small amount of the crystal that remained inside. "Fuckin' greedy bitch," he muttered and reached behind him and slugged the sleeping girl hard between the shoulder blades.

"Get up, you cunt. Get out! Steal my shit!" She winced, but didn't move fast enough. Toby dropped his jeans and got up on his knees over her. His penis flapped back and forth between his bare legs as he hit the girl four or five more times in the back. She screamed and tried to shuttle off the side of the bed away from him. He went after her and grabbed her hair from behind.

"No, stop. That hurts, you maniac!" she screamed and swung on him, scratching at his face. When she missed, he kicked her between her legs and she went to the floor. He kicked her again in the face and heard bone crunch.

"Fuckin' cunt! How much did you take last night? Didn't leave me shit. Get out!" He threw clothes at her as she scrambled to her feet and ran naked out of the room and then out the front door of the trailer.

Toby was breathing hard and had to lean against the door frame to stop the room from spinning. He staggered back over to the bed, retrieved the bag and took it into the bathroom to shoot up. The girl was in the front yard trying to put on her shorts and called back toward the trailer, "Okay, Toby. I'm sorry. I'll call you later, sweetie." He couldn't answer; he had a shoelace in his mouth trying to shut off the blood flow to his left arm to produce a visible vein.

~ * ~

If you were some distance away, the two would sound an awful lot alike. In the hills and valleys around State College, the drumming of the male ruffed grouse's wings against a log to attract his mate and the thud, thud, thud of the John Deere tractor moving down the grass taxi strip of the gliderport were very similar. Jack Conner sat on his prize 1940s tricycle tractor, slowly pulling the Schweizer 2-33 two seat glider from the tie down area to the end of the runway near the small office. His almost ninety year old eyes scanned the sky and he smiled a wrinkled grin at the whiffs of white cumulus beginning to take shape out of the northwest. If this kept up, the ridge would be working and boomer thermals would be popping before noon.

Jack lied about his age to join the army air corps in 1942 and then survived the hedgerows of Normandy in 1944 and earned a Purple Heart and a Silver Star for the heavy fighting he took part in after safely landing his glider full of infantry in a flooded field. A real tough kid who had to grow up quickly. He returned home after the war and had a few different jobs that paid the bills so he could teach the subtle art of flying sailplanes to several generations of eager students.

Forty five years ago, he bought the land and carved out his small airport to take advantage of the almost solid ridge that ran from near Williamsport to the northeast all the way southwest into Tennessee. Flights of several hundred miles in a glider were possible from his little airstrip if the wind hit the ridge at the proper angle and forced an updraft of air over the mountain that could keep a sailplane riding the crest. He moved past the line of power planes and gliders resting at their straps and waved at the father and son getting their small sailplane ready for the day's flight.

Sam watched his old friend on the green tractor pull the trainer past and wrung the wetness out of the cloth he was using to wipe the wings of his and Ken's shiny 1-26.

"That tractor sounds like it's still new," Ken said to his dad. Ken was bent over in the cockpit slipping in a fresh battery for the aircraft radio. The bubble canopy sat on a mat on the ground next to Ken and glistened as the rising sun reflected off the clean Plexiglas.

"I put in an extra bottle of water and a couple packs of cheese crackers to hold me over." Ken at eighteen, was an experienced pilot. He'd been flying, actually hands on, with his dad since he was six. His last year at General Varnum Military Academy had been in the preparatory program for the Air Force Academy and he had been flying twice a week, weather permitting, at school and every chance he got with his dad on weekends and holidays.

"These cloud streets line up the way I think they're going to, you'll be sitting in the Airport Diner in les than five hours after takeoff. Or, I could be digging you out of a field somewhere in the mountains. What do you think, hot shot?" Sam smiled at his son. They had been looking for this weather set up since mid April. Each spring they brought their single seat glider from its fall and winter quarters on the ridge to the farm field surrounded airport at Kutztown, one hundred and twenty air miles to the southeast.

"I think we launch in an hour, hour and a half. I want the thermals cooking good for the first half of the trip," Ken said. Landable fields were few and scattered in the mountainous area southeast of Jack's airport. Ken needed lots of uprising air in the thermals generated by the sun warming the ground to give him distance and options. Once released from the tow plane, he would have to find and circle in the rising columns of air to regain the altitude he would lose when flying straight ahead.

"Go on in and call Flight Service again for the latest weather, Ken. I'll finish up and pre-flight the Citabria," Sam said. The day before, Ken had earned enough 'credit' with Jack by flying tow plane to finish paying for most of the hanger fees for the 1-26. Sam added to that by flying backseat in the 2-33, giving rides and instruction to Jack's customers and today would fly the Citabria tow plane up until he had to leave to follow underneath Ken with the Pathfinder and trailer.

If Ken didn't make it all the way to Kutztown and had to land in a pasture somewhere, Sam would be close by to help take the wings off the glider and put it on the trailer for the rest of the trip. The 1-26 was ready to go, and Sam slipped the canopy back on its hinge and stowed the cleaning gear in the bag behind the seat. One last visual of the cockpit assured Sam that Ken had everything he needed for the flight. All Ken needed to do before launch was release the ropes holding the wings to the ground and pull the ship to the starting line.

Sam walked past several other privately owned sailplanes in the tie down area and made his way to the end of the line where Jack kept the little tail dragger used for towing. The two seat Citabria was a climber and did an excellent job pulling the gliders up to two thousand feet above the ground where they would release and either catch the ridge lift, a thermal, or make their way back to the field and enter the landing pattern. There was no tower at this field and both glider and power pilots used the glider frequency at 123.3 megacycles on the aircraft band to announce their takeoff and landing intentions.

Sam found the routine of the pre-flight to be reassuring. Since his Naval R.O.T.C. training at Villanova and navy aircraft carrier qualifications and flight operations, he had learned a lot about pilots and airplanes. He was patient and paid attention to all the little things that kept him and the aircraft safe. Pre-flight was how he made sure everything that could be done to make the flight routine, was taken care of.

Other owners and glider crews were arriving and setting up for the day. Jack didn't fly by himself anymore and depended on Sam and a few other good friends and customers to help him around the place. There was always a fresh supply of eager glider nuts from Penn State University up the mountain that would work to earn tow fees and rental time. In the busiest times of spring and fall when the cold fronts brought strong northwesterly winds and cooked the ridge into a glider highway, Jack would break down and actually pay a tow pilot and back seat glider instructor to fly the trainer and sell rides and lessons. Broke his heart, though.

It had always been tough to earn a living running a small airport. Anything that had the word 'aircraft' in it just plain cost more and was harder to find. Insurance and taxes bit in to the rest. Jack didn't grumble too much anymore, though. His partner for the last ten years was only in her early sixties and still made his eyes glitter. He hooked up with her at some resort he got talked in to going to on a rare vacation and she moved in two years later. She had a heart of gold, loved Jack, and could keep a set of books well enough to fend off the IRS and the County Tax Collector.

June Bea was known to everyone as just Bea. She was from Baton Rouge, Louisiana and retired from nursing. Jack parked the 2-33 and wheeled the John Deere around back of the wooden office building. Bea stepped out onto the covered porch and plopped down on one of the eight big rocking chairs overlooking the grass runways. She sipped on a cup of apple cinnamon tea and counted six glider owners and crews prepping to run the ridge. She could see Sam under the cowl of the Citabria checking the oil and inspecting the engine.

The first student for the 2-33 was due any time now, and one of her regular instructors was just pulling into the parking lot. Sam and Ken were part of her family here. She knew all the names of the customers' kids and grandkids and most of their dogs, too.

"Gonna miss me, Bea?" she heard the young voice say just behind her. "I won't get back here until next year." She turned to see Ken standing next to her.

"Oh, my yes, Kenny. Your dad better not be a stranger, though. When will you take the 1-26 out to Colorado?" Bea asked.

"Not until my second year, if then. No way a plebe can get off campus for personal flying for the first year. Dad says we'll put oxygen in it and fly the wave. I'm gonna miss it around here. Once I graduate, they'll ship me all over." Ken knelt down next to Bea and put his arm around her. "You and Jack have been real special to Dad and me. I want you both to know how grateful I am for all that you've taught me." He kissed her on her tanned cheek.

"Hey, two timer. Sneakin' 'round with the young bucks again," Jack caught them as he stepped up onto the porch from the side steps, wiping tractor grease from his well weathered hands. "Only gonna' be left with this old fart when the young one here runs off to college on ya."

She turned to him and said, "He's not the only one I got runnin'. Whole college full of them up the hill. You just be thankful I can still bat my eyes and bring them in. You old crust." They all laughed and Jack plopped down beside her in the next rocker.

Sam clipped the cowl closed and began his walk around the tow plane. He watched the young glider instructor walk up to the office from the parking lot and knew he would be towing the first flight of the day within the half hour. Bea had another tow pilot lined up to take Sam's place after he left to chase Ken.

Sam inspected each control surface and the pins holding them in place. Jack kept the Citabria immaculate and in all the tows Sam had run in it, it never even coughed. He reached the rear of the plane and connected the two hundred foot tow rope to the release under the tail. The rope was new as of yesterday. Ken had handled the situation without any trouble.

Ken was in the tow plane towing a heavy fiberglass high performance sailplane the owner had weighted down with water in the wing tanks. At about seven hundred feet above the ground, the glider bumped into a strong thermal and strained the tow rope beyond its capacity. The few seconds that followed the rope break caused much concern among the glider pilot's crew on the ground, but no one got hurt, and the surprised pilot followed his training by dropping his nose for a turn into the wind and did a one-eighty back to the field. It was quite a sight to witness the low level return of the long winged white bird dumping water from its wings and dashing for the end of the runway.

Ken maintained his climb after the rope break and allowed the glider to make the emergency landing before he entered the pattern and touched down. The glider owner refilled his wings with a little less ballast and got back in line for, hopefully, a less exciting tow.

Sam remembered his first rope break. When he returned from the navy to raise Ken after Ken's mother was killed in a wreck on the turnpike, Sam got several civilian ratings, including his glider and later his glider instructor ticket. The last ride with a glider instructor before solo is the test of all the safety training the student has been exposed to. After the tow plane pulls the trainer out over the end of the runway at about three hundred feet, the instructor in the back seat pulls the tow rope release to simulate a low altitude rope break. The surprised student is expected to turn quickly back to the airport to land.

Sam was smart enough to realize he would be put to the test and wasn't really surprised when his turn came. It still was a bit of a shock when he felt the pop of the release. The noise triggered his reaction, and at the sudden loss of speed, Sam dropped the nose of the trainer and built up his airspeed before turning back toward the runway for the landing. He soloed on the next flight and had built up hundreds of hours since.

When he finished preparing the Citabria, Sam walked over to the office and sat next to Bea. "I can give you about two hours this morning, sweetie. You going to be okay after that?" he asked.

"Yep. Tommy is coming in from Harrisburg. Should be here about the time Ken launches," Bea said.

A college age boy and girl walked in from the parking lot and said hello to everyone on the porch. The girl had her blue covered log book in her hand and then walked over to the 2-33 to start her pre-flight with the instructor.

"Time to get to work, hot shot. Give her a good thermal, Sam. She's almost ready to solo."

~ * ~

"Okay, I'll be there." Toby ended the call and sat back to feel the speed rip through his system. He reached to his left and opened the drawer in the battered end table next to the couch he was stretched out on. The black revolver lying in the drawer was worn and the silver metal showed through around the cylinder and at the end of the barrel. Toby didn't like the semi-automatics they used on TV. Too many parts to get broken. Too many buttons to remember. The old .38 was his grandfather's and worked every time he needed it to. Besides, it was too old to be registered and could never be traced back to him if he had to dump it. Once he stood up, he stuck the gun into the back of his jeans and pulled his black Harley t-shirt out over it. Between the meth and the gun, he felt like he could take on almost anything. He bounced out the door of the trailer and stumbled down the metal steps, crashing face first to the ground in a cloud of dust. Not a good start for his adventure today.

He was broke again. He had fifteen dollars and change in his pocket and needed gas for his Chevy pick-up. The old truck ate gas and he wouldn't get far, what with prices these days. Well, if everything went as he had brilliantly planned, he would have plenty of money by the end of the day. He brushed the grit from his shirt and pants and climbed into the truck for his ride south.

~ * ~

"Ozzie, would you cook chicken on the grill for us, please?" Marie asked.

"Yeah, Dad. You make the best chicken!" the twins chimed in unison. They crinkled their noses at the thought of saying something at the same time. They couldn't help it, though. No matter how much they tried to be different.

"Please, Daddy, good chicken, yum, yum," chirped little Katie.

Ozzie was really Walter. He didn't let anybody call him Walter, though. Only his beautiful wife, Marie. But she usually called him Ozzie too. Except when she got mad. Then she used Stanislaus, his middle name. Ozzie came from Ozliewski. Big and blonde and Polish on both sides, mother and father. Marie was dark haired and Italian on both sides. The six kids were a mixture. The new baby, Vinny, came out blonde like his older brother, Walter Junior.

Trooper Ozliewski was off duty and driving his tribe home from nine o'clock mass. During the warm months, their traditional Sunday morning after mass brunch often turned into an early picnic on their deck with Ozzie cooking mass quantities of food on the grill.

"Just so happens old Dad stuck a bunch of wings and legs in a vat of sauce before we left for church. You guys help your mom with the baby and the salads and we'll be eatin' with our fingers afore ya knows it!" Ozzie winked over his shoulder to five year old Katie and she tittered happily at her funny dad.

Marie heard the first grumblings from Vinny's car seat behind her in the van and hoped he stayed quiet until they got home. "I'm going to feed him as soon as we get home. Connie, you and the twins peel some potatoes and make up a tossed salad. Junior, you supervise and get out the things to set the table." Connie was ten now and Junior just turned sixteen. The only thing on his mind, besides girls, was the learner's permit burning a hole in his wallet.

"Hey, Dad, after lunch can we drive over to the shopping center and practice?" Junior pleaded. The twelve year old twin girls laughed together in the back seat as the smell of the baby's diaper reached them.

Connie gagged. She and Junior straddled Vinnie's car seat between them in the van's middle seat. "Ewww! He stinks. Roll down the window Daddy, save me from the fumes."

"I got a better idea, son. I'll let you drive me over the back roads to Sam's to feed Molly. Won't be too much traffic today and you can drive slow. How's that sound?"

"Yep, that'll do, Dad!" Junior hadn't expected that.

Ozzie was real proud of his boy. Starting out to be a good driver and real careful. Ozzie couldn't wait to get the insurance bill, though. Junior would have to work that off helping with Ozzie's remodeling business he ran on the side. "Sam and Ken aren't due back until tonight. We'll let her run a bit and see if we can catch a few minnies in the creek to fish with this afternoon at the lake on the way back." Ozzie worked with Sam Deland at the barracks. They were also good friends and tomorrow they had a very important court date in Philadelphia.

~ * ~

It was hot and sticky. Even at this time of the morning the humidity slung itself across the pastures and hammocks like an invisible fog. Air so thick you felt like you were breathing water. Jimmy needed a bath. Today's sweat was running down his back over last night's dried up crust and he couldn't get the last spark plug out. The socket didn't seem to fit in between all the hoses and wires plastered all around the engine block. "Shitty little cars," muttered Jimmy. The wrench finally took hold and he skinned his knuckles twisting out the old plug.

"Wanna beer?" Russell called from the porch. "Gonna be hot agin' today."

"Fuckin' hot ever' day, big brother. Yeh, gimme 'nother cold one. I'm almost done with 'er," Jimmy called back over his dirty shoulder.

His brother, Russell, stepped back across the bowed and uneven boards that covered the porch of the small wooden house and went inside. Little or no white paint remained on the outer walls, and the two windows on the front side had torn screens that didn't do much to keep out the hoards of biting insects that lived in this part of rural Florida.

This was the second house the Santees built on the family plot. The first stood fifty feet to the east and was even more run down. They had let it stand even after they had to get out of it because of the termite damage. They used it for storage now. The "new" house didn't look much better. At least the bugs hadn't eaten out the floor yet.

"Hey, get outta that beer. That's mine!" Momma yelled from her bedroom at the back of the house.

"Shut up, old woman. Me and Jimmy got work to do today. We'll bring you back some more later. Old witch." Russell grabbed two cans out of the refrigerator and walked through the living room and back out to the yard where Jimmy was working on the ol' Mustang.

The only good things about this miserable little bit of palmetto and sand were the three big live oak trees that provided shade to this part of the yard. They spread up and out like ponderous green umbrellas to block out the scorching Florida sun. Jimmy had the car parked out under the shade. It helped a little, but he was still miserable from the bugs and the heat. Russell and Jimmy Santee were both coming off nasty divorces and had moved back in with Momma. Jimmy just recently. Momma bothered them some, so they tried to keep her in beer to shut her up.

Jimmy took the cold can from his brother and drank half of it with the first gulp, "I gotta get outta here. She's drivin' me nuts. Worse'n my ex-old lady."

"She don't mean nothin'. Ya get used to it after a bit. Specially about the third o' the month when her check comes." Russell laughed a goofy hee haw like laugh and Jimmy grinned at him. Russell was a little slower than most and even though Jimmy was younger, he looked out after Russell.

Their nearest neighbor was a few hundred yards down the sandy dirt road. Their granddad settled on this piece to farm it years ago, and over the years they had to sell off parts just to pay the taxes. Drank up the rest. Didn't do any farming anymore. Just a few half wild chickens. Now they hustled a bit. Sold some grass and whatever they could steal.

Jimmy wasn't satisfied any more. He wanted things. He wanted people to stop looking down at him. But with no education, no real skills and a record, it made it difficult. Lately, they figured a new one. Lots of new construction along the Gulf and it was spreading inland. Half built houses just full of copper pipes and brand new stoves and refrigerators. Most construction companies couldn't afford to hire nighttime security. That made it easy for Russell and Jimmy. All they needed now was a good truck to haul the stuff. Jimmy knew buyers in Fort Myers, Fort Lauderdale and up north in Tampa.

That was today's job. Jimmy was trying to wring some life into Russ's old Ford in case they had to make a fast exit from one of the stops they had to make later.

"Hand me them new plugs there, big brother, and go get me 'nother a them beers."

~ * ~

Ken was on the right wing and Bea was on the left dragging the 1-26 up the line behind a Nimbus and another 1-26. Ken heard the engine of the tow plane wind up and watched his dad pull the 2-33 down the runway. Ken looked up at the building lines of puffy clouds and felt a twinge of excitement inside. Flying cross country in a sailplane is an exercise in skill and faith. The success of the flight depends on the shifting air and the pilot's ability to put the glider in the right place to take advantage of the lift generated by the sun heating the ground.

Today, streets of clouds were being generated by long lines of continuous lift shaped by the northwesterly wind. If Ken could put his 1-26 in the right spot, he could ride the lines of lift under the clouds downwind in generally up rising air. That would let him cover ground at a relatively fast rate without having to stop and circle in any single thermal for too long. Heaven to a glider driver.

The 2-33 towed by Sam in the Citabria was turning downwind over them and would run a bit that way before turning back into the wind and climb to the release point upwind and two thousand feet above the ground. Then, even if the student flying the front seat didn't catch a thermal, she could easily glide back to the airport and enter the landing pattern.

Bea dropped her wing and said, "Okay, Kenny. You're set. I called Margie and Will in Florida. They'll have a 2-33 ready for you on Thursday. Good flight. See you soon, I hope."

"Thanks, Bea." Ken couldn't say anything else. He felt a little choked up. He didn't think he could get back up here before he had to report to the Academy later this summer. She walked toward the office but turned and jogged back to him for a last hug.

"You...you...just do good, Kenny. We'll miss you." Bea squeezed him and turned back to the office. She needed to get busy doing something before she cried all her eye makeup off.

~ * ~

The gas station had only one set of pumps. It had just opened and there was a teenage girl inside behind the counter. Her belly fat surged out over the top of the tight pink jammie bottoms she wore. Her hair had streaks of blue in it and needed a good brushing and her eyes were rimmed in blackness. A small silver ball was stuck in her lower lip.

Toby's Chevy lumbered up to the island and he got out. His problem was, he needed thirty dollars' worth of gas and worse, cigarettes. With only fifteen dollars in his pocket, he was stuck. He fiddled with the pump for a minute and then trudged into the station.

She was playing loud street rap on her little portable CD player stuck up on the shelf behind the register. This far upstate, she probably didn't even know anybody from the big city, but she thought it was cool. She didn't really understand what the guy, yelling against the thumping background noise, was so mad about or even most of what he was saying, she just liked the repeating beat and the sound of it. When Toby came through the door, she looked up at him and turned the stereo down just a bit.

"Damn pump ain't workin' right. I must not be hittin' the right buttons or somethin'. Ya wanna come out and get me started?" he asked.

She shrugged her shoulders and said, "Yeah, you gotta hit the little red button, I'll show you." *Dirty, skinny tough man can't work the friggin pump*, she laughed to herself.

She came out from behind the counter and Toby started to follow her out of the door. She stepped into the lot and he stopped with the open door in his hand, "Oops, forgot my keys on the counter. Be right out," he told her and swung back inside. Before she could suspect anything, he came right back out and followed her to the pump. She couldn't see the four packs of Kools and the two Slim Jims in his pants.

She smirked at him and pushed the little red button. The pump jingled and cleared to all zeros. Toby handed her his last fifteen bucks and started pumping. He thought about stealing gas from her, too, but didn't. At least he had some smokes now.

~ * ~

"You look funny, Daddy. That's Mommy's apron," Katie shook her little stubby finger at her dad. He did look funny. Over six three and two fifty-five with a little strawberry covered frilly apron stretched tight around his middle, standing at the grill turning the smoking chicken pieces. Ozzie drained the beer from the bottle and wished he could have another. He could, but he wouldn't. He was the on call trooper and could be yanked out if anything big happened. It usually didn't.

Ozzie worked in the crime room, what most police agencies would call the detective squad. Pennsylvania was a little set in its ways. Ozzie was still a trooper and could be put back into uniform if the bosses ever decided to do that. He didn't think that was a great idea. Straus Valley barracks covered the area west of Allentown out to near Reading. Mostly farm country and a few small towns. The cities were moving west and east, though. Several shopping centers were already built and a new mall was in the works. All that money being spent by hard working decent folks attracted some that weren't quite so decent. Ozzie kept real busy, but if he was lucky, not today. Sunday was his family day.

Ozzie worked hard. Both at the barracks for the state and on his own too. He and Marie had a few rental properties and Ozzie did kitchens and bathrooms for paying customers. They planned on sending their kids to college. Ozzie never got to finish at Kutztown University. A decent football player, he quit in his junior year to support his wife and new son. He never regretted it. He figured he earned the equivalent of a doctorate in the years he put in on the state police. He wanted better for his kids, though. As long as Junior didn't become a cop or a lawyer, he would be happy.

"Katie, honey. Run get me the squirter, would you? Mom keeps it on the washer." The chicken was dripping and flaring a bit. Marie came out onto the deck with a table cloth and a basket of silverware and napkins.

"How much longer, Oz? The kids'r starving. All except Vincent, he's full and asleep." Ozzie caught her pleasing profile as Marie bent over the table. She still had some pounds to lose after Vinny was born, but Ozzie didn't mind her fullness; she needed to feed the baby. Her walk was up to three miles a day now. Having the older girls to help out freed her up to burn off the calories.

"'Bout ten minutes more. Start rounding up the girls. Junior is out in the garage getting our fishing stuff ready. I'll get him in when it's done," Ozzie said.

Katie appeared with the water bottle, and Ozzie saved the meat from burning up. With all the joy surrounding him, he should be happier than he was. He was worried about tomorrow. Most cops don't like going to court any more than they have to. None of them ever figure they would be going as the defendant.

~ * ~

Sam checked back over his shoulder at the big two seater behind him. He was trying to pull to the right with the tow plane just a bit to center up on a bubble that seemed to be a decent thermal. The glider was at the release point, and Sam wanted to drop them in the middle of the lift. He felt the sudden release of the tow rope and visually confirmed the glider pulling up and to the right behind him. He chopped the throttle with his left hand and mashed the left rudder with his foot. The stick followed to the left and he dropped into a steep turn back toward the field. Pressure back on the stick and some right rudder and he descended through a thousand feet, leveled his wings and entered the downwind leg of the landing pattern.

"Citabria tow plane downwind, Nittany," Sam reported on the radio to let anyone in the area know he was landing. Sam could see the pilot and the line boy standing at the wings of the white fiberglass sailplane that was next in line. They remained off to the side of the runway so Sam could land before they pulled the long winged bird out to set up for the tow. Ken was next to their 1-26 and a second 1-26 was between Ken and the glass bird.

"Badger, Kestrel. It's jumping, you ready?" Sam called Ken on the radio using their call signs.

Below, Ken watched his dad start his base leg turn and reached into the cockpit of the glider and grabbed the radio microphone, "Roger, Kestrel. I'm more than ready." Ken heard two clicks of the radio and knew his dad was acknowledging the transmission.

Sam turned final and Ken could see the Citabria cock on its side as Sam side slipped the plane down as close to the end of the runway as safely as possible. Putting planes down on a precise spot was something Sam had plenty of training to do. Jets didn't side slip as deftly as the light tow plane, though. Sam greased a three point landing, straightening out just before touchdown. The tow rope dangled behind him and the tow plane slowed rapidly once on the grass strip.

The next glider was pulled out and lined up on the runway and the pilot climbed in. Sam turned left off the runway and taxied back toward Ken and the others. The young kid working the line stepped out as Sam spun across in front of the gleaming white sailplane and retrieved the tow rope. He ran back and hooked the rope to the release under the nose of the glider. Sam slowed and waited until the canopy closed and the pilot nodded to the kid now holding the glider's left wing. Sam looked left and right for any pattern traffic and, as the line boy signaled for him to take up the tow rope slack, pushed the throttle forward and rolled out onto the center of the runway. He took a quick glance at the engine instruments and then looked back at the glider for the rope to tighten and the sailplane's rudder to waggle. Another look above for approaching traffic, just to be sure. Once he got the signal, he moved the throttle full forward and started his takeoff.

Slow at first, he gained speed and felt the drag reduce when the glider cleared the ground. A few more miles per hour and he was up also. He kept the Citabria moving straight down the runway as they gained altitude and as they cleared nine hundred feet, started a left turn downwind. Sam knew the Nimbus pilot and appreciated his skill at keeping the big sailplane tight in behind the tow plane. Some less skilled pilots yanked and pulled the tail of the tow plane all over. Sam felt several good thermals on the downwind and judged his turn back into the wind trying to reach one as they went through two thousand feet. The Nimbus released and Sam dove back for the field. One more, then it was Ken's turn.

~ * ~

"Shoulda' done the front brakes, too, Russ. Don't jam 'em too hard. We'll take care of 'um soon as we get ahead a bit," Jimmy wiped his face with the dirty rag. "I'm gonna wash up and we'll get on down the road."

Russell didn't get up from the beach chair at the base of the oak. He nodded that he heard his brother and sipped on the warming beer. He was a might slow, but he knew they were going to move on up once they got them a truck. Jimmy had it all figured out. Just slip in to the houses and take what they wanted; sweet deal. He wondered why Jimmy insisted they keep Grandpa's Winchester in the trunk. *Just in case*, Jimmy had said. *Just in case*.

It was even hot in the shade now. The sun was full up and even the bugs wouldn't go out in it. The air conditioning didn't work in the Mustang and Russell knew it would be miserable even with the windows down. The wheel wells were starting to show a little rust here and there. This wasn't one of the real powerful older Mustangs. This one only had a six cylinder and was more like a Pinto. Good thing Florida got rid of its inspection program a few years back. Gave a clunker like Russell's extra life on the road. The brakes were worn out and the muffler was just a shell, but it got from here to there.

Jimmy shot out through the front screen door and crossed the sandy weed covered lawn. He tossed the keys to Russell and went to the passenger door to get in, "We gotta get her some brews, gettin' bitchy in there. Come on, It's almost noon."

Russell unfurled himself from the chair and made his way to the car. Jimmy usually drove, but he was suspended and on probation for driving drunk, again, and didn't want to push the issue in case the motherfucker state trooper that arrested him the last time was sitting between them and the store out on the highway. A cloud of blue smoke sputtered out of the exhaust as Russell fired up the tired six and eased them down the rutted drive to the hard road.

## Chapter Two

"Ladies and Gentleman, this is the captain once again. Please remain seated until the aircraft comes to a complete stop at the arrival gate. If you need any assistance in retrieving your carry on bags, please ask any of the cabin crew to help you out. Thanks for flying with us today, and we hope to see you all again real soon."

It was all becoming quite routine for Grace. She could see the impatient ones already unbuckling and trying to get into position to jump into the aisle and pull their things from the overhead storage bins. It never ceased to amaze her the huge bags and cases people tried to drag onto the planes with them. Every flight, the crew had to juggle for space to keep the customers happy. Passengers didn't want to pay for checked baggage, so they brought it all with them into the cabin. They really got ticked off when Grace or one of the other crew made them set aside for checking into the hold a bag that was oversized.

Once the flight was over, it all started again when they all tried to pull the overstuffed articles down and waddle through the narrow center of the plane to get out. She shared a frustrated look with Mark, her partner in the coach section, from their jump seats at the very back of the plane. The good news was that even though she had less than a year of seniority, the turnover rate was such that she finally was able to bid once in a while on routes and schedules. It didn't always work out, but this week she was lucky. By Tuesday she would be in Philadelphia with five days off in a row and Ken all to herself. She got that little tingle in that certain spot just thinking about it.

"Behold, the herd moveth," whispered Mark into her left ear. "To the fray, my lady." They popped the belts in unison and got back to work.

~ * ~

Toby crossed the bridge and made the left to climb up the mountain. He could almost see the gas gauge falling toward empty as he climbed higher and the road seemed to narrow a bit. It wasn't much farther and the houses got more space between them as he drove away from the town. He was cranking as good as he could with what little dope the bitch had left him now and lit his next cigarette from the butt of the last one. The radio blasted heavy metal music, and the static from the Scranton station cleared as he gained altitude. He pounded his hand on the outside of the driver's door to the beat and could just picture himself on stage grinding out the music.

*Concert tickets, yeah, I'll get some good concert tickets, shoot up real good and feel the live music. Yeah.* He popped the glove box and took out the pint of whiskey he had stashed there. It was still half full and he stuck it between his knees and unscrewed the cap with one hand. He glanced in the side mirror to see what was behind him and drained what was left in the bottle. The burn went all the way down to his toes. *Feels good.* Nothing could hold him back. He turned the radio up as far as the speakers could stand and howled out the words to the song as he drove.

~ * ~

The 1-26 ahead of Ken was climbing in the solid thermal Sam dropped him into as Ken settled into the cockpit at the end of the runway. Sam was turning the Citabria onto the strip from the taxiway and gave a thumbs up as he passed. Ken arranged his maps and water and tucked everything in tight for the tow. The line boy hooked the tow rope and called for Ken to pop the release to test it. Once they both felt the solid snap, the kid reset the ring at the end of the rope and Ken slid the release lever back forward to lock in the tow rope.

It was getting hot and stuffy in the cockpit, and Ken adjusted the air intake to blow up to his face. He would risk a few pieces of runway grass from the Citabria's prop wash just to get some air moving. The line boy jogged out to Ken's left wing, picked it up and leveled the glider. Sam eased out onto the runway and pulled the tow rope tight. When Ken saw the slack gone, he glanced over his left shoulder looking for planes in the pattern, and when he saw it was clear, waggled his rudder back and forth to signal his dad he was ready.

The light 1-26 single seater bounded down the runway and after only a few steps, the kid on the wing let go. Ken felt the stick respond to his touch, and he kept the wings level in the churning air. The glider rumbled and bounced on the grass then lifted off the runway. Ken pushed lightly forward on the stick to keep the sailplane within a few feet of the ground so he wouldn't pull up the tail of the tow plane and rub the prop into the grass. Sam pulled the Citabria into the air and the climb was on.

Out over the end of the runway, Ken felt the first good bump of a thermal. His dad pulled him through several more on the upwind run and Ken pulled the release a bit early at eighteen hundred feet into the middle of a four hundred feet a minute up lift. He banked into a tight right turn and watched the variometer indicate his climb up toward cloud base.

Sam smiled when he felt Ken release. Even though he hadn't made it to two thousand feet, Ken was smart enough to know to drop into any good thermal above fifteen hundred. Sam settled into the pattern and landed. As he taxied back toward the office, he watched Ken dancing in the lift above. This time together had to be made the best of. Before much longer, the young man would release the father son tow rope and be on his own.

Ken kept adjusting the bank to take advantage of the lift. Thermals are rising columns of air, but the columns are never completely symmetrical. They bulge and shift, depending on the wind and moisture. This one was pulling Ken up to a cloud street that stretched out to the southeast for many miles. The ridge below wouldn't be needed today. He could see the 2-33 skimming along the ridge working the lift along the face. The student pilot getting in a good day's practice. Ken placed the other 1-26, but the Nimbus was already gone; streaking at high speed south toward Maryland.

Ken knew the landmarks and as he neared cloud base, he marked his exit point to the southeast on each revolution. The first twenty miles weren't too bad. Although mountainous, there were several airports and fields scattered along his route. A small strip to the southwest and the big airport at

State College. Beyond that, though, the ridges up and across Mifflin and Snyder Counties offered little but places to crash.

Sam parked the tow plane and set the switches. The pilot that would take over for him was walking out from the office and Sam knew he would want to do his own pre-flight. Once he gathered his flight bag, Sam slipped out the right side of the plane and greeted the younger man.

"Ken's going to give you a good run today, Sam," the new pilot said.

Sam shook his firm hand and said, "Doesn't look like Jack will be selling too many second tows today; the lift is all over. Just pick your thermal and go." Sam told him the plane was running smoothly, as usual, and moved off toward the office to check out with Bea and Jack. He looked up to where Ken had been circling and watched as his son rolled out from under the cloud and put the nose on course.

Ken let the lift pull him up under the curved dome of the cloud. The bottom of the graying cloud wasn't flat like most people thought but domed up from the outer edges to the middle. Technically, Ken shouldn't be this tight to the base, but he allowed himself the extra few hundred feet up into it before he leveled out to the southeast and put the nose down.

He skirted through the mist at the outside edge of the cloud he was under and went straight into the edge of the next cloud in the street. He was still showing lift and put the nose of the little sailplane down even farther, gaining speed and taking advantage of the almost continuous up draft. The street didn't follow his direct path to Kutztown and he would have to jump south to the next one to stay on course. He decided he would ride this one just short of the heavier mountains and try to run to the next one over the last landable fields.

Sam took the steps up onto the porch and caught Jack's eye over the gathering crowd. Customers had arrived in groups and Jack was trying to stay out of Bea's way while she juggled tows and rentals.

"Ken's off on course. Gotta go now. Give me hug," Sam said in Bea's direction.

Jack lumbered over toward him and grabbed Sam up in his still strong arms, "Little darlin', I thought you'd never ask," Jack laughed. Bea held up her hand to the couple in front of her and made her way to the red faced Sam.

She slipped into his arms and kissed him on the cheek, "We'll see you before football season, won't we?" she asked. A little tear was starting to form at the edge of her right eye.

"Sure, Bea. Once I get Ken out to Colorado, I'll be looking for company. You'll see me," Sam assured her. He returned her kiss and reached around to shake Jack's hand. He pulled away from Bea and left them standing on the porch as he walked quickly across the grass to the edge of the tie down area where the Pathfinder was parked with the 1-26 trailer hooked up.

"Badger ground, you rolling yet?" Sam heard the aircraft receiver in the truck snap.

Sam reached through the driver's window and said into the microphone, "I'm leaving now. Where are you?"

"Passing north of the big airport. Eighty indicated and only two hundred down. This street is cooking!" an excited Ken exclaimed.

Sam knew that if Ken was moving that fast down the cloud street, he had better get moving, faster. He drove out on to Route 220 south and into the left lane. He had to run south for about six miles and then pick up U.S. 322 to pass around State College. The light trailer didn't slow him down too much and stayed tight in behind the Pathfinder as he fed the gas to the engine and wound up to seventy in a hurry.

"Badger ground. Looks like I can stay on this street to Route 26 and then run south to leapfrog to the next one, give you a chance to catch up," Ken radioed. Sam knew it was eleven miles from 220 to where 26 crossed and more than a few stop lights until he could get on the bypass.

"Don't worry about me; just keep me posted where you are. If these conditions hold up, you'll have to order for me at the diner." Sam snuck a peek over his shoulder up toward the mountain, but couldn't spot Ken. He made the turn onto 322 and made the first two lights before he got stuck.

Route 322 ran around the town sweeping to the north out near the hard runways of the familiar airfield that served this college town. The Pathfinder worked hard up the mountain and things smoothed out on the bypass. Ken let him know he had left the street and was punching through the heavy sink. A thermal boosted his altitude and he made the next street to the south with plenty to spare. Sam was within a few miles of him and caught a glimpse of the white wings circling up under the line of clouds. The test would come about fifteen miles farther on when the road turned south and

Ken's course would take him over State Forest and the Mid State Trail. Only a few roads ran up into the woods and those all seemed to run across the course line and not with it.

~ * ~

They had to wait for several slow customers before the clerk got to them to pay for the three six packs. Russell passed the time picking his nose deep and hard. Jimmy got disgusted with him and found some shade off to the side of the small crossroads country store and smoked what was left of a joint. Once they had the beer, they hauled the eleven miles back to the house and dropped off one of the six packs to Momma.

What fine sons they were. She was still in bed under a floppy old ceiling fan that spun wobbly and sounded like it was ready to fall off. Russell told her the beer was in the fridge and piled back out of the front door to the car where Jimmy was tossing his second empty out the window and studying an old Exxon map. It looked like a foreign language to Jimmy. He grumbled under his breath and tossed the map into the back seat.

"Which way, little brother?" asked Russ.

"Over toward Arcadia, then north on 17," Jimmy said and started on his third beer. He was pretty sure he had this all worked out. Another twelve ounces would help him keep it straight.

Russell got them down their sand lane and onto the hard road then out to the state road and turned east. He liked this ride. Narrow, long and mostly straight, he didn't have to think too hard about where he was or which turn to make until he was near Arcadia. The state road passed through flat, endless pasture land dotted by swamps and palmetto thickets. Here and there, live oak hammocks and clusters of thin, tall pines broke up the open landscape. A few cattle could be seen beyond the barbed wire barriers that lined both sides of the desolate road.

Large ranches owned every bit of this land and few private homes even existed for the twenty odd miles to Arcadia. Their own family plot and a few others on their side road were now surrounded by the big landowners that seemed to be the only ones able to still make a profit from the swampy sandy center of the state.

Jimmy had them headed deeper still into the middle of Florida to an area that still looked like 1965 in a lot of corners. The Mustang sounded a bit smoother today after Jimmy had fiddled with it some. He would check the oil when they stopped for gas and more beer in Wauchula. Russell kept it at about sixty; no hurry and no need to attract attention from the yellow and black Highway Patrol cars. Nice Sunday drive.

The state road merged with the one coming into Arcadia from Bradenton and flowed into the small town. Tired cement block houses with sand spur yards circled in cheap chain link fence lined the street. Some of the older homes had wide porches and were kept up, but many were not. In the center of the town a few of the stores and shops were closed up. Out of business and not needed anymore. The chain stores were here now with lots of stuff and lower prices. Life moves on. Only the gas stations and mini marts seemed to have business happening mid-day Sunday. Russell turned north on U.S. 17 and in less than a mile they were back up to speed.

The beer started to kick in and Jimmy said, "Find me a hole to piss in, Russ. We got some business up ahead. I need to empty out first."

~ * ~

The inside of the pick-up seemed to shudder from the rumble underneath Ozzie. Junior looked over at his smirking dad and rolled the window all the way down, "Can you hold it until we get to the farm, Dad?" Junior sounded a bit annoyed. He was trying to concentrate on his driving and avoid the critical comments of his teacher. "Is this some kind of a test? Driving while your eyes water and try to focus? Jeez, Dad."

Ozzie squirmed a bit and let another one go, "Ahh, there. Had to make some room," he laughed out loud and it infected Junior who laughed with him. They were easing along the south side of the mountain and stopped at U.S. 309.

"Okay, first time on a four lane, Junior. Make sure you watch the traffic coming from the left. Give yourself plenty of time to get up to speed. Don't be in a hurry. If you're not sure, wait.

A car passed and another was just coming in to view over the last hill. Junior gave the truck the gas and out they went. He swung a bit wide, but got it back into the right lane and brought it up to fifty. Within a half mile, they were climbing and Junior had to push harder on the pedal to keep his speed up. The truck responded and they crossed over the ridge past the sign for the Appalachian Trail and started down the back side. Junior learned to feed in some brakes to keep the truck from going too fast around the sweeping turns as they moved north.

The turn off to Sam's farm was up ahead, and Junior felt much more comfortable once they got back onto a two lane road. This one twisted a bit and Junior kept his speed down, trying to feel the truck come into and out of the turns. Ozzie offered advice and was real pleased with how Junior was doing. Ozzie and Junior had made this trip many times, but this was the first time Junior had driven it.

"I never realized it before, but those big maples are real close to the road. This would be tough with some snow on," Junior thought out loud. Between two of the old maples up on the left, a small gravel drive met the hard road. Junior turned in and followed the winding path with grass growing between the tire trails up a rise and around a blossoming apple orchard that looked to be a hundred years old. The gravel crunched under the wheels, and he had to keep it slow as the drive dipped and then rose again through huge oaks that ran up and off to the right following a creek bed.

"Listen to her. She hears us coming." Ozzie cocked his ear out the window and picked up the howl of the beagle. "She's gonna be glad to see us."

As they cleared the oaks, the building started to take shape ahead. They passed by the foundation of what used to be a stone farmhouse from long ago. Now spring growth was sprouting and coming up all around the remaining stones. Black from the fire that destroyed the original house still showed on some of the stones and a few pieces of timber that remained embedded in the site. The new house was really the old barn. When Sam bought this place, it was supposed to be just a hunting camp, but Sam started fixing things and then enlisted Ozzie to supervise and ended up with a beautiful home from the converted barn.

The old German raised barns built of stone and timbers still stand in numbers in this part of the country. Ozzie and Sam stripped out the tired parts of the old barn, and with decks and glass had fashioned a work to be proud of.

Junior saw her white tipped tail first, flopping rapidly back and forth as fast as she could wag it. The little beagle howled with delight and jumped into the air, restrained only by her leash clipped onto an overhead wire as she saw the truck crest the last small rise and pull into the open yard.

"Look, I gotta hit the head, quick," Ozzie said with a pained face. "Can you see to Molly?"

Junior watched his big dad cross the space between the truck and the stairs up to the back kitchen door in swift strides. When his dad had to go...

Molly settled a bit as Junior rubbed her lovingly, scratching her ears and giving her the tummy rub she expected whenever she saw him. She yipped at his heels as he walked over to her bowls and scooped them up for a trip up the hill to the old milk house that served as a yard shed and storage for Molly's food and water. Junior unclipped her and let her run a tight circle around the yard. He knew she wouldn't go far when food was about to appear.

The white wooden door was held shut by a wooden latch. Junior opened it and could hear the trickle of the natural spring as it poured out of a pipe and splashed into the galvanized tub at the lower end of the milk house. The dented gray metal once kept the cans of the farmer's fresh milk cold while they were submerged in the frigid water until the truck could get by to pick them up. Junior rinsed her water dish and filled it from the pipe sticking out of the side wall. Molly's food was sealed in a thick plastic drum meant to keep out the various critters that would help themselves if they had a chance.

She stood in the door watching Junior's every move and wagging that tipped tail as hard as ever. Next to Sam and Ken, Ozzie and Junior were her best pals. Whenever Sam was off doing the many things that kept him busy, Junior looked after Molly. It was the best part time job a kid could have. He topped off her dish with dry food and carried the bowls back down next to the old whiskey barrel that was her outside dog house.

While she attacked her food, Junior walked over to the truck and got his net and minnie bucket from the back. He heard the kitchen door slam and saw his dad bounding down the steps to the yard adjusting his zipper and belt.

"Feel like a new man!" Ozzie shouted. Molly didn't even look up.

"Let's get us some bait."

Junior fell into step with his father and they started up and around the barn toward the stream that ran down toward the hard road east of the house. Molly wasn't far behind and passed them with her nose down searching for bunnies. The path rose up and over the bank as they went into thicker woods. Bright green dotted the edges of the path in shades from nearly translucent to dark. Each of the different kinds of plants and trees, as if on timers set by an artist, jumped out with new growth. Fresh, clean, spring was meant to be this way. Ridding the brown and gray earth of winter's icy grip. Defiantly and with purpose.

Though most of the big mature trees lacked color and were still shrouded in gray and black, the little ones closer to the ground and thorny were getting a head start. They went down toward the stream and the path twisted along the bank on well used game trails. A pool the size of a basketball court stretched out behind an old stone dam or what was left of it. Years ago the farmer tried to slow up the little stream, but time had given back most of the independence these mountain brooks seem to have.

Ozzie and Junior moved slowly up to the edge of the water, and Junior stabbed the net into the cool surface. "Yep, got a few!" he exclaimed. Ozzie brought the minnie bucket over and filled it from the pool. Junior dumped what he had into the bucket and was after more.

"Listen to her," Ozzie held up his hand as the sound of Molly yowling reached them. "She's on one."

The little dog sounded off as only beagles can when their nose fills up with rabbit scent. "Right near where we got a couple last fall. She'll be bringing it around. I'll get us some more minnies. Why don't you cut her off; meet you back at the truck."

Junior listened for a few seconds and figured his course to intercept the dog. He knew the rabbit would lead Molly in a loop that would come back to a safe hole, probably close to where she had jumped it.

"Okay, see you there in a bit." And he was off through the woods on a trot toward the beagle noise.

~ * ~

There were already two cars and a Harley in the short dirt driveway below the house. Toby bumped the truck over the edge of the road and into the shallow ditch in front of the house, just missing the rusted black mailbox. It didn't seem to sink so he figured he could drive it out again. *Close enough.* He was still just a bit wired and half buzzed on the whiskey and shrugged it off. He bit off the last of the Slim Jim and pitched the wrapper out on the road for someone else to pick up.

The house was really a trailer, with a hard roof and porch tacked onto the front, perched on the side of a fairly steep hill and tucked up under large pines. As he walked up the drive, he heard the big dog start barking deep and mean from under the porch. *I hope the fucker is tied up. I'd have to shoot it and waste a good bullet.* He hated the thing but put up with it.

This was the only place his "partner" would meet on days they had a job to do. The driveway was rutted from the runoff of rainstorms sent tumbling down the hillside. Tree roots protruded up through the gravel and made for bumpy footing. Toby managed to stumble around the bigger ones and made his way up toward the porch.

The wide porch on the front of the trailer looked old and tired. Up on the decking, a rotten couch with torn fabric sat crooked and sagging along with an odd collection of wooden and plastic chairs in various states of disintegration. Above the sound of the dog he could hear blaring music, almost the same stuff he had been listening to on the way here. Loud, shouting singers barely heard over even louder and hard edged guitars.

In the front door of the house stood a tall and imposing figure dressed in the uniform of the day; black undershirt and jeans. His hair was long and straight and his face covered in beard and a mean look. Tattoos overtook the tanned skin on his heavy arms and a silver semi auto pistol in his belt pushed up against his gut.

Toby called up to him, "That shithead dog a theirs tied up, Head?"

When he grinned back at Toby, Thomas "Flathead" McCall revealed the missing top left incisor that gave him a lopsided smile. The rest of his teeth seemed a bit yellowish green and appeared to be headed for the same fate. "He don't want none of your nasty skinny little ass anyhoo, Turd. Where the fuck you been? Supposed to be here an hour ago; we got things to talk about," Flathead snarled through his grin.

Toby didn't like it when Flathead called him Turd. He didn't want that as his nickname. He had been called a lot of names by those that knew him. Shithead, dickwad or just Toby. He tried to call himself "T-bird," but that melted down to Turd so he gave up.

"Damndest thing, actually fell asleep last night. I think I drank too much," Toby explained as he clogged up the wobbly steps to the deck. "Listen, I'm kinda dry. You got anything to help me out?" He watched as Flathead opened the ratty screen door and walked out to meet him.

"You are a lucky little Turd today. Boys came up last night from Jersey and brung me a nice present. In on the table. You got your own shit, don't you?" Flathead nodded toward the inside.

Toby just licked his lips and slid past the big man into the house. To the left was the living room, more an oversized hallway running back toward the rear. The only furniture was a slab of plywood set up on cement blocks in the middle of the room and two sets of car seats, one on either side. The woman was in one of the seats and some old guy Toby had seen around here before in the other. To the right was the small kitchen with a half table stuck to the side of the trailer and two chairs. The table was piled with food boxes and dirty dishes.

The picture hung on the wall between the living room and the kitchen table. Toby was looking between the rubbish for the dope but couldn't help himself and took a long look at the fading oil painting. The young naked woman had flowing blonde hair and large breasts that didn't droop. Her nipples were a rosy pink and not too wide. She had dark pubic hair and her firm full legs were spread just a bit to tease the viewer with what was between. Toby was always puzzled why the picture still hung there. After all, the woman sitting in the living room had aged terribly since she posed for it. *To each their own,* he thought.

The plastic bag was nearly full. Toby knew Flathead didn't use the stuff very much. It was really for the woman and her customers. The old guy was probably getting some of it too.

Flathead came in through the door and said, "Do your thing then come on out for a sit down. Go over it again before we go get our ride." Toby took the bag and went past the woman and into the bathroom. In a few minutes, the methamphetamine would surge through him and rebuild his false strength and courage. Toby unpacked his needles from a black leather case and set to work.

~ * ~

"Come on, old man, we're rolling now!" Ken urged from his perch at cloud base above the forest. The 1-26 was dancing in the lift like it was one of those dainty fiberglass high performance sailplanes. That's what made flying it challenging. You had to work for every mile. It didn't have all the sleek wingspan and technology of the $200,000 plus European models. But today Mother Nature was providing the difference. Ken had slipped south to the next cloud street and was using the lines of lift to streak ahead at up to eighty miles per hour airspeed and with the tailwind that converted to almost ninety-five over the ground.

"Crossing Bear Gap now. I'm going to stay with this street until I get on the other side of the mountain. Plenty of breathing room," Ken added.

Sam had struggled along the two lane portion of 322 behind a couple of slow campers. He broke out and passed them on the four lane section as he crossed over the southern end of the same ridge Ken was crossing ten miles northeast of him. Sam caught up each time Ken stopped to circle in a thermal as he jumped between the cloud streets. Sam did a quick map check and scratched his plan to run northeast toward Ken on the narrow mountain roads. At the speed Ken was traveling, Sam thought it would be better to risk losing radio contact and run ahead to Lewistown and pick up the wider U.S. 522 for the run back to the northeast.

The radio quieted down, losing the chatter from the locals back at the airport. Sam drove up and down the ridges and finally lost Ken as he entered the outskirts of Lewistown. There was still very little traffic and Sam managed to avoid the campers and log trucks, slipping onto 522.

Within ten miles he heard Ken again, "Badger ground, you copy?" Sam heard the confidence in his voice and reported in.

"Loud and clear. Ten miles northeast of Lewistown. What's your status?"

"Hit heavy sink jumping streets near Walker Lake. I'm okay now.

Running on course about halfway between the lake and the river," Ken called.

Sam knew the river was about the halfway point to Kutztown. That meant Ken would be way ahead of him by the time he drove all the way north to Sunbury to cross the river. His other option was to turn around and go back south to 322 and cross the river at Duncannon. Farther from the course, but better roads and quicker.

He pulled over into the lot of a gas station near the top of a hill and got the map out. "Help me decide where to cross the river, Ken. I'll be closer to you if I run north, but once I cross, it's slow going from there and I don't think I can keep up." Sam let the microphone button go.

"Easy. Go back down 322. I'm going to run south before I get to the river and jump two or three streets. I want to run over the hills on the other side without having to stop and thermal," Ken said.

Made sense to Sam. He got the Pathfinder and trailer turned around to retrace his path.

~ * ~

Jimmy spotted what he was looking for as they drove through Zolfo Springs. The repair garage was closed and the lot had ten or fifteen vehicles parked outside next to the building and tucked in front of a cluster of trees. A couple had for sale signs, but the rest looked like they were waiting to be fixed. Buried three deep on the side of the building was a Ford half ton pick-up covered with a layer of dust.

"Drive 'round the back, Russ. Slow up and let me out and then circle. Take me just a minute or two and ya can get me again." Jimmy stuck two screwdrivers in his side pocket and as Russell pulled behind the building, Jimmy stepped out of the still moving car.

Russ pulled ahead and disappeared around the corner as Jimmy dropped between the cars and worked his way up to the back of the truck. He was lucky today. The tag was still good and was on with two straight head screws. Jimmy quickly worked the tag off and slid it into the back of his pants. He only had to wait a bit for Russell to come back around and they were back out onto 17 and going north without anyone seeing them.

"Still got five months on it," Jimmy said, showing the truck plate to Russ before he pushed it under his seat. "Never miss it before we're done with her."

"We need gas, little brother," said Russ.

"Stop at the big station up in Wauchula," Jimmy ordered. He reached behind him and grabbed a beer. It lasted three gulps and was gone. Jimmy sipped on the next one for the short trip to the next town.

Wauchula straddled U.S. 17 and was just starting to come alive. Church was out and folks were moving between home and the stores or to Grandma's. The gas station was busy, but Russ found an empty pump and shut off the Mustang.

Jimmy handed Russ a couple of twenties and told him to get two quarts of 10W-30 and another six pack. Jimmy got the gas pump going and raised the hood. He was right. The dipstick showed it was a quart low. The second quart would get them home later on. He stopped the pump and grabbed paper towels from the island. Russ ambled out the door with a couple of grocery bags and Jimmy met him at the car.

"Wanna burrito?" Russ offered the sack of burritos to Jimmy and tried not to drop the one he had in his hand.

"Fuck no. Make me have to shit. Gimme the oil," Jimmy said.

Russell shrugged and tried to jump back out of the way of the greasy blob falling from the rolled mess. He didn't make it and ended up with a big stain on the front of his shirt.

"Jesus, Russ. Try getting some of that in your mouth."

With the car gassed and new oil inserted for the tired engine to burn, they headed north. At Ft. Meade, Jimmy told Russ to go west on a county road and then north again a few miles farther. The pasture land of Florida cattle ranches started changing over to barren stretches of gray sand and little vegetation. In the distance, on both sides of the road, they could see huge digging cranes reaching up into the sky.

The phosphate industry supplies huge amounts of fertilizer dug from open pits and stored on artificial mountains built up to be hauled by truck and train to the port at Tampa or across to Jacksonville. The gray-green dirt contained the remains of the oceans that used to cover Florida. The paved road they were on was intersected by white sand drives leading off through the scrub back toward the phosphate mountains. Jimmy made Russell slow up each time they came to one and they turned onto a couple only to have to retreat out of the sugary sand before they got stuck and had to dig out.

They came to one of the drives that had shell spread over the sand. Russell eased onto the road and followed it almost a half mile back into the pits. The palmettos on the sides of the narrow driveway reached out and snipped at them in spots as they passed. The tips of the fan shaped leaves showed where they had been bruised and ripped by passing vehicles. Around several bends, they came to an open parking lot. At the far end was a lopsided office trailer that sagged at the roof and appeared to be sitting in a hole at one end.

Several dust and phosphate covered Mack truck tractors sat at the south end and half a dozen Ford and Chevy pick-up trucks were parked at random angles at the opposite. A chain link gate blocked the path into the mine next to the office. Signs warned any and all to beware of the danger and not to trespass. The Santee brothers ignored the signs and scanned the office for any movement.

Space for parking in front of the office was empty and Jimmy said, "Swing around like we're lost and pulling back out. Stop by the end of the lot and let's see if anyone stirs."

Russell had to think about what Jimmy said, but it clicked and he did a turn around and started back the way they came in. Before he left the lot, he stopped and Jimmy got out and walked around to the rear of the Mustang, looking at the rear tires. He looked back at the beat up old trailer to see if anyone was looking at them. He stood there for almost five minutes, leaning his butt against the trunk and fiddling with the Exxon map he pulled out from the backseat.

"What the fuck, Jimmy? What are you doin'?" Russell sounded frustrated. There was no shade and no air moving in the stopped car. "Fuckin' hot out here."

Jimmy made Russell shut off the car and listened for another minute. He walked back to the passenger side and leaned in. "Pull over by the pick-ups, let's see if they made it easy for us."

Russell started the car and turned back through the lot to where the pick-up trucks sat. They both got out and started checking the driver's side doors. The third one Jimmy tried was a white Ford four wheel drive and Jimmy found it unlocked. He pulled it quickly open and dropped the visor over the steering wheel. He jumped back and almost got stuck in the eye by the keys as they fell.

"Got one!" he shouted to Russell. Jimmy hustled back over to the Mustang and slipped the tag he had stolen from the truck at Zolfo Springs and the screwdrivers out from under the seat. He met Russell at the back of their new truck where they took off the tag and put on the one they brought. They set to work swapping tags on the other trucks until they had switched several, putting the tag from the soon to be missing truck on one of the other Fords. Jimmy folded the left over tag twice and pitched it twenty yards out into the swampy thick brush just beyond the lot.

"Take a few days to figure this out," Jimmy snickered. "I'll folla you. Stop at the road and honk if it's clear."

The truck still had just over half a tank of gas and started right up. Knucklehead that last drove it was too lazy to run the keys back to the trailer; all the better for the brothers. Russell drove ahead and Jimmy stayed back about thirty yards. As they neared the paved road, Jimmy stopped and waited. He could see Russell pull up and stop where he could see both ways. Russell tooted the horn and waved his arm out the window for Jimmy to follow. Jimmy got the truck moving and got in behind Russell. Before they went much farther, Jimmy passed the Mustang. They turned west at the county road and headed the opposite way they had come in.

It burned some as he slid the needle out of his left arm. He tolerated this bit of discomfort for the buzz to come. The dope he had done this morning was just too little to really get him off. This gift from Flathead would launch him into his zone. He put his works away before he got all zippy and pissed before he went back through the living room. The woman was dressed in a red flannel shirt over pink sweat pants. Her bare feet were crusty with dirt around her toes and were a little yellow. She watched him pass and then turned back to the television playing country music videos with no sound. Might drown out the heavy metal roaring from a beat up stereo in the corner. The old man had left and Toby caught sight of him out of the front door walking down the drive to the road.

"He got no need to know anything," Flathead said when he saw Toby watching the old man. Toby glanced back at the woman and Flathead picked up on it, "She won't be any problem. Keep her mouth shut. Out on the porch?"

Toby nodded and followed the big man to the far end of the deck, "Your guy come through?" Toby asked.

McCall fished into his left front pocket and came out with a car key, "Stylin'. Toyota 4 Runner. Tinted windows and CD player. Says the used car manager let him have it for the weekend 'cause he sold over his quota for the month. Got it parked down at the Travel Stop. We'll switch there. If we have to dump it, he'll report it stolen."

Toby let all that sink in around the speed bubbling up through his insides. He pictured the hotel lot that was tucked in behind a burger joint next to the interstate. They could go in any direction from there. *Drop the Toyota and split; me in my truck and Flathead on his Harley. Change shirts or jackets, stop for some stuff in Lehighton, run back up the mountain, split up the take.*

Flathead hit him on top of the head with a metal ashtray, "Pay fuckin' attention. You and your fucking crank. Snap out of it, Turd." McCall took a long drink on a bottle of beer and waited for Toby to settle himself into a chair. Toby couldn't sit still now that the dope was working, but he tried to at least look like he was listening to Flathead.

"Sorry. Just running it through my head," Toby said.

McCall went over the plan and Toby told him that the place would have a wad of cash. By the end of the day, only the owner and one or two of the employees would be left. As long as they did what they were told, they'd be poorer, but alive.

Flathead tossed the bottle into the weeds growing below the end of the porch and said, "You want a beer to ease off the edge. We got a couple hours to kill off."

~ * ~

Sam lost radio contact with him a couple of times, but as Ken made his way down the river, it was less critical. "Lots of real heavy sink spots between thermals, but six hundred to eight hundred up to cloud base once I get centered. Go on ahead and start up toward Tower City. I shouldn't have any problem. One more thermal and I'm crossing the river." Ken sounded like he was really enjoying the work.

"Badger ground, copy. Moving on," Sam replied and pulled into the left lane on 322. He had hesitated on a high spot to make sure he could talk to Ken and now could make time on the highway. Sam hoped they could do this again before Ken had to report to the Academy. Maybe run a cross country up to the gliderport at Beltzville or down to Morgantown.

Their last outing didn't work out so well. The previous November was a busy time for both of them. Thanksgiving weekend followed two weeks of misery for Sam. The holiday was supposed to be ridge running from Jack's gliderport, but rain and clouds limited their ridge running to one day and then kept them grounded until that Saturday. The clouds broke, but the winds were too light to push over the ridge and create lift for sailplanes. They decided to take the rented Cessna 182 and fly northeast to Wellsboro and have a delayed Thanksgiving with Grandpa and Grandma Deland. During the flight, Ken finally got Sam to talk about what had happened in Philadelphia with Ozzie.

*"Life's too short, Ken," Sam told his son over the intercom as Ken piloted them over the farm field covered valleys and sparsely populated forests 3500 feet below. "I'm not real sure how much longer I want to stay on The Job. Ozzie and I were damned lucky. It could have gone the other way and I don't ever want to have to look into Marie's eyes and tell her bad news." Ken thought about that and a bit of a chill shuddered up his back and into his neck.*

*Sam told Ken how he and Ozzie survived a shootout in Philadelphia with a wanted murderer. The bad guy got the worst of it and ended up in a body bag. Both of them had never even shot at anyone before. It was a good shooting, though. They dodged fire from a .45 Colt and saved the life of a Philly cop in the process. But what felt like endless hours of questioning by Philadelphia Homicide and the Bureau of Professional Responsibility, the state police version of internal affairs, was grueling.*

*Sam knew one of the BPR sergeants asking the questions, but the other one, the homeliest woman he'd ever seen, twisted everything he said and tried to play him and Ozzie against each other. She picked at every detail of the week long investigation of a double murder that led Sam and his troopers to Philadelphia to arrest the shooters. Finally, when Sam turned on her and made her admit she had never conducted a murder investigation and had only made traffic or misdemeanor arrests, it got tense. Taught Sam a lesson about himself and how poorly he suffered fools.*

*In the end they were cleared and went back to work. Sam's lieutenant, a real dickhead named Harman, wanted Sam and Ozzie gone and wore out several red pens sending back reports that didn't meet his standards and harassed them constantly with administrative bullshit. Sam still wasn't out from under the prick's thumb. The holiday came just in time; gave him a little break.*

*"I have a hearing in Philly on Wednesday, but we can get in a day of deer hunting before you go back to school," Sam told Ken. Ken saw the wind drift was weaker than he had planned and turned a few degrees east, adjusting his course and resetting the trim.*

*"Grandpa said we can get a bit of pheasant hunting in this afternoon. Both he and the dog need the exercise," Ken said. Grandpa Deland had a pretty fair Brittany and, when he wasn't driving his fuel oil truck, in the spring and summer farmed leased fields that they could hunt. Saturday was the last day of small game season. The first day of buck season, nearly a state holiday, was the Monday after Thanksgiving. Pennsylvania public schools closed that day and Varnum Military Academy went along, giving the cadets a long weekend.*

*Sam said, "Forecast says we can fly back tomorrow. No low clouds until Monday afternoon. Shouldn't be too cold for opening day. Ozzie and Junior will be over early. They're anxious to find that nice big buck they've spotted lurking on the mountain."*

*Sam's converted barn sat on a couple of hundred acres and backed up to a couple of thousand on the mountain owned by a university. Sam was the unofficial "warden" for the university property and was allowed to hunt on it for his watchful eyes the rest of the year. Ozzie's big buck had survived a few hunting seasons on that tract and Sam's cornfields kept him fat and healthy.*

*Sam, Ken, and Ozzie planned to try to push the wily deer past Junior on opening morning.*

*Movement on the instrument panel caught Sam's eye. Ken was right with him and brought the single engine plane a few degrees to the right and watched the needles move on the dial. Wellsboro had no tower and Visual Flight Rules applied. Ken knew the light winds were generally from the north and northwest, so it would be a mild crosswind landing on the small paved strip, probably runway 28 back to the west. He would decide when he got within sight of the airport. Less than a half hour later, Ken reached forward and reduced the throttle setting and let the nose drop. The altimeter slowly unwound until Ken leveled at two thousand feet. Within minutes, he could see the airport ahead on the left, crossed over the runway and turned to parallel it for his downwind leg.*

*"28's the active," Ken said over the intercom. He picked up the radio microphone and announced his arrival on the Unicom frequency. Ken fed in flaps and activated the landing gear. This plane had retractable gear which allowed it to have a much higher cruising speed.*

*Sam confirmed the green lights for the landing gear, and Ken turned base then final. Only one other plane in the area, well off to the east and of no concern for his landing, Ken eased down on the pavement and when the main gear settled, lowered the nose gear to the ground and got on the brakes. Sam spotted the big red GMC pick-up parked by the office and thought he saw his dad's meaty arm waving to them.*

*"Your grandpa's already here. Looks like an empty tie down near the end of the line. Head for that," Sam said. Ken turned off the runway and taxied back toward the east end of the airport and into the tie down space. It only took a few moments for Ken to shut everything down and set the switches. Sam climbed out the side door and began pulling their gear from the rear. Ken followed him out and slipped the tie down ropes into place at each wingtip as Grandpa walked over from the parking lot.*

*"Nice landing; you or Kenny?" asked the older man. His handshake and hug of Sam was strong and genuine.*

*"Genius dropped it right on the centerline. This country will be a lot safer once they put an F-22 under him," Sam grinned to his dad. "How's Mom?"*

*"In heaven, cooking the last two days for you fellas. You don't eat it all, I'm gonna gain ten pounds before Monday," he laughed.*

*"Hi, Grandpa!" Ken jumped at his grandfather and was picked up off his feet by him. Ken reached down and poked his grandad's sides and was dropped back to the ground, "You're getting soft. We need to burn some of that fat off. How you been?"*

*"Bored. Got the last of the corn in and fuel oil deliveries have been slow with this warm weather. Need some snow to pry open their wallets. Glad you two are here, it's been too long." Grandpa helped with the bags and the shotguns and they went over to the parking area and dumped it into the bed of the truck.*

*"Grandma was up at five this morning putting pies in the oven. She's gonna be real happy to see you. We'll get her to feed us lunch and visit then we'll take Brush out to the fields, let her push up a rooster."*

*His Brittany was a pretty good bird dog, but more of a pet for the last few years. Ken hadn't been back here since summer. It was a Deland family tradition that Ken spent the summer in Wellsboro and helped Grandpa with the haying and other farm work. Ken drove a tractor for three years before he ever got to drive a car, but knew his next summer would be cut short. Other obligations in Colorado Springs.*

*After many hugs and kisses with Grandma, they ate too much lunch and got caught up on the family's news. Before the food put them to sleep, they got into hunting clothes and put the excited bird dog into her travel box in Grandpa's truck. Some of the fields Jacob Deland farmed were out west of town a short ways. They parked and let Brush down. She moved into the harvested field and worked through the left over corn stubble. Sam and his dad spread out and put Ken in the middle. The dog was out about twenty five yards, and they followed her into the field.*

*Sam missed the first pheasant Brush nosed from the edge of the field. Grandpa and Ken let him hear about it, and Ken dropped the next two that flew.*

*"That's my limit, Dad. You can shoot at the next one," Ken said as he unloaded his shotgun. "Tough getting old, isn't it? Eyes aren't what they used to be."*

*At that, two birds flushed and split above the elder Delands. Sam and*

*Grandpa both shot at one and dropped both. Brush was frozen for a moment, trying to decide which to retrieve, but went to Grandpa's first then found Sam's several rows into the corn stalks. They hunted hard for the next hour, but only launched a couple of hens; too far for a shot. The day ended early so they could get back to spend some time with Grandma.*

*Ken had that look in his eye. Grandma picked it out and dropped down next to him on the couch. "Potatoes will be a few more minutes," she said, wiping her hands on a dishtowel. "Your dad's cleaning the pheasants with Grandpa Jake. I'll send a couple of them back with you. Sooo...when do I get to meet her?"*

*Her hazel eyes still had that twinkle Ken remembered from when he was just a little bit. She and Grandma Landis had helped raise him since his mom died when he was two. Summers and most holidays here in Wellsboro and the school year was with his other grandma, until seventh grade when he went to Varnum.*

*"M...m...meet her?" Ken stuttered.*

*"Yes, I said when do I get to meet her? Grandmas know these things. Your dad mentioned you had a good trip out to the Penn State game in Illinois two weeks ago. Something about a girl. Out with it."*

*She melted him with her smile. Ken told her about Grace and how they met when he and his dad flew out to Champaign.*

*"She's just a real nice girl. It clicked when we met. Something about her. Even though she's older, I don't think that matters. She lost her dad a couple of years ago, and I can talk to her about how I feel about losing someone. I can talk to her about anything." Ken took his grandmother's hand and kissed it. "I'll see how it goes, Grandma. I'm hoping to see her at New Year's. If Penn State makes it to the Orange Bowl, Dad will be flying the rich guys down to Miami. Grace's grandmother lives there, and she might be able to shift her schedule to meet. If not, her mom lives up in Sarasota and we might meet there instead. You know I can't get too wrapped up in this. Not with the Academy coming up." Ken watched as Grandma cleared her throat and turned directly toward him.*

*"I know you're about the smartest thing this family's seen since your dad. You'll do just fine. I waited for Jake until he came home from his second trip through Vietnam. It seemed like a long time then, but it really wasn't.*

*Keep busy and don't give up on your dream. Make these things fit into it." She planted a kiss on his forehead and bounced back to the kitchen. Ken walked through behind her out into the yard and spent the next half hour pulling burrs from Brush's legs and chest.*

*The next morning, Ken was up at dawn and took his morning run through the streets of the small town. From the quiet street at the edge of town where Grandma lived into the worn, but clean downtown. The old brick buildings still stood and although the faces changed here and there on the storefronts, there were still shops that Ken remembered from years ago.*

*He was worried about his dad. The Philadelphia shooting had started to change him. He rarely used to talk about work but now seemed to be burdened by it. Ken listened to him complain about the stiff management and pettiness of his bosses. Very unusual. Ken ran back past the house and out of town. The road steepened and he pushed himself hard up the grade and out past the damp and quiet fields until his heart seemed to want to jump out of his chest.*

*At the top of the second hill, he turned and cruised back down, walking and cooling down the last half mile. He spotted the lone figure jogging toward him from town and recognized his father slogging along in heavy sweats and hiking boots. Ken waved and they sat together on the grass in front of the house.*

*"Town hasn't changed too much since I was your age," Sam said as he pulled off his hooded sweatshirt and wiped his face. "Nice and quiet, no hustle and bustle. Makes me think what might have been different if I'd stayed. No Villanova, no navy, no state police. Yep, a lot different."*

*"No me," Ken put an end to Sam's feeling sorry for himself. Sam started to say something, but stopped and just tilted his head and looked at Ken.*

*After a ridiculously huge breakfast and the obligatory packages of food to take home, Grandpa drove them back to the airport. "She expects you for Christmas, son," Jacob Deland told Sam.*

*"You bet, Dad. We'll be here. Probably be going to Miami for New Year's, though. Lovestruck youth yonder is counting the days."*

*Sam and his dad both laughed and Ken, who was untying the plane, just looked at them funny.*

"Badger ground, you copy?" Sam heard the radio bark. He had been thinking about Thanksgiving and must have been driving on autopilot. He was just coming into the town of Lykens tucked in between rows of hills running southwest to northeast east of the river.

"Ground copies, go ahead," Sam replied.

"I'm crossing Interstate 81 at Pine Grove; plenty of lift. Might as well head direct to Kutztown; I'm not going to need you," Ken advised.

"Roger, Badger, I'll cut cross country, but you'll probably beat me there. Order me a Pepsi and the stuffed peppers." Sam smiled at how well Ken had handled this flight. Good conditions and good planning added up to a great time. He made the turn at the next town and cut up and over the ridges until he hooked into Interstate 78 and headed east at 70. He heard from Ken twice more, both good reports and was forty miles from Kutztown when Ken reported he was running for the airport and had it in sight.

~ * ~

The county road stopped at State Road 37. Jimmy turned them south and then west to I-75. They got off at the airport exit and pulled into an industrial park near the end of the runway. The rented spaces held a variety of businesses that were all closed. At the end of the road was a small frame house with a broken front porch. Behind the house was a fairly new, steel double garage. The bay doors were closed, but they could see through the window that the lights inside were on.

Jimmy parked their newly acquired pick-up in front of one of the doors and Russell stopped the Mustang behind him. Before they could get out, the side door of the house flew open and the double barrels of a shotgun preceded its holder out of the door. Jimmy stopped halfway out of the truck and shouted, "It's Jimmy Santee, Miss Ellie. Just here to see the boys. They in the shop?"

The shotgun lowered and a woman, bent over from arthritis and well past seventy, squinted at the arrivals. Apparently recognizing them, she spit a gusher of black tobacco juice in Jimmy's direction and nodded toward the garage. Without saying a word, she shuffled back into the house and slammed the door. Welcome.

Russell followed Jimmy to the side door and they went in. Inside the air was misty and filled with the heavy plastic smell of automotive spray paint. Jimmy could hear the hiss of the sprayer over the drumming roar of the air compressor driving it. The small man with the sprayer was bent over the front fender of the car he was working on and had only a set of goggles and a blue bandana over his face.

"You're gonna die from this shit, Popper. Eat up your liver. How you been?" Jimmy shouted. The sprayer stopped and when the figure stood up, he was only just over five feet and thin as a matchstick. It took a few moments, but the compressor finally caught up and shut off.

"Fine and dandy, Jimmy boy. Hey, Russell. Whooee that paint makes me zipped. Come on outside, we'll roll one." Popper was a good old boy. His mom, Miss Ellie, was born in the little yellow house and intended on dying there too. The industrial park tried to buy it from Miss Ellie, but she wouldn't hear of it. Popper snapped the goggles over his head and walked over to a row of paint cans stacked on a single shelf on the back wall. He pulled a plastic bag of pot out of one of the cans and followed Jimmy and Russell back out of the side door.

"That part of the last batch we did?" Russell asked.

"Gettin' low. 'Bout time for you to make another run down to Naples. What you hear from our friends in Miami?" Popper turned to Jimmy as they went around the back of the garage to a small yard walled in on three sides by seven foot hedges of Brazilian pepper trees. The overhanging branches and twisted trunks formed a thick barrier from the dumpsters at the end of the parking lot next door. A small, rusted, round metal table sat surrounded by six different colored and shaped lawn chairs. A sixty year old oak shaded the spot and the temperature was five degrees cooler in the vegetation ringed alcove.

Popper dropped into one of the chairs and produced rolling papers that quickly turned into a fat joint. Between hits, Jimmy told Popper he had a paint job for him and needed to get some cash together so they could do another load of grass. They were pretty small time and the dark haired dudes in Miami only dealt in cash, no upfront dope.

"We got somethin' cookin' with the truck. Soon as we get ahead, we'll run down south and do a deal," Jimmy looked back at the stolen truck. "Navy blue. Yeah, I think I want it navy blue. Pick her up on Tuesday, Okay?"

Popper squinted through the smoke of the last hit on the joint and said, "Yeah, Tuesday, late, though. After supper."

The brothers left Popper to mellow on the paint fumes and reefer and turned the Mustang south toward the beaches. Some of the colleges were out and the scenery was outstanding.

~ * ~

Flathead thought about taking the Low Rider down the mountain but didn't want to leave it in the motel parking lot for even a little while. He knew how often Harleys got stolen; he'd gotten his that way. Toby didn't argue when Flathead took the keys to Toby's truck from him and drove. Before they had gone out of sight of the trailer, Flathead began bitching about the truck being out of gas.

"You stupid asshole. You knew we were doin' this thing today. You blow all your money on broads and dope like some teenager," Flathead growled and yanked the truck around the curves down toward the river.

"Aww, give me a break. Things been real slim lately. Spot me twenty and take it outta my share. Okay, Head?" Toby whined. He was too wired to be afraid that McCall was going to put the Chevy into the rocks hanging off the mountain just feet from the door next to Toby.

McCall ignored him, horsing the pick-up out onto the highway and then into the lot of the gas station at the next crossroad. "Pump the gas, Turd. Stay with the truck." Flathead slammed the door and marched into the store to pay, hoping nothing else went wrong the rest of the afternoon.

"Gonna blow up yer truck." McCall didn't get it at first. The plump little gray haired man punched the cash register and looked back out the window toward the pumps where Toby stood next to his truck. "He retarded or something?" the man said to McCall.

Flathead dropped money onto the counter and shot a look out to where Toby stood over the hose pumping gas into the truck with a lit cigarette hanging loosely in his mouth. McCall winced and tried to grin at the man behind the counter, "Don't read too well and not very bright," he mumbled and spun for the door. *Nosey little prick.*

He cleared the step down to the paved lot and made for Toby. "Stop at twenty and ditch the butt. Fuckin' jerk inside thinks he's the smoking police."

Toby's mind was somewhere else at that moment and could only respond, "Huh?"

## Chapter Three

Debbie and Hank Wellenhoffer worked well together. She had the head for business and he loved to play in the dirt. What started as a part time tree nursery had grown into a well-stocked and very popular home and yard supply store. The fields around them used to be farmland. Now, housing developments and office parks shared the available space with huge truck shipping terminals that took advantage of the road networks and hard working locals for employees.

Allentown was only a few miles to the east, and after the steel mills cut back in the seventies, the area reformed itself into a prosperous and diversified business community. Debbie began by growing dogwoods and flowering crabs on the one hundred and fifty acres that had been her grandfather's small dairy farm. Hank was a salesman for a company that made springs and wire for the steel trade. He lasted only a short year after the mills began to shrink before he got laid off and found himself in one too many screaming sales meetings at the Lincoln dealership where he had ended up selling cars.

Daydreaming one day about a new mix of potting soil for Debbie's seedlings, the sales manager appeared before him frothing about the monthly quota, "Hank! Don't you care? Don't you have any pride? How can you sleep at night? You have to push harder, close the deals! Now, the way I see it, you've got to move an additional..."

The sales manager was looking at a printout and was standing so close to Hank that Hank could smell the stale smoke on the manager's clothes. Hank stood right up from his seat and slid past the manager, who looked up from the papers in surprise. Hank pulled at his necktie and dropped it in the trash can at the door. The receptionist watched him cross the showroom. Hank could hear the conference room door open behind him and the manager yelling something at him as he hit the side door and walked toward his car. Cheap bastards didn't even let them have demos.

Hank never looked back and only spoke briefly on the phone to the owner later the next day to tell him it hadn't worked out and he was going to pursue other options. Debbie was worried, but the farmhouse was paid for and they could make out somehow. They laughed about it now; Hank hadn't moped around at all. He started retailing spring annuals and fall mums from a roadside stand and now they had three pole buildings and ten plastic covered greenhouses clustered at this end of the farm. Debbie designed the sales areas and sold crafts and country art along with the lawn and garden stuff. Business was real good. Especially during spring planting season. The parking area filled up with mini vans and sport utility vehicles, and each Monday they had trucks delivering extra plants because they couldn't grow enough by themselves.

Saturday and Sunday were the big days of the week for them. It started early and the last customers stayed until nine Saturday night and until five on Sunday. More than once, Debbie would be running receipts in her little office in what used to be her dining room when a horn tooted and some desperate housewife wanted her to open up and sell a tray of petunias. All in all, life was good and they were happy and getting rich.

All this required them to put in long hours. Debbie wanted kids, but it never worked out. Finally, they went to a special doctor and found out why. She didn't seem to mind and put even more effort into the business. She mothered her two Labrador Retrievers, Salt and Pepper, and they followed her around as she waited on customers. Salt was the yellow Lab and Pepper was, obviously, the black one. Litter mates that Hank had brought home from a trip to Chester County to buy impatiens seedlings. Debbie loved her "boys" and dressed them in matching red bandanas. The boys wandered among the customers and slobbered over the kids. They withstood the ear twisting and tail pulling and the parents seemed to appreciate the distraction so they could shop.

When they really got going, Hank hired local kids to work part time at the garden center. As they grew, they decided to have at least two yard boys full time from May to November and went through several, always seeming to be short-handed. Hank got a call from a former steel salesman buddy who was now working for county probation asking if Hank would consider putting some of the troubled youth to work as part of their rehabilitation. Hank and Debbie finally agreed, and with few exceptions, found the kids to be more bluff than bad and got them to put their energy into tossing bales of peat moss rather than each other. Most had crappy home lives and the spare bedroom upstairs in the old farmhouse was often occupied by one or two of the more desperate kids. Hank would hear Debbie talking to a customer or a supplier and sometimes didn't know if she was talking about the Labs or the help when she used the word "boys."

This beautiful Sunday afternoon was busy for them. Debbie had to empty the cash register several times, stuffing the twenties, fifties and hundreds into paper bags and taking them into the house where she hid them in the freezer she kept in the mudroom next to the kitchen. She never really thought seriously about anyone stealing it; never happened before. Everyone around here seemed to be regular folks, and she was sure the cash would be safe until she could make up the deposit for Hank to take to the night deposit after they closed.

Salt and Pepper followed her back out to the customers and she could see Hank and one of the boys loading landscape timbers into a truck at the end of the lot. The boy and Hank worked well as a team, and that made Debbie feel happy. She treated the yard boys more like family than employees. The other kid was watering flats in the next greenhouse connected by an archway with the main pole barn where she had her checkout area. Debbie heard him whistling something.

This summer was going to be a good one, she thought. New houses going up all around making for plenty of customers and two good helpers for her and Hank. She never thought about the ones that hadn't worked out. Like the kid three years ago who they had to let go because he just couldn't seem to show up every day. The skinny kid with the drug problem. She never wondered about what happened to him; too busy with everything else.

~ * ~

Grace slipped into the stark empty hallway beyond the security door and hurried to the open door on the left. She brushed a stray strand of black hair away from her dark eyes and wrinkled her nose at the smell of stale coffee. The small crew office at the hub of the terminal provided little privacy but did have a computer to give her access to e-mail. She hated typing on her smartphone and couldn't afford a tablet yet, so the terminal would have to do. She got a pre-packaged salad from the oversized vending machine and sat down at the computer table in the far corner to write Ken.

Her schedule changed and she would be arriving in Philadelphia earlier than she had thought. Between bites of the limp salad, she typed a few lines and then hit a wall. She had to sit there for a few minutes so she could think of what to write. She knew she would have Kenny for five days and was trying to save the more delicate thoughts she was having for their time together. She decided to keep it short and sent the message off into cyberspace. The rest of the salad got pitched into the trash, and she started a second note to her mom in Florida.

She was real anxious to see Ken and wanted her mom to finally meet him. Their last time together had been at New Year's in Miami. A brief twenty hours together, four of them spent visiting her Cuban grandmother. Thank goodness her grandma never asked Ken if he was Catholic. Although Grace really didn't go that often to mass herself, Grandma would have expected her to only be involved with a good Catholic boy. Both of Ken's parents had been Protestant, his dad descended from French Huguenots and definitely not Catholic.

*Grandma Echaverria couldn't hear too well, so the conversation was limited and they spent most of the time talking about Grace's dad and how it was in Cuba before Fidel. Ken was staying in a hotel with Sam, who had flown a group of wealthy rabid Penn State football fans to the Orange Bowl to watch them squeak by Florida State.*

*Grace told Grandma about how she met Ken at the Penn State game in Illinois last November. When Ken excused himself to go to the bathroom, Grandma leaned over to Grace and said in Spanish, "Handsome young man. He has honest eyes and a strong chin. You can trust him. Do you love him, my little flower?"*

*Grace almost spoke, but paused and looked at her hands. Grandma reached and took them into her own and squeezed. Grace smiled and said, "I do, Grandmother. But he has much to do before we can go on. I love him that much. I have to let him make his place in his life. If we belong together, it will be easy."*

*Grandma then said in English, "Then I will pray to live long enough to hold my great grandson and tell him about his grandfather, great grandfather and the island." She straightened up and her eyes cleared. She was smiling broadly as Ken came back into the room and she made them both black bean soup with rice and fresh shaved onion before they left.*

~ * ~

Heck of a day. That's about the best way to describe it. Up early and in the woods with Ken, Sam was feeling it now. Pushing the Pathfinder and empty trailer east along I-78 toward the Kutztown exit, he was getting just a bit sleepy and had to roll down the window to let the fresh air howl around him to keep awake. Then it happened. The big rig in front of him whipped left without a signal and jumped into the median lane where Sam was ready to pass. He jammed the brakes and just missed losing the front of his truck. The rig drifted left over the line and gravel shot up and out from the big wheels, pelting Sam's windshield before Sam could slow enough to put some distance between him and the crazy trucker.

Sunday afternoon was a busy time on this road. Trucks heading into New York for Monday morning loads crowded the highway all the way back to Carlisle. The rest areas and truck stops between the Jersey line and greater New York would be packed tonight and empty out by early morning.

Sam cursed several times out loud to himself and decided to exit early and run Old 22 to get away from the tractor trailers. The two lane ran right next to the Interstate and even though it was slower, it was less hectic. Sam cruised at forty five through the farmland and could catch a glimpse of I-78 now and then between the trees. He didn't need to hurry, Ken was down at the airport and probably setting the 1-26 into its tie downs in the grass next to the paved runway.

The close call with the truck stirred Sam's thoughts. He thought about Ken's mom. Her young life had ended tragically when one of the hard driving, hard headed idiots that push trucks around for a living got all whacked out to stay awake longer and drove over a line of cars stopped on the turnpike. He walked away from it, but Linda and several others didn't. Ken was only two at the time and although his mom had been running around on Sam and was never happy in her marriage, a kid still needs his mom.

Sam came home from flying EA-6Bs off carriers and left the navy to take care of Ken. The fuel oil business in Wellsboro didn't seem to be what Sam wanted to do, so he wound up at the State Police Academy in Hershey. They were a bit displeased that Sam wasn't interested in flying their planes for them and sent him to Philadelphia instead of back upstate after graduation.

Later, the state police tried to make a big deal out of Trooper Sam Deland becoming a multi-millionaire from the accident settlement but failed. Sam dumped the money into the hands of a trust for Ken and only thought about it when the dividend statements came in the mail. Ken didn't find out until the background investigation for the Air Force Academy forced Sam to finally tell him the whole story. Didn't seem to change Ken any. Like it didn't matter. Sam hoped it would stay that way. Smartest thing he ever did, though, depending on how court in Philadelphia turned out tomorrow.

The big German shepherd jumped when the phone rang. He had been sleeping peacefully on the floor near the feed sacks at the back of the store while the pretty dark haired lady sat at her desk doing paperwork. Once Dutch decided his skill as the supreme protector of the woman he viewed as the alpha female wasn't needed, he dropped his ears and slipped his black and tan muzzle down between his front paws and went back to sleep.

"Hi, Kenny. Where are you?" Eileen Matthews said into the phone. Her liquid brown eyes sparkled when she heard the young voice on the line. Able to convince almost anyone she was under thirty, even though she wasn't, she had met Sam Deland at her country store when her town had been sent into a spin by the brutal shooting of her neighbors. Since then, Ken's dad had gotten himself involved with her and she with him. Nice involved, that is. Real nice involved.

Ken liked her too. She didn't push too hard on Sam. Sam had his own way of dealing with his lady friends. Since Ken's mom, Sam had a lot of hurt inside to put somewhere. Not getting in too deep with women was the usual path. That seemed to be slipping aside for Eileen, though.

"At the airport in Kutztown. Just flew the sailplane in from State College. Dad's behind about forty-five minutes with the trailer. You want to join us for supper at the diner next to the airport? Please?" Ken said from the airport office phone. Eileen lived in the little town of Porter fifteen miles from the airport. "Surprise him and cheer him up. He's got court in Philly tomorrow. The lawsuit."

Eileen stood up, holding the phone, spun and stuck her face in the mirror on the shelf behind her. *Not too bad for a working woman.* She brushed her denim shirt off and shrugged, "Oh, alright. I've got Dutch with me, okay to bring him?" she asked.

"Heck, yeah. I'll sneak a piece of pie out to him. Come on, it'll be fun," Ken pleaded.

"On my way, sweetie. See you in half an hour." Eileen hung up and grabbed her keys. At the first jingle, Dutch popped up to his feet and the tan dots over his eyes bounced back and forth between the door and Eileen. "Load up, big dog. Goin' to see Sam." The dog woofed and jumped straight up in the air. He had become pals with Sam and Ken, too, and raced to the door, nails scraping on the worn wooden floors. Eileen closed up her little grocery and feed store and they piled down the steps to her SUV for the ride over to Kutztown.

~ * ~

"Oh, baby. I'm in love again." Russell watched the teal blue bathing suit float by, barely covering the firm college girl within it. Jimmy watched, too, but didn't seem to be enjoying himself. Brooding over another beer, he wasn't getting into it. It was hot and they weren't dressed for the beach in their jeans and work boots. The last six-pack was getting warm and they needed ice.

"Let's go on down to Siesta Key. This place is too crowded," Jimmy growled. He watched the city police car cruise the parking lot for the third time since they'd been there. Russell started the Mustang and they slowly cruised back out onto Ben Franklin Drive and away from Lido Beach. Russ had to pick his way around St. Armand's Circle through all the tourists anxious to spend big bucks in the little shops packed onto the island. Finally, they picked up speed and crossed the causeway back into Sarasota.

The air was getting thick with humidity as the day got older and any air moving was better than nothing. Russ turned south on U.S. 41 and they drove quietly in the thick stop and go traffic to the south end of town where they turned west toward the beach again. Siesta Key was outside of the city, and the beach there was more wide open. Better beach, better parking areas and fewer cops. Jimmy told Russ to pull into the next store they saw and they got two fresh six-packs and stuffed the cans into a bag of ice on the floor of the back seat. Messy but effective. They made a second stop then went on to the beach.

It only took a little over a half hour before a pair of doe eyed girls agreed to hang out and have a beer. They were a shade under twenty and put up with the older rednecks for the free drinks. Neither was really pretty, and the blonde needed to lose fifteen or twenty pounds. Jimmy perked up and they actually had him laughing a couple of times. The girls loosened after the second beer and it looked promising. The parking lot was only about half full and no one seemed to notice.

"Come on, you can have one more can't you? You're not wimpin' out on us are you?" Jimmy told the girls. He let them fiddle with the radio and put on their stupid music. The third beer went down real quick, and they couldn't stop giggling at the stuff the jerk on the radio was saying between songs. Jimmy shot Russell a grin and the bottle of Jim Beam came out for the real party to begin.

~ * ~

"Shit, look at this traffic. All the big city folk headin' back to the asphalt and concrete." Flathead had to slow to sixty behind a line of cars before he could pass and ride the left lane through the tunnel. The turnpike was the main feeder to the Poconos from the Philadelphia area. Friday night it was packed northbound, and on Sunday everything was going back south again. Years ago, before the state opened a second tunnel through the zinc mined wasteland of a mountain that divided the Pocono plateau from the Lehigh Valley, traffic would back up past the exit for six miles. McCall and Toby had just gotten on there and although the traffic was thick as they drove south to the tunnel, it wasn't nearly as bad as it used to be.

Toby was restless. The dope Flathead gave him was good stuff. Had Toby wired up and feeling the push. He fiddled with his stringy hair, messed with the radio and rolled his window up then down then up again. Flathead noticed, "Jesus, you're makin' me nervous. Can't you sit still?"

"Wha..? Ahh... ahh, I'm okay. Yeah, okay," Toby didn't sound convincing. "You sure they won't be able to tell who we are? They ain't no dummies. You sure?"

Now Flathead was getting really annoyed. "Asshole! You just have to stand there and watch my back. Don't say a word. They never seen me and they ain't gonna see nothin' with us wearin' them hoods and big glasses." McCall had been to the surplus store and bought two double X large, hooded black sweatshirts and tinted ski goggles for their disguise. He told Toby they would just toss them in a dumpster after the robbery.

The turnpike flattened out a bit south of the tunnel, and they got off at the Allentown exit and went west on 22 and onto I-78. The Travel Stop motel was at the next exit tucked in behind a couple of fast food joints and a big gas station and mini mart. Flathead eased into the motel lot and was glad to see it was well over half full. The Toyota was in between a van and a Buick. Flathead pulled past and crossed into the next section of cars before he parked Toby's truck.

McCall didn't even look at Toby and said, "Here's the keys. Pick me up over at the burger place. Take the bag with you." Toby picked up the athletic bag with the sweatshirts and goggles and got out of the truck. He walked as slowly as his speeding system would allow and found the Toyota. Flathead waited a minute then locked up Toby's truck and walked across the lot to the restaurant.

Toby had to fumble with the key but finally got the door open and started the 4 Runner. He sat there and thought about what he was supposed to do next. *Did Flathead say to wait two minutes or ten?* He couldn't remember. Flustered, he tried to start the truck again and jumped when the starter emitted a shrill grinding sound.

"Shit," he mumbled. Toby hit the button and rolled down the window and took in a few gulps of fresh air and tried to calm down. He'd dealt dope, shoplifted and stolen from hunting cabins many times, but this was the first real stick up he'd been in on. The old revolver in his pants didn't give him much courage right now. Everyone who dealt speed carried guns. Toby had gotten used to that. Nearly caught stealing diapers and soda pop cases from the unlit back loading dock of a grocery store, he'd shot at a security guard one night just to scare him off but didn't hit him and didn't like the idea of having to actually shoot anyone. He hoped Flathead knew what he was doing.

McCall came back out with a drink in his hand and was pissed when he didn't see Toby. He waited for a minute then saw the black Toyota bump over the parking lot curb and lurch up to where he stood.

Flathead walked around to the driver's door and snatched it open. "Get the fuck out and let me drive, you fucking idiot!" Toby meekly slipped past him and walked around to the other side. Flathead threw the drink out into the parking lot and slammed the door behind him. Once Toby managed to move the bag and get into the seat, McCall wheeled the truck out of the lot and turned south on Route 100.

Marie watched them for several minutes. They had their backs to her and she could see her men busily cleaning the fish and yakking with each other while they worked. Her girls were here and there and Vinny was squealing happily with Connie in the family room. She pulled herself away and answered the phone that no one else seemed to hear. That meant the twins were outside or they would have been diving for it on the first ring. She wrote the information down for Ozzie. A quote on a bathroom over in Slatington for a lady they did a deck for last year. Ozzie had plenty of work and with Junior starting to help more, they were doing real well.

Her men were still at the bench next to the garage hosing off the scales and guts when she got back into the kitchen to work on the rest of the meal. During the week she didn't make a big dinner every night and she usually made a pot of soup or stew on the weekend to fill in on busy school nights. The kids all had spring fever now that it was staying light later into the evening and sometimes supper didn't get finished until after eight. Ozzie worked almost every night at one remodeling job or another after he got home from the barracks, and she sent soup and sandwiches with him to eat on the run.

She figured the fish for one night this week and the pot of ham and bean soup she was stirring would cover at least two other meals. She kept a calendar up on the fridge in between Katie's colorful artwork and it was covered with appointments and events her busy family had obligated themselves to. Marie stirred the big kettle of soup, replaced the cover and turned down the burner. A stuffed chicken and baked potatoes were in the oven for Sunday night dinner.

She slipped out of her apron and dropped into one of the kitchen chairs to lace up her cross trainers. "Connie, watch Vinny and Katie. I'm going for my walk. Daddy's outside if you need anything." She heard what sounded like an "okay, Mom" from the noise in the family room, and she banged out of the kitchen door and down the steps of the deck toward the garage.

"I'll be back," she called to Ozzie.

He spun and caught the pleasant sight of her caboose going down the driveway and whistled. "Go, baby, go!" he teased. She shot him the bird and then remembered Junior was there and let her other four fingers join the middle one in her salute.

"Mom!" Junior scolded and laughed with his dad. Junior scooped up the bucket with the cleaned fish and went into the house to wrap them and stick them in the freezer. Ozzie finished washing down the bench they used for cleaning fish, pheasants and rabbits and dropped the hose back into its pile next to the garage. The two car structure was separate from the house and was Ozzie's sanctuary.

The first bay was actually his workshop, and he had borrowed the other space today where he usually kept Marie's van to set up sawhorses. He had strips of baseboard trim stretched out and needed to put a coat of polyurethane on them so he could start installing them at the job he was finishing up on Monday night. He grabbed a tack cloth from the shelf over his painting bench and started rubbing the strips free of dust and grit. Junior bounded back out of the kitchen door onto the deck bouncing a basketball and followed closely by Katie.

He stopped at the bottom of the step when he saw his dad working and said, "Dad, you need any help with that?"

Katie looked at Junior and then at Ozzie and Ozzie just waved them off so they could shoot some hoops. Junior lowered the net and rebounded for Katie in her version of HORSE where she kept shooting until she decided it was Junior's turn. He made her laugh by stuffing several through the lowered net. Ozzie could hear them bantering and although that made him feel real good, he couldn't help but think about tomorrow. He rubbed the trim pieces and worked the sticky cloth into the grooves. The back of his mind was churning and even though the lawyers assured him it was all going to be fine, he still worried.

He tried to follow the psychologist's advice and keep it all in perspective. Ozzie figured he would never go to a shrink, but after the shooting, the bosses forced him. He tried to joke with the guy at first but listened and learned a little. That flickering movie reel playing over and over in the brain would not stop. Ozzie still saw the room and the muzzle of the big .45 pointed right at him, and he was still amazed that he didn't remember firing his own gun. But he had. So had Sam. They had no choice, really. That didn't make it any easier or make it go away. He had to deal with it and he did. Stubbornly and with great effort.

He still didn't like it when someone would come up to him and ask him about it, but he learned that if he just told it like it happened, it was better for him. Lawyers, that was the problem. Greedy lawyers and greedy relatives dragging him and Sam to court trying to wring money out of them and the state. *Screw 'em.*

~ * ~

The chubby blonde decided Jimmy was hers and the other one, who turned out to be nineteen, had latched on to Russell. Jimmy's dark mood was long gone, and they were all splashing in the cool salt water drunk as skunks.

The beer and bourbon had narrowed the age difference between the girls and the brothers, and they chased each other back and forth in the small chop until Jimmy finally got the blonde in his arms and dropped down into the shallow water with her sitting on his lap.

She leaned forward and planted a tongue filled kiss on him and slipped her top down around her waist. Jimmy popped an almost instant erection through his wet jeans when her soft slippery breasts melted against his chest. He kissed her back with a lot more interest now and let his hand move down the back of her thin suit bottom and found a handful of fleshy ass.

Russell and the redhead finally noticed the other two and that seemed to be all the girl needed to jump into Russell's arms and follow the leaders. The alcohol insulated them from the temperature of the springtime Gulf, but eventually they had to get out and warm up.

Jimmy went to the Mustang and got the old blanket that the Winchester was wrapped up in out of the trunk and spread it out on the white sand for them to lie on. They sipped on the Jim Beam, washed it down with warming beer and felt the sun. Russell was in love and Jimmy was trying to figure if he had enough money on him for a motel room.

~ * ~

For the first time that day, Debbie didn't have someone wanting something from her. She stood in the shop and looked around at all the plants out of place and started to straighten up. Hank was moving bags of fertilizer out to the front from the back barn, restocking the displays. There were still a few customers milling around in the sales areas and a bit of a cool breeze swept through the building around her. She glanced at her watch and wondered where the day had gone. So busy the last four hours, it had seemed like only one.

One of the yard boys, Mattie, came in to help get organized for Monday. He was a cute kid, just eighteen and had been staying upstairs for the past month. Both parents were either dead or long gone, even he didn't know. He got messed up with acting tough and growing up and only recently started putting things where they belonged in his life. Debbie and Hank offered him the room when his older sister got married and left for Arkansas. He worked hard and so far had stayed out of trouble. Mattie was trying to save money to buy a used car. He even borrowed a book to read the other day. Left Hank and Debbie staring at each other.

"I'm getting my hair cut tomorrow," he said. His long and thick brown hair was always pulled back into a frizzy pony tail. "Tired of it and it's too hard to keep clean in all this dirt."

Debbie smiled to herself and remembered Hank in his college pictures had a huge mop of hair and a scraggly beard. Now, he looked like a drill sergeant with his close cropped and just starting to gray top. "Sounds like you've thought about that a bit," Debbie replied.

Mattie turned to her and pulled a wrinkled scrap of magazine from his pocket. He unfolded it and handed it to her. The ad was for a technical institute in Allentown. "I...I...I think I might try to get in there to take some classes. It says I can get my G.E.D. and learn how to fix computers. If it doesn't cut in to my time here, that is," he looked at her and waited for her to say something.

Debbie read the ad for a second time and said, "I think it's a great idea. We can work your hours around it if we need to. Don't worry about that. Great idea." She smiled and reached over to him and gave him a hug. He didn't seem to know what to do, but eventually hugged her back and thanked her. He put the ad back into his pocket and started gathering up the orphan plants left out of place by the customers and put them back in the correct spots. Debbie got her straw broom and began clearing the floors and feeling all warm inside.

The next farm he passed was set back off the road a ways. In the big garden in the side yard he could see two barefoot Amish teenage girls walking out toward the barn in back of the house. In the field past the barn, a team of beautiful bronze draft horses grazed peacefully on their day off from the hard work required of them by the Amish farmer. Sam knew how demanding farm work was even with tractors and power machinery. He couldn't imagine the effort it would take to run a farm without electricity or a well-tuned John Deere.

Even his own place, though he leased the fields to a nearby company owned farm that planted and harvested them for their own dairy herd, required a lot of work keeping the grass cut and bringing in his winter wood supply. He needed his small Ford tractor to plow snow and haul the fire wood and wouldn't get it all done without it.

He was cutting cross country now and knew this area quite well. It was at the western end of the territory covered by Straus Valley barracks and he had been at some of these farms and small towns doing the state's work. When the road would straighten out, Sam snuck glances up at the crisp blue and white sky looking for movement. The radio had been quiet since Ken checked in last, but the 2-32 out of Kutztown just exchanged a pilot weather report with a glass bird coming in from Bucks County. No word about any 1-26s landing out.

If tomorrow turned out okay, he would be able to enjoy Ken's graduation on Wednesday. Ken, of course, didn't seem too concerned about anything but Grace coming in on a Tuesday afternoon flight. Sam and Eileen were going to cook them all dinner at Sam's and then let the kids go out somewhere by themselves. Then he and Eileen could act like adults.

Ken was excused from the mandatory practice sessions at Varnum but had to be there all Wednesday afternoon for the final run through before the ceremony. Ken made scholastic honors for all of his junior and senior year and had been selected for Honor Staff. That included a promotion to Cadet Major from 1st lieutenant and relief from drilling his platoon for the final parade. He would be standing in front of the reviewing stand with the other staff officers as the brigade marched past. The big deal was that he was excused from his finals and received leave through the weekend. Ken made good use of the time flying with his dad and counting the hours until he was meeting Grace.

As Sam neared the airport, he spotted the tow plane banking down from releasing a glider and floating into the downwind leg of the approach. The airport came up on the right and Sam slowed as he passed and turned into the lot on the far side of the office to pull into the taxi area. Their 1-26 was parked safely at the end of two lines of power planes in an open area private glider owners used to assemble their gliders and store trailers. Sam spotted the big black dog romping out from between two empty trailers chasing a well-worn tennis ball. It startled Sam for a moment, but he quickly recognized the shepherd and stuck his head out of the driver's side window and hollered, "Hey, Dutch!"

The dog's black ears shot straight up, and he whipped his head toward Sam, grinning at him from the Pathfinder's window. Now the dog couldn't decide if he was supposed to take the ball back or go see his pal, Sam. Eileen put him straight by walking up and taking the ball and telling Dutch to go get Sam. Sam stopped the truck and got out, knowing the big dog might just jump through the window if he didn't. Dutch ran like a mini locomotive at Sam, and the two grappled to the ground and wrestled for a couple of minutes until Sam gave up and ordered the dog up into the cab for the short ride to where Ken and Eileen had the 1-26 parked.

"Hey, lady. Wanna buy a dog, cheap?" Sam laughed as he pulled up. Dutch climbed over him and stuck his nose out of the window at Eileen and slobbered spit down the side of Sam's truck. His tail thumped against the passenger seat headrest as he vigorously wagged at the sight of his mom. Dutch didn't wait for Sam to open the door and bounded out, landing nearly ten feet from the Pathfinder.

"Surprise, sailor. Thought you two would like some intelligent conversation after being trapped together all weekend." Eileen took Sam's outstretched hand, and they came together for a quick kiss. Ken had Dutch's heavy leash and clipped him by the collar. The four of them visited for a few minutes and then Sam pulled the tie down stakes from the Pathfinder and they got the 1-26 secured and covered the canopy. Ken backed the trailer into a space opposite the glider and they all rode back out to the lot where Eileen put Dutch in her SUV and followed them across the end of the runway to the diner next door.

She left the windows down a bit and ordered the dog to stay. He watched anxiously as the three of them left him alone and went in to eat. The diner had rows of windows across the seating area for customers to watch the comings and goings of the small, but fairly busy airport next door. They got a booth with a good view and where they could keep an eye on the shepherd too.

Ken finally asked Eileen if he was being a bore talking to Sam about the flight and how well it had gone. She said no but changed the subject to Grace. "You going to be able to keep your mind on school?" Eileen sounded like a big sister.

Ken smiled and stirred his chicken rice soup. "It's not like that with us. I think about her all the time, but I still get everything done. If anything, I'm even more focused now." Ken hesitated and glanced at his dad then back to Eileen. "Grace doesn't play any of the little games girls sometimes do. She told me she regrets not always being honest with her father before he was killed. She's not going to do that with me. We both have a lot to get done and there will be plenty of time for an us later. We just enjoy each other while we're together. It's hard to explain but..." Ken ran out of words and Sam squirmed a bit in the seat.

"We're going to stay real busy while she's here then I'm going to soak up the Florida sun with her for a few days before I come back to get ready for the Academy. I promised the guys at the airport I'd help them do an annual on the Lear and I have at least four books to read, plus the physical training."

"You're making me exhausted just talking about it. Oh, look at the lost soul out there." Eileen nodded her head in the direction of her truck and the saddest looking dog they'd ever seen watching the door of the diner. Dutch was in the back of the SUV with his muzzle stuck out through the rear window. Sam wrapped several pieces of roast beef in a napkin and set it aside for the dog, and they finished up before his heart broke any more than it already had.

From where they sat on the small street between two big car dealerships, they could see the front of the garden center a quarter of a mile down the highway. A few customers had come and gone and a few were still milling about. "That's the husband with the wheelbarrow," Toby told Flathead. Toby handed the binoculars to McCall who took a long look and then caught sight of a matronly woman carrying a tray of flowers out to her green van in the parking lot. When she left, there was only one vehicle left in the lot, and it was twenty minutes past the closing time.

"Fuckin' straggler," McCall mumbled. He was back on the binoculars again and saw the husband wave as a young guy drove out from the back lot in a beat up Corsica and went past them on the highway heading for Allentown. "Help's leavin'. Just one more customer to go."

After several minutes, a blonde in tight jeans marched out of the pole barn dragging a screaming two year old boy. She manhandled him into a car seat in the rear of her Explorer and after digging in her purse, found her keys and drove the opposite way toward the new homes out in the country.

"Finally," McCall mumbled again and put the field glasses on the floor between the seats. "Give it fifteen minutes for them to clean up then we move. Get the shit outta the bag, Turd."

Toby reached behind him and zippered open the athletic bag. He handed one of the big hooded sweatshirts to McCall and then tried to get into the other one himself. Somehow he managed to get the sleeve twisted inside out and struggled while Flathead looked at him like he was crazy. Flathead scrunched the sleeves up around the hood and in one quick motion had the hood over his head and pulled the waistband down around him.

"Too fuckin' complicated for your meager brain, Turd," he snarled. Each took a pair of the dark amber tinted ski goggles and slipped them over their heads and around their necks where they could pull them up quickly.

McCall adjusted the silver automatic resting on his right side and pulled the Toyota out onto the road and drove toward the target. As he drove past, he could see the man standing inside the main building talking to a small woman. Toby leaned across and said, "That's her. It's just the two of them now. Pull past and turn in the side lot behind the piles of mulch. There." He pointed toward a small driveway angling into the property and McCall pointed the black SUV into the gravel and stopped behind the brown musty piles.

They both quickly got out and Flathead had to grab Toby by the dangling hood of Toby's sweatshirt and force him to put up the hood and slip the goggles onto his eyes. Toby fumbled the old revolver out into his right hand and Flathead pulled the automatic. The only sound was of the grit crunching under boots as they went through the open back entrance to the pole barn.

Flathead's vision went dark. He took one more step and crashed into a display rack of seeds, knocking it over to his left. Toby was right behind and didn't see McCall stop. Toby piled into the big man and let out an "Oohff!" They hadn't figured on the tinted goggles being so efficient at blocking the light.

The interior of the barn wasn't really that dark, but the goggles were meant to block out glare off the snow. Flathead reached up and tried to pull the goggles down where he could see and finally got his bearings. He could see movement at the front of the building and realized the two figures advancing on him were the man and the woman. Flathead sidestepped to his right between two aisles and found the man facing him at the other end about fifteen feet away. He couldn't see the woman and didn't know where Toby was either.

"Freeze right there, asshole!" Flathead yelled, pointing his gun at a very surprised Hank. Hank was in mid step and it took two more steps before he registered what was happening and managed to get stopped. Debbie appeared behind him and stared wide eyed at the looming figure in front of them.

Toby appeared on Flathead's left, pointing his revolver at the owners over a display of marigolds. Hank looked at Toby and then back at Flathead who was rapidly advancing on Hank.

"Turn around and move back up to the register, folks. Don't be stupid, your money ain't worth dyin' for. Move!" McCall emphasized his words with a wave of the pistol and Hank and Debbie kind of shuffled in reverse until Hank stumbled into her and they both turned around and walked slowly to the sales counter. Flathead's eyes were beginning to adjust to the light he could get through the goggles and followed closely behind. "Keep movin', keep movin'," Flathead urged.

"Don't shoot, please," Hank finally blurted out. He tried to catch Debbie's eye, but she had her back to him now and didn't turn completely around toward him when he spoke. When they reached Debbie's check-out station, she stopped short, unwilling to enter the small space behind the register. McCall came up behind them and pushed past as Toby closed in and covered the now silent couple.

"Fuck!" McCall roared looking at the open cash register and its empty drawer. There were only a few empty penny and nickel wrappers in the tray and the sectioned part that held the money was gone. Flathead turned to

Debbie and screamed, "Where's the fucking money?" he shoved the silver gun into her face and she lost all her color. Her eyes rolled up into the back of her head and she collapsed with a thud at Hank's feet. He started to move down for her and Flathead came down swift and hard onto his head with the barrel of the handgun. Hank didn't go down, but staggered in place and when he straightened back up, blood was flowing in a warm red stream down from his scalp and onto Debbie's shirt. McCall leaped from behind the counter and scooped Hank up with his free hand and shook him. "Answer me, you little fuck. The money!"

Hank tried to say something, but couldn't. He was almost off his feet and the bright little lights squirting back and forth across his eyes seemed to draw all his attention. He couldn't figure out where they were coming from.

Flathead raised his gun to swat Hank again and they both heard a squeak from below them, "In the house. It's in the house, don't hurt him, please don't hurt him. Take it." Debbie had come to and was struggling to sit up, holding her head with one hand and her stomach with the other.

Flathead immediately let Hank come back to earth and scooped up Debbie instead. He pushed the gun roughly up into her nose until blood started squirting out and held her where Hank could see what he was doing.

"Let's go," Flathead ordered, nodding toward the stone farmhouse behind and off to the side of the pole barn. Debbie pleaded with her eyes to Hank and he started slowly through the aisles toward the house. Flathead switched the gun from her bloody nose to the back of her head and had her by the neck as he followed her and Hank.

Toby's heart was pounding so hard and loud he actually looked behind him to see what the noise was before he finally realized it was coming from him. He gulped in air and tried to tell himself it would be alright and this would soon be over. He followed behind Flathead along the dirt and gravel path until they came out of the barn and walked the twenty yards to the side door of the house.

"Stop there," Flathead told Hank at the steps. McCall turned quickly and told Toby, "Check inside."

Toby didn't want to go in by himself but didn't want to make Flathead any madder. He cautiously slid up the steps and in through the storm door to a small mud room. The kitchen door was closed but not locked, and he opened it slowly. The hinges creaked and he smelled something good cooking as he went inside. The oven was on and clicked as he passed, making him jump slightly. He went through the kitchen and into the dining room where he saw the register drawer sitting on the dining room table among papers and credit card slips. The drawer looked full and he hollered, "It's here, in here!"

Flathead didn't know at first what Toby meant, but jabbed Debbie in the back of her head with the automatic and said, "On up and in, folks. Let's get it over with." Hank trudged up the steps and went into the kitchen where Toby was standing with a hand full of bills.

His gun was tucked into his belt and a big grin was on his face showed under the goggles, "Lookey here what I got!" Toby burbled. Happy they'd found what he'd told Flathead would be here.

McCall stopped them in the kitchen and said, "Have a seat here on the floor up against the cabinets. Sit!" Hank and Debbie sat down next to each other and she put her hand up to his still bleeding scalp. McCall produced a half roll of duct tape from his jacket and tossed it to Toby, "Hog tie 'em."

Toby handed the money to Flathead and started wrapping Hank and Debbie's arms and hands with the tape. He looped it through their legs so that they sat bundled and unable to get up. Flathead engaged the safety and slipped his gun into the space between his jeans and the small of his back and started counting money.

In only moments, he was back in the kitchen with four scraps of paper and waved them in Hank's face. "Holdin' out on me, you little shithead. Where's the rest?"

Toby asked, "What's wrong? The money's there on the table."

"Couple a hundred is all," McCall waved the papers again. "850, 1100, 1050, and 1500. They pulled cash out and put markers in." McCall was turning red and purple between the anger and the greed. He pulled the pistol back out leaned over and shoved it up between Debbie's legs causing her to wince and cry out in sharp pain.

"Stop!" the young voice blurted from behind Flathead. In a quick turn, he rose and spun to his left, pulled down on the safety and fired two shots into the stunned face of Mattie standing barefoot next to the dining room table. The room shook from the packed in sound of the explosions and Mattie crumbled to the floor, shaking from muscle spasms and gurgling through the blood trying to breathe. Debbie let out a loud cry and burst into tears at the twitching shape helplessly convulsing and struggling to live.

McCall froze as he watched the kid drop and then looked at Toby and then bent down and pointed the pistol into Debbie's face. She stared into the orange plastic of Flathead's goggles and spit a glob square into the space between his eyes. He flinched even though the plastic blocked it and then brought the pistol down onto her face opening a gash on the bridge of her nose with the blow.

"Fuckin' bitch! Where's the rest of the money?" he reached forward and grabbed her right breast with his free hand and roughly twisted the soft flesh through her shirt and lightweight bra. She screamed again and tried to pull free, but he turned it harder, dragging her down to the floor where she started sobbing in pain.

"It's in the freezer, please just take it and stop hurting her," Hank managed to say between his own sobs. "It's all there."

McCall heard him but didn't stop. Toby hadn't moved from his spot near the door of the mud room and now quickly went to the freezer and opened it up. There he found four paper lunch bags sitting on top of plastic bags of meat and boxes of green beans. He looked in the first one and saw green bills and knew he had what they were looking for. In his excitement and the confusion of how quickly McCall had become so enraged and violent, he grabbed the bags and jumped through the door and back into the kitchen. "Flathead, I got it. Four bags of cash, let's go!" Poor Toby didn't even realize what he had done.

McCall let loose of Debbie and just stood up over the couple looking at Toby. "You dickhead. You got a big mouth." Toby couldn't see McCall's eyes and would have been very afraid if he had been able to. McCall swung the .45 down to Debbie and pulled the trigger. Before the roar of the shot died, she folded onto the floor from her half sitting position. Hank jumped at the sound and the concussion so close to him. When he realized that the big man had just shot Debbie, his mind went blank with rage. He struggled against the tape, screaming a guttural roar deep from inside. Flathead raised his pistol again but instead kicked Hank in the ribs, silencing him.

McCall shook his head and looked at Toby standing there with the frozen money bags. "Your fault, you shoot him." Flathead flipped the safety on his automatic and slipped it into his belt again. He walked out past Toby and took the bags from him as he passed. "Make sure he's dead, Turd," Flathead growled as he passed.

Toby thought he would piss himself right there. This was supposed to be quick and easy. No fuss, no problem. It finally hit him that he had blurted out Flathead's name and now things had changed. He turned to say something to McCall, but he was gone down the steps and into the pole barn. Toby looked back at Hank struggling to breathe on the floor next to the still shape of his wife. He gave it a quick thought to just leave, but then he would have to face Flathead.

Reluctantly he half stepped over to Hank and said, "I'm sorry. This wasn't supposed to be this way. I'm sorry."

Hank opened his eyes and saw the goggles staring down at him blankly. He thought he could see where the dark was worn off the gun the man with the goggles was pointing at him. Worn off around the muzzle.

Toby pointed the .38 at Hank's head and tried to stop the shaking of the front blade sight as it wobbled back and forth. He took another half step closer then turned his head to the side. He closed his eyes and felt the gun buck in his hand as he pulled the trigger twice, then again. When he opened his eyes, he saw Hank motionless and draped over Debbie. Toby simply turned and left, the image burned into his mind forever.

~ * ~

Jimmy felt the tingle of the beginning of a sunburn on his back. And he needed to piss, right now. He had been sleeping for a while and the girls were off with Russell getting burgers at the concession stand. The water had cooled him off and rewound his buzz where he could start over and feel the edge of the alcohol without losing it. He rolled over and sat up. The breeze off the gulf was warm but fresh. Summer hadn't really got hold of them just yet and until it did, you could still breathe without drawing too much moisture into your lungs.

He gathered the scattered shirts and shoes and wrapped them all into the blanket. The empty whiskey bottle and beer cans were left where they lay.

Jimmy dumped the sand out of his boots and started toward the beach shack where the bathrooms were. He spotted his brother and both girls sitting on the low cement wall that separated the beach sand from the parking lot. Jimmy dumped the blanket and its cargo in front of them and turned, without a word, for the building. The blonde said something about snoring and the girls laughed together. Russell knew better and kept his mouth shut. Jimmy let it pass and went about his business. Once he had drained what seemed like a gallon, he walked a little easier back to where the rest of them were.

"I need a fresh beer. You girls wanna take a ride, maybe get some real food?" Jimmy asked.

The girls exchanged a look and the blonde, Jimmy thought he heard the other one call her Patsy, said something like "for sure, baby" and they dug into the blanket to get their shoes for the walk across the hot pavement of the parking lot. Russell lagged behind and told Jimmy they were ready to party if they could get some coke or grass. The girls had a place at one of the cheap motels out on 41 where they could crash for a while.

"Why don't we run up to Newtown and see if we can scrounge up some blow, little brother?" Russell suggested.

Jimmy figured that if they didn't have to spring for a room out of their meager cash, they might could swing a bit of the white stuff to go with the beer. "Let's go see Booger, if he ain't at church," said Jimmy. "Come on, girls, got a little stop to make up town and then we can have us a party."

Jimmy grinned at Patsy who then winked at the redhead. They trudged over to the Mustang and Jimmy climbed into the backseat with Patsy who immediately ran her hand up his thigh for a handful to keep her busy for the trip north into Sarasota.

~ * ~

Ken laughed to himself. Up ahead the black dog wasn't satisfied with sticking his nose out of the half rolled down back seat window and kept bumping the back of Sam's head to get at the better air of the front passenger window. Apparently, Sam wasn't too upset because Ken could see his hand come up and rub Dutch's muzzle. Dog heaven: an open window in a moving car.

Eileen and Sam were just in front and Ken was following in the Pathfinder. Ken wished she would go faster so he could get home to check his e-mail. He hadn't heard from Grace since Friday and figured he would have a note waiting for him when he got back to the farm. His dad said they were only stopping at Eileen's for coffee and a piece of her pineapple pound cake and then heading home to get caught up on laundry and rescue Molly from loneliness. Ken figured he could last a little longer.

~ * ~

"It's sticky, Daddy." Katie held up her finger for her dad to see. The smudge she left on the trim piece was at the very end and before he got upset with her for touching it, Ozzie realized he probably would cut the end off anyway before he fit it into place.

"Shouldn't touch, sweetie. These are for one of Daddy's customers. We have to keep them real nice so they don't get mad at Daddy, okay?" Ozzie saw her milling that around in her head and then she looked at her finger and then back to her dad.

"Let me get that off you, honey." Ozzie picked one of the mineral spirit soaked rags out of the little Franklin stove in the garage and wiped the polyurethane from Katie's finger. She seemed happy with that and bounded for the house. Her mom was back and feeding Vinny before the rest of them sat down for dinner. Ozzie tossed the smelly rag back into the stove and then lit and pitched a wooden kitchen match in after it. The rags poofed and quickly burned. He left the garage door open to air the place out and went in to wash up before supper.

## Chapter Four

Trooper Timothy Adams was proud of himself. He made it through another meal without giving in to the temptation. The other trooper he met for his meal break insisted on the taco place next to the interstate and Adams had to watch him wolf down a couple of super burritos while Adams settled for a salad with lo-cal dressing. He could have a protein drink later but had to be real careful about his fat intake.

Most of his off duty time was divided between sleeping and lifting really heavy weights. His neck and arms showed the results of it too. Didn't do much for his social life, except for the redhead at the gym. His shift work schedule kept his sleep clock permanently screwed up, and he always seemed behind on sack time. Just off probation and his last evaluation was even better than he expected. His corporal was always on him about something but had given him high marks in almost every category. The guy was hard to figure out.

He turned his shiny marked unit out onto Route 100 and headed north for a ride through the shopping center and then to the spot where he could run radar on the southbound traffic. It had been a quiet Sunday. Since he had come on duty at three, he handled a minor wreck in Fogelsville and dirt bikes in the park. Not much going on. Maybe write a couple of tickets and then start cruising from bar to bar and try to catch a drunk. The radio told him the corporal was signing on from the barracks, and one of the Bethlehem cars was stopping a tractor trailer on 22.

"Straus Valley 4, 9-1-1 call possibly a phone left off the hook. At the garden center, Old Dairy Road and Victory Highway," the radio clipped. The new civilian radio operator had a bit of a feminine voice and it seemed to irritate most of the guys, even though he was married and had a kid.

Adams picked up the microphone and replied, "Valley 4, 10-4. From 100 and 78." Adams knew Corporal Dickson liked them to give their location so everyone knew from where they were responding. He made his left turn into the shopping center and spun a U-turn right back out again and punched the big V-8 in the Ford Crown Victoria as he turned onto the four lane Route 100 southbound.

He calculated the turns and distance to the call. He knew the place but had never stopped there. A quick glance at the digital clock on the dash and he figured they probably were closed by now. Likely the cat dumped the phone. He pushed the cruiser up past sixty and made the last light easily. Traffic was thin and he managed to pass the few cars in his way.

Within four minutes, he was turning onto Victory, "Straus Valley 4, 10-23." Adams passed the last crossroad and slowed as he pulled into the dirt and gravel parking lot. It was empty. The building closest to the lot had a glass door with credit card symbols on it and was standing propped open by a bucket of geraniums. Adams got out of the police car and slipped his 'Smokey' hat on before he walked deliberately across the lot from his car to the door.

He stopped just outside and listened for about ten seconds before stepping through. Just inside the door was a sales counter to the left with the cash register open and empty. Lots of merchants would do that to discourage a thief from smashing open the machine. It could cost more to replace or repair the register than it could hold. Adams noticed a phone on the counter next to the register. The desk top phone had several buttons, one of which was lit. The handset was firmly sitting in place and didn't appear to be off the hook.

Through big windows at the back, Adams could see other similar but somewhat smaller buildings and greenhouses situated on the property. He walked through and down the aisle toward the rear door. Just inside that door he noticed a display rack of seeds knocked over and the packs scattered from the fall. Tim's heart rate accelerated rapidly, and he instinctively flexed his knees and quickly scanned left then right. He listened but could only hear his heart thumping within his chest. Closer now to the back of the barn he saw the house for the first time.

The stone and cream sided old farmhouse was about twenty yards off to the rear and left of the main barn and was connected by a walkway of the same crushed stone and grit he was standing on. The front of the house faced the road and had a small front porch covered by an overhang just a bit wider than the step. On the right side of the house toward the pole barn was a deck and landing made of pressure treated lumber leading to a side door.

The two Labs were perched at the top of the steps staring into the house through the porch door. The storm door was closed, but as Adams went out the back of the barn, he could see the inside door was open through the glass of the outer door. The dogs alarmed him a bit, but they made no move toward him and only gave him a glance and went back to watching the door. Still no one around so Adams walked slowly toward the house, his boots crunching on the stone with each step. The portable radio was chirping with the trooper from Bethlehem running the driver's license and wanted checks on the driver he had stopped. Adams reached down and lowered the volume to where it was just audible through the speaker/microphone clipped to his left shoulder flap.

When he was about ten feet from the side door steps, Adams stopped and stared at a spot on the top step. At first he thought it was where something had spilled, like a soft drink. A couple steps more and Adams could make out another of the marks on the bottom step. Adams leaned down and looked at what now appeared to be a partial shoe print of red paint. He saw another between the top step and the storm door and that caused him to hesitate once again.

*No, not again.* Adams whispered to himself. The two murdered bodies he discovered last November in Porter had caused him many fitful nights of sleep since. Although he got to play at being a detective when he was pulled off the road to help Corporal Deland and the other crime troopers with that murder investigation, he was glad when it had ended and the routine of the barracks had quietly returned. He was now convinced the footprints were blood and what was beyond the door meant things might be getting real dizzy, real quick.

Tim took two deep breaths and softly crept up the steps and onto the landing. He released and drew his Glock .45 and held it at waist level covering his front as he turned and stepped to the side of the glass upper half of the storm door. The yellow Lab had to scoot aside and both were anxiously wagging their tails looking up at the trooper. He turned the black knob of the aluminum storm door and once the latch released, Adams moved his head and took a quick look through the glass to the inside.

He could see someone in the dining room. A person sitting at the table leaning forward with their head down. On his second look he could tell it was a young man at the table wearing a white t-shirt and shorts. The whole left side of the guy was covered in blood staining his shirt and leaking over onto his shorts. Adams didn't see anything in the dim light of the kitchen and decided he had to go in.

Squaring his feet, he yanked the door open, leaped into the kitchen and yelled fiercely, "Police, don't move!"

The young man didn't budge and Adams advanced toward him watching for anything like a weapon to appear. On his third step, he yelled again not quite as loudly, "Don't move, don't..." Before he got the last word out, he felt himself tripping and fell forward, hard, breaking his fall with his outstretched left hand. The noise of his fall settled in the room and he heard a soft groan from underneath him. Tim realized there was another person there and spun around to find Debbie and Hank in a heap next to the cabinets. Both were trussed in silver tape and the man had blood covering the front of his upper body and in a puddle beneath him.

Adams looked back at the guy sitting at the table and he still had not moved. Keeping the Glock pointed at the dining room, Tim carefully checked the man on the floor for a pulse. A faint beat could be felt in the man's neck. Tim then did the same for the small woman but couldn't feel anything. He gathered himself up to his feet and crossed quickly to the young man at the table, and as he reached down to the man's neck, the man moved, trying to raise his head.

Tim could see him breathing and the blood was still coming out of the guy's left ear. The whole top half of the ear lobe was gone, replaced with a pulpy, bloody mess. The guy wheezed and gave a wet hoarse cough. A cordless phone was on the table next to him and was covered in a bloody hand print. Adams stepped back and reached up to the microphone for his portable radio with his left hand to transmit, "Valley 4, I need an ambulance, no check that, better send a couple of them to the garden center. Three victims, possibly shot..."

He released the button trying to think what to say next and heard, "2's with 4. 6 start this way." It was his corporal, Brad Dickson. He had been rolling toward the call and just pulled up in front when Adams called for the ambulance.

Now Adams didn't know what to do next. He was standing in the middle of a crime scene, but he had three injured people and even though the injured man at the table looked to be hurt pretty bad, did he get hurt while hurting the other two?

"Adams! Where are you?" the corporal was calling from the pole barn.

Keeping the table guy covered he yelled back over his shoulder, "In the house!"

"Debbie?" Adams jumped even though the voice wasn't loud at all. The tied up bloody man in the kitchen was straining at the tape and trying to get a response from the woman. Adams decided none of these three were a threat and holstered his pistol. He moved back into the kitchen and knelt down next to the man and woman.

Adams unsheathed his buck knife from his pistol belt and slit the tape in several places to free up the man's hands. "What happened, who did this?" Adams asked just as Corporal Dickson came banging through the kitchen door.

"You okay, Tim?" Brad asked.

"Debbie, are you alright? Debbie, Debbie?" the bleeding man stripped the tape off his hands and reached across to the woman, gently cradling her head. Adams carefully cut her tape, but she didn't move. He could see the gash on her nose and an obvious bullet wound just below her left eye. Just a round red mark. Dickson went to the dining room and started grabbing the napkins from the center of the table and pressed them against the young man's bleeding ear. Brad could tell from the bubbling sound the kid was making the ear was the least of his problems.

Dickson glanced at the stairs and then said to Tim, "You check upstairs yet?"

"No, just in here." Adams turned back to the man and asked, "What happened, can you tell me?"

Hank blinked and mumbled, "Two of them shot us, just shot us. Why did they do that?" he started to cry and sobbed while he stroked Debbie's hair. He startled a bit as his hand came away from the back of her head covered in her blood and pieces of light colored tissue.

The siren in the distance penetrated the silent room and Adams pressed, "Try to tell me what they looked like. Try. Please, sir."

~ * ~

Their first stop was for fresh beer and ice and then they split onto 301 at the newspaper office and worked through the lights of the city as they moved north. Past 12th then 17th and finally right on 27th and across the tracks to several single story rows of apartments surrounded by dirty sand and pieces of broken plastic tricycles. Russell turned into the lot in front and left the engine running.

The four buildings were mostly brown and worn out. Screens were ripped and everything seemed to need a good washing. At least fifteen black kids from two to twelve were yakking and running through the bits of grass that had survived the foot traffic between the units. Groups of two or three adults sat in front of the doors of the apartments smoking and listening to music. One group had brought a color television outside tethered to cable and power cords and were in animated enjoyment of a baseball game from Atlanta.

Jimmy pulled a wad of wet bills from his pocket and handed it forward to Russ, saying, "Booger's Lincoln is here. See what he's got for us."

Russell saw the big white car at the other end of the parking area. Its windows were down and a pair of white fuzzy crosses hung from the rear view mirror. Booger was the Reverend Reginald McKenzie, pastor of the Light of Jesus Divine Savior Church. He also worked at the Ford dealership rebuilding transmissions and sold cocaine.

Usually it was Jimmy and Russell selling grass to Booger, but the girls wanted some coke so here they were. Several of the adult groups spotted Russell as he climbed out of the Mustang and quick words were exchanged until someone recognized him and things settled back to normal. Russell trudged through the soft sand and made his way to the third building. Booger met Russell at the door. Booger was resplendent in his Sunday evening preacher outfit. A gleaming white tux with ruby shirt studs and a deep purple bow tie. He was still in his socks and his coat hung on a hanger from the top of the open door. Behind Booger the stereo in the living room of the small apartment was pouring out the rock and roll sound of a lively gospel group singing, "Goin' to meet my Lord, my Lord and Savior..."

"Hey, Booger," Russell said as he walked up to the screen door.

"Russell, you sinner. Come to join the congregation on this beautiful Lord's Day?" Booger opened the door for Russell and led him into the room and through to the small kitchen. Russell could see a tiny girl scamper down the hallway in a fluffy dress and black shiny shoes. Booger opened the refrigerator and took out a green wine bottle with a thin neck. He took two juice glasses from a cupboard with no door and poured them almost full, handing one to Russell.

"To my heathen friend," Booger offered and slugged back the rosy drink. Russell did the same.

"Jimmy wants some stuff," Russell said, offering the wad of soggy money to Booger. "We met some girls at the beach, gonna get laid and stoned."

"Or vice versa, no doubt," grinned Booger with a brilliant smile. Russell didn't get it. Booger counted the bills and said, "The church thanks you for your generous offering."

The preacher reached into a green diaper bag on the counter and fished around a bit, coming out with a clear plastic baggie of white powder. "A bit more than my competitors would give you for the price. Remember that the next load of weed you get for me."

"Great. Thanks, Booger. Me and Jimmy'll take care of ya, don't worry." Russell followed the preacher back out to the front door and they vigorously shook hands before Russell walked back to the car.

The blonde squirmed and giggled when she saw Russell hand the dope back to Jimmy. "Let's do it," she squealed. "Come on, Jimmy."

Russell eased out and started back toward 301. Jimmy slipped the bag into his jeans and slugged the last half of his beer down. "It can wait a bit, girls. Relax. Ya'll wanna get somethin' to eat?" The girls looked at each other and agreed. Jimmy told Russell to take them to the chicken place below 12th

Street. They could eat at the picnic tables and didn't have to leave a tip.

~ * ~

Neither said a word as Flathead drove the black SUV toward the motel parking lot. Toby was sick. He had never felt like this, ever. All the bad stuff he had done since he could remember ever made him feel like this. No drug or drink had ever fucked him up this bad.

Two lights away from the motel, Toby suddenly had to vomit. He didn't have time to punch the electric window; he jerked the door handle open and spewed out the opening toward the road. Gushes of liquid came out. He felt like his asshole was coming up through his insides and out his throat. McCall stared straight ahead figuring his next move. The couple in the Buick behind them didn't find it a bit amusing.

~ * ~

"In the name of the Father, Son, and Holy Spirit, Amen." Ozzie finished the prayer and reached for the steaming fat bird on the platter in front of him. Marie had already sliced off the drumsticks and the white meat from one side. Ozzie took a leg and several slices of breast and passed the platter to Junior on his right. He flared his nostrils and took in a deep sample of the delicious odor just as the phone rang.

Eileen closed the screen door to the back yard after she let Dutch out for his pee run and moved across the kitchen to her well used coffee maker on the counter next to the stove. "Regular or sissy stuff?" she asked Sam. Sam was about to answer when the cell phone on his belt began to vibrate then chirp and distracted him. One look at the call back number on the display told him what he suspected. The barracks. Ken came in from the bathroom and walked to the back door to watch the big German shepherd searching the corners of Eileen's fenced back yard.

Sam looked grim as he ended the call. "Kenny, I need you to drop me at the barracks. Keep the Pathfinder and run on to the farm. I gotta go in to work. Sorry about the coffee, Eileen, something's come up." Sam turned sharply on his heel and marched out through the house to the front door. "Come on, Ken, let's go. Thanks for coming down to meet us, Eileen. I'll call you tomorrow."

Sam sidestepped Ken and let his son pass out onto the porch, and when she got to the door near him, Sam squeezed Eileen around the waist. He planted a warm kiss square on her lips and whispered, "Sorry, but this is important." With that, he bounded down the steps and jogged to the Pathfinder at the curb.

Sam streaked around to the driver's side and got a look from Ken who apparently thought he was going to drive. "I'll drive," said Sam. "This has to be quick."

Sam dropped the Pathfinder into gear and roared through the stop sign at the end of Eileen's street. Another two blocks and they were on the main road through the little hamlet of Porter and streaking south toward the interstate.

~ * ~

Corporal Dickson had the next trooper that arrived check the rest of the house and made sure everyone got latex gloves on to handle the victims. Adams stayed with Hank and got enough pieces of what happened to put out a radio call about two men in hoods and goggles. Township cops from neighboring jurisdictions also arrived, and Brad asked them to block off the road and start contacting the nearest neighbors. Through it all, the Labs sat on the porch watching the door, waiting for their mom to come out.

"She's very critical. Don't know how she's lasted this long," the paramedic said in a low voice to Brad. "We've called for the chopper for her and the kid. She may not need it."

Young Mattie had a bullet in his shoulder blade that nicked his windpipe on the way, but the EMT wasn't positive that it missed the artery. Blood was clogging his lungs and he was barely breathing. Hank was the luckiest of the three. Besides his busted head, he took one bullet to the right thigh just above his knee. Two others had slammed into the cabinets beside his ear. "Can't say for sure, but the husband will be out in a week at the most."

Brad figured he better plan for the worst and got one of the troopers to start a scene log listing everyone who was in the house. He just had to keep the lid on until the crime trooper and corporal arrived.

~ * ~

Ozzie's gun was in its holster on the front seat of his truck amid a pile of pens, papers, handcuffs and a spare magazine. The big man's attention was on the drumstick he was attempting to remove every morsel from as he barreled around turns on the two lane road. The steering wheel had a good lather of chicken grease by now, and the one piece of paper towel he had wrapped the chicken leg with on his way out of the house was soggy and not much help.

Finally down to bone, he tossed it out of the window. Now he had to deal with the mess. The front of his short sleeved dress shirt was a disaster. Ozzie tried to remember if he had a clean one in his locker at the barracks, but guessed not. He fished a stained rag from under the seat and worked on his hands and the steering wheel. He would worry about his shirt later. Only a few minutes out from the station now, he tried to recall what the sissy dispatcher had told him on the phone. He wasn't exactly sure where this garden center was but knew the area pretty well. Must be bad if Brad Dickson called for Sam to come in too. Ozzie hoped Marie put up some of the stuffing and gravy for later.

~ * ~

He didn't have to tell Turd to open the window. McCall used the window controls on the driver's side to roll Toby's window down to air out the Toyota. They entered the motel lot and parked at the end nearest to the interstate. McCall dropped the keys onto the floor board. Stripping off the parka, he stuffed it and his ski goggles into the empty duffle bag and tossed that into Toby's lap.

"Wipe your face off, pussy," Flathead growled. McCall scooped the cash bags from between the seats and stuffed them into his shirt. Toby glanced toward Flathead but didn't say anything. "Wait here until I get the truck started." McCall was out of the door and moving across the lot toward Toby's truck.

Toby's head was pounding and he needed a drink. Mechanically, he tugged at the hooded sweatshirt and pulled it and the goggles off all at once. He picked up the bag and added his disguise to Flathead's and feebly stumbled out of the 4-Runner and onto the parking lot. But now he didn't know where to go. He couldn't remember where his truck was, so he started in the general direction he last saw McCall moving.

"Get in the truck, you idiot!" Suddenly Toby's truck appeared in front of him. Toby opened the door and swung the duffle bag up onto the seat and followed it into the cab. McCall hit the gas and moved them quickly across the lot toward the exit onto Route 100.

"Asshole, look, your fucking gun is hanging out of your pants!" Flathead snapped. Toby looked down and saw the .38 stuck into the front of his pants. He pulled his shirt out over it, a bit late if anyone had seen him walking across the parking lot.

"You didn't have to do them like that," Toby said to McCall. "We shoulda just took the money, man." Toby never saw it coming. He did see the stars dancing as Flathead cracked him across the forehead with the .45. Toby's vision cleared just enough to look left and see the automatic pointed at his nose.

"You're next, little fucker. You better get it fixed in your weak brain what's happened, s'happened. Ain't nothin' we can change now. You keep your pie hole shut, understand?" Flathead returned the Colt to his belt and drove north on 100 back toward the mountains. Toby felt sick again but didn't have anything left to throw up.

~ * ~

"It was a black truck, an SUV, Corporal," the township officer said to Brad. "Lady was watering her flowers in the side yard and saw it parked over there," he said, pointing to the side of the garden center property. "She went in to turn down the stove and when she came back out, it was gone. The first marked unit pulled up a few minutes later."

"Well, it's something. Grab one of the troopers and put some tape up to block off the drive so the crime scene fellas can have a look." Brad broadcast the description of the black truck and put in the call for the crime scene troopers to respond to photo and collect what evidence they could. He could hear a helicopter approaching from the east and hoped it was from the hospital and not from Channel 6. A landing zone had been hastily designated in the field next to the car dealership. Local volunteer fire police were arriving and had traffic stopped in both directions so one of the ambulances could move the shooting victims quickly across to the field. Adams looked ashen.

~ * ~

Ken snuck a peek at his dad from time to time but kept mostly quiet on the mad dash over the country roads toward the barracks. Other than, "Some folks got shot down below Fogelsville," Sam was silent. He pushed the Pathfinder and once on the interstate, really opened it up. In just a few minutes they were approaching the exit at Route 100. It was actually out of the way to drive up to the barracks; the garden center was the other way, but Sam didn't want to drag Ken to the scene.

Sam braked hard and dug into the exit ramp. The Pathfinder's tires wailed at the friction of the turn and Ken had to put his hand on the arm rest to keep from sliding across the seat. As they neared the bottom of the ramp, Sam spotted an unmarked state car passing southbound and let out a "Shit!"

Sam quickly moved to the left lane to turn into the shopping center a block north of the exit and was dialing his cell phone with one hand and steering with the other. "This is Sam. Call Ozzie on the radio and tell him to pull over, I'm coming up behind him. Have him wait for me at the Wawa," Sam didn't bother to make the left, instead doing a U-turn on three tires around the median.

~ * ~

"Straus Valley 16, Straus Valley," the radio barked.

Ozzie unhooked the microphone from its holder and replied, "Valley 16, go ahead."

"Meet the corporal at the Wawa."

"Valley 16, 10-4," Ozzie had already passed the store by then, but spun around at the skating rink and went back, pulling in off to the side near the air hose.

~ * ~

"Well, sweetie. You ready to go for that drink now?" The three gold stripes on his sleeve were smudged with a coffee stain and his breath smelled like he had just sprayed in one of those antiseptic fresheners. Grace continued typing on the computer in the airline crew lounge trying to finish the note to her mom before the van left for the hotel. She suffered the stale coffee and perspiration smell that filled these small spaces where airline ground and air crew could escape the rush of travelers in the terminal.

A good looking guy, the first officer, persisted. "You told me 'Sometime, maybe' I quote you accurately, correct?" he asked.

Deliberately, she typed the last two words before hitting "Send." She sighed and without turning from the screen while it acknowledged her mail, said, "I'm flattered, again, Simon. But no thanks." The guy had been really trying to start something with her. He asked her out every time he ran into her and if he was lucky enough to end up on the same aircraft with her, followed her as much as the captain would let him. "But just not interested, okay?" she looked up at him blankly and then gathered her bags and moved toward the door.

"Think about it, Grace. I don't bite…much," he gave her a weak grin and stepped aside to let her pass through the door. Without another word, she pulled her carry-on bag down the hall through the security door and out into the airport. She quickly forgot about Simon; her mind was on someone else.

~ * ~

She just picked at her food and drank easily from the paper bag wrapped beer. Her vision was a little foggy, but the bag in Jimmy's pocket was all that occupied her mind. The redhead was stretched out on the picnic table bench with her head in Russell's lap.

"Let's get goin'," said Jimmy. They left the trash behind and went through the other tables to the sand and shell parking lot. "Now where is this luxurious palace you girls have?"

"Down South Trail, past the Mexican joint," the redhead said. "Mango Grove Motel."

Jimmy winced. He knew the place. He and Russell had done a few dope deals there and in some of the other dumps along that stretch. Only a few of the small motels remained. Whores and dopers were being replaced with mini malls and fifty dollar a meal upscale restaurants. But it was out in the county, and there were fewer cops than in the city limits.

~ * ~

Ken said a quick good bye to his dad's back as Sam piled out of the Pathfinder to get in with Ozzie. Sam stopped and turned, "Sorry I've got my head up my butt. See you later tonight," and was gone.

The ride over the mountain to home was quiet for Ken. He sorted through thoughts of graduation, Grace and the summer of basic at the Academy. He knew it would be physically and mentally challenging. The upper classmen would be harsh breaking in the plebes. Ken had endured a similar time when he was younger and entered the military school but had been promoted steadily over the years and the chicken crap slowed. He was determined to be in the best physical shape he could be and decided a long run was on the schedule for the morning.

~ * ~

Flathead avoided the turnpike and followed the thinner roads through the small towns and through the gap at Palmerton. Once past Lehighton, he pushed onto the back roads, watching his rear view mirror until they got back to the house with the naked lady picture.

"Go home and stay there, I'll come by later with some dope and we'll split the cash," McCall growled. Toby stared at him, not really focused but nodded. Flathead walked quickly to his Harley, kicked it to life and roared down the hill. Toby sat for a minute and then fumbled out a smoke and lit it. The nausea wouldn't go away.

He didn't want to go home, but he didn't want to stay here. He walked around to the driver's side of the still running truck and backed out onto the road. It took a few minutes for him to gather enough awareness to drive away in the general direction of his trailer. A drink, no he needed many drinks, but he had no money. The girl whose name began with a K lived over the next couple of ridges. Maybe she was home.

~ * ~

"She's dead," Brad quietly told Sam, "They're still going to chopper her and the kid out, but she'll be DOA. The kid may not make it either. Took a shot through his neck."

Ozzie was furiously writing in his notebook while Adams told his tale. Sam looked out through the storm door and watched the two Labs staring at the stretcher as the ambulance guys loaded their dad.

"Let's clear out of here, guys, let the lab folks work it," he said. They stepped over the evidence and moved outside. "I'm making the calls, Brad. Your guys can string as much tape as they need to." Sam watched the helicopter lift off and transition east toward the hospital.

Ozzie went to the back of the ambulance and stuck his head in to speak to Hank before they took him away.

The lieutenant was drunk. Sam tried to tell him what was happening, but Lt. Harman would not stop interrupting. He was arrogant and acted ignorant while sober, lit up he was impossible. Sam ended the call and punched a speed dial number on his phone.

"Hi. Sorry to bother you, but Harman is being his usual shitty self." Sam described the situation and said, "I need Johnny and Calvin and would you call the DA and let him know?"

The Captain was understanding. She went back a ways with Sam, but he had been avoiding contact with her other than work. Complications with his current female situation.

"Thanks, Jess." Sam kept punching numbers and started the overtime money rolling for his two other crime troopers.

~ * ~

Johnny Bonner had just finished supper and was on the porch smoking when Sam called. Calvin Livingston was at the gym working on rehabbing his hip. It was going slowly. He was back to work after recovering from two gunshot wounds last November. Sam and Ozzie had to go to court in Philly tomorrow to deal with the aftermath of gunning down Calvin's shooter.

"On my way, Sam," Calvin said and smiled at the young girl on the machine stepping next to him. She ignored the good looking black man or at least tried to look like she was ignoring him while watching his butt walk quickly across the gym and out the door.

~ * ~

The Labs looked lost as the ambulance pulled away. They hesitated and then began to follow Ozzie as he walked toward Sam. "Can I use your phone, Sam? Left mine at home," Ozzie asked with a sheepish grin. "The husband heard them use what sounds like AKAs. Gonna run them through the computer. We need some people at the hospital to keep an eye on him. They left him for dead and he ain't."

Sam was well aware of Ozzie's lack of cell phone aptitude. Ozzie never got up to speed with technology. He still had trouble with the computer system at the barracks. He missed his electric typewriter.

~ * ~

The redhead was on top of Russell and the sweat flipped off her nipples as she worked up and down. Jimmy was buzzing from the coke, but was having difficulty with his sexual concentration in the small room with two double beds. Too much distraction.

"Come on, Jimmy," the blonde laughed. "That limp noodle ain't gonna fit in sideways." Her flabby belly shook as she laughed at him.

Jimmy rolled off and sat up on the bed, facing away from Russell's bouncing. He reached over and picked up the baggie lying on the nightstand and licked the inside of it with his tongue. The blonde giggled again.

A switch went off in Jimmy's head. He spun and slapped the girl. That stopped her giggling, and she reached out for his arm and sunk what nails she had into his bicep.

"Yoww!" he squawked. He pulled his arm away, swung a powerful roundhouse fist hard into the girl's neck. She grabbed herself and choked. She gagged and tried to breathe. Jimmy bolted up and grabbed his jeans.

"Fuckin' dumbass bitch."

The blonde was gasping for air and then vomited. She managed to roll over and spit more supper onto the bed.

"Hey, you!" the redhead yelped. Russell looked lost. The redhead jumped off and moved over next to the blonde and put her arm around her. Jimmy was stepping into his boots and picked up his shirt as he opened and went out the door.

Russell lay naked on the other bed for a moment before he started to move and said, "It's okay girls, I'll talk to him."

The redhead spun to him and snarled, "Get the fuck out, get out!" Russell was hesitant, but the redhead threw a pillow at him and was reaching for her shoe to throw next. Russell jumped and scooped his pants, shirt and shoes as he moved toward the door. He left his socks on the floor and a red sneaker thumped into his back before he could escape.

Outside, he hopped down the landing one foot at a time trying to put on his pants. He trotted barefoot down the steps and found Jimmy in the Mustang smoking a tiny joint. Jimmy said, "Get in, we're done here."

Russell scrunched up his brow and replied, "I wasn't done. What the hell did she do?"

"Shut up and drive us home," Jimmy said and flicked the roach out onto the parking lot.

~ * ~

Ken heard her yip as he pulled the Pathfinder down the gravel drive through the orchard. The big barn converted to a home appeared ahead as he got closer to the barking beagle. He saw her straining at her lead and that tail was moving fast. He spent a few moments with her before he mounted the steps up to the deck and went in the kitchen door. He searched the refrigerator and came out with some frozen yogurt. He marched into his room on the first floor and immediately turned on his computer. He needed some Grace time.

~ * ~

Flathead rode through the gates and stopped to go back and lock them up behind him. He checked the dirt drive and saw that no new tracks had appeared since he left earlier in the day. His small house sat back off the road on just over five acres of woods. The house belonged to a cousin on his mother's side. The cousin was in federal prison for a few years, and Flathead kept the place from falling down and paid the taxes and utilities.

He drove the Harley past a new black Dodge four wheel drive truck and stopped to pull a remote control from his saddle bag. The bike went into the garage and Flathead wove a heavy chain through and around the machine, locking it to a metal I beam buried in cement. This part of the country was not for suckers. In the house, he pulled a beer from the old refrigerator and went to the cluttered dining table. He unloaded and started cleaning his Colt. He considered tossing into the Lehigh River on his way home but decided he had more use for it and would keep it a bit longer. He reloaded the magazine and slipped it back into the pistol.

Flathead took a cell phone from his back pocket and turned it on. He sent a brief text message and returned the phone to his pocket. He would check it later for the reply he expected.

~ * ~

Grace worked the heavy beverage cart down the narrow aisle, working with one of the older girls. The flight had started out bumpy, but the pilots had moved up in altitude and out of the layer of turbulence. She spotted camouflage and moved up next to a young soldier wearing earphones and staring at the seatback in front of him. He noticed the movement next to him and looked up into Grace's pretty dark eyes. He smiled and took out the earphone closest to the aisle.

"Coffee?" he asked.

Grace couldn't help but think of Ken in his school uniform. She had a great picture of him in his dress grays on her smartphone. She served the young soldier and then continued with the other passengers, but her mind was elsewhere. Another day and a half.

Johnny got to the barracks first and found the keys for the unmarked car. He was dressed in slacks and a dress shirt but no tie. His light jacket covered the pistol and cuffs on his belt. He checked out a portable radio and got a cup of coffee in the kitchen. Calvin appeared about ten minutes later, resplendent in an immaculate gray suit and gleaming black wingtips. He wore a shimmering deep blue tie and limped slightly into the squad room.

"Well, well. His assholiness in person," Johnny quipped in his Georgia drawl. "Still shittin' in stereo?" Johnny grinned as Calvin glared at him.

"Doing much better than your stale cigarette smelly self, redneck. Healed up nice and neat. The girls love to caress my many wound scars. Turns them on," Calvin said. Calvin took a round to the chest and one to his, well, posterior last fall in Philadelphia. Johnny had been there and saved Calvin's life that night. Johnny figured he had an obligation to wring every bit of squirm possible out of his partner. They had known each other from their first day at the Academy and had been close friends since.

"You ready?" Johnny asked and held up the keys.

"Let's go." Calvin turned to the back door and moved outside ahead of Johnny.

~ * ~

"Two Bethlehem troopers are on their way. Meet with hospital security and see how best to protect the husband and the kid, if he lives," Sam said to Calvin. Calvin put in a call to Sam once he and Johnny were in the car leaving the barracks. "Ozzie is staying with the scene for a while to see if the crime scene guys come up with anything. We're waiting on the intelligence people to run the nicknames through the database. Some of the older ones are still on paper so it may be a while. See if hubby can remember anything more. I'll be down to give him the notification shortly."

"Damn you, Johnny!" Calvin yelped into the phone. Sam shook his head and listened to the sound of the big V-8 Crown Vic roaring in the background. Johnny was a race car driver in his misspent youth and could still move a big car about smartly and fast. "Gonna die before my time," Calvin growled.

"Nine lives, Calvin. You still have a few in the bank," Sam said and ended the call.

~ * ~

The rescue unit EMT bagged the blonde on the floor of the motel room. She had passed out when she couldn't get enough air down her damaged windpipe. The EMT covered her nakedness with a blanket from his kit and got an IV started. One of the other firemen pumped air into her while a third came in with a backboard and they carefully strapped her on. The deputy outside with the redhead was getting the names and vitals of the girls and trying to coax the redhead into giving him a better description of who had almost killed her friend. He could tell she was stoned and scared. Every time his portable radio spoke out, she visibly jumped. He reached down to his belt and lowered the volume.

"Do you want to go with her to the ER?" he asked her.

"Can I? We ain't got no car. We come down here on a bus," she said.

"Sure, she'll need someone there with her. Look, she's not doing very well. It's important we get all the help from you we can. The creeps that did this need to answer for it. We can't do our job without you. It may be a while before she can say anything. You have to speak for her." The deputy wasn't sure these were not working girls but suspected they were just dumb kids in town to party.

"I told you, they were just two guys we met on the beach. Kinda plain lookin'. They had a...a old, ah, ah Chevy, I think," she lied. Afraid and just wanting her friend fixed up and then get out of town. She didn't need another drug arrest either.

~ * ~

It was dark now and Ken finished reading and writing to Grace. He had hinted to his dad that he wanted a cell phone. He had not been allowed one at school but figured the Academy would tolerate it. Grace seemed to always be on a plane, but he still wanted to actually talk to her more. He walked outside into the cool spring air and let Molly loose to come inside for the night. She would have been very comfortable in her barrel, but he needed company.

~ * ~

Toby found the girl at home. She was cool to him at first, but when he promised to get her stoned later, she warmed. She made him a frozen pizza, but he only looked at it. He drank the half bottle of Calverts she had and two wine coolers, but his stomach was still tossing. He had stuff in his mind he could not shake out. They left her place and he drove her back to his trailer to wait for McCall.

~ * ~

Ozzie stumbled over the black dog that was right behind him. The Labs had not let him out of their sight. He tried to pet them now and then, but was very busy directing everyone. Every time he turned around they were there; sad eyes staring. Sam was standing next to him when Sam's phone sounded off. Sam listened and then took Ozzie's pad and began to write,

"Okay, keep on it. Thanks."

Sam showed Ozzie the name, address, DOB and State ID Number on the pad. Ozzie read, "Tobias Ezra Diamond. AKA Turd. Our boy. Any luck on the Flathead name?"

"Not on the computer. They're checking the paper, but won't be through it all until more people come in tomorrow. Still stuff out in the Troops that's in a file folder or in some trooper's desk."

"Address in Lehighton." Ozzie felt a nudge on his leg. Salt was looking up and wagging his tail. He put his paw on Ozzie's leg, and Ozzie tried to move aside. Pepper came up on the other side and sat there.

"They're hungry, Ozzie," Sam said. "Let's find their food." Sam stuck his head in the mud room and found a huge bag of dog food. The bowls were on the porch and were licked clean. Sam filled them and the Labs were in them instantly. They ate fast and hard. "Slow down, boys. There's more tomorrow," Sam laughed.

"Jeez, Sam. I just thought. What are these dogs gonna do. I mean, what are we gonna do with them?"

"The county will put them up temporarily in the pound," Sam said, "Seems a shame no one can take them. They are real people dogs."

"I don't know, Sam. How long before hubby gets out and can walk around to take care of them. No, they can't go to the pound, it's not right," Ozzie sounded sad. "You got that big farm, Sam. Molly would love the company."

"Oh, no. Ken's got graduation and no one will be there," Sam quickly said.

Ozzie was quiet for a bit and said, "She'll kill me, just kill me dead."

Sam threw up his hands and said, "It's the right thing to do, but I didn't say that. I don't want Marie coming after me."

It was settled. The boys were temporarily added to the Ozliewski tribe.

~ * ~

Calvin was able to get Hank to tell him the gun had a shiny end. Calvin finally figured out what the groggy husband was saying. He was still sitting next to Hank when Sam and Ozzie walked into the room. "I see the uniforms are out in the hall. Where's the kid?" asked Sam.

"In the morgue," said Johnny quietly. "Flatlined right after they brought him in. Didn't say another word. Probie working off his shoplifting pinch at the garden center."

Sam motioned them out into the hall. "Looks like two guys and two guns, a .38 and a .45."

Calvin filled Sam in on the new information he received from Hank, "He's out of it now. They doped him up. Not a good time to tell him about the Mrs."

Sam thought a minute and said, "We have an address on one of them in Lehighton. We're gonna meet a Troop N car and pay him a visit. Vests and extra mags."

Calvin groaned, "Mess up my good shoes, man."

"Oh, you can sit on your pillow in the car if it's all too much for your prissy self," Johnny said dryly.

Calvin just cocked his head at Johnny and headed for the car, "Make him follow you, Corp. Slow his cracker ass down."

When they got to the parking lot, Johnny burst into laughter. Ozzie's car was parked next to Johnny's and two wet noses were sticking out of the rear window. The big bag of dog food was on the floorboard and the back windows were stained and covered in dog snot, "Holy shit, Ozzie. You brought the K-9 corps with you!"

"And more dog hair than you can imagine!" Sam added.

## Chapter Five

Detective Christie O'Shea didn't like Sunday nights. She never made any plans because she knew from her twelve years on the sheriff's department that Sunday night was disliked by a lot of other people too. They then took out their frustrations and weirdness on each other. That's when her phone would ring. She was a "Persons" detective and any crime where a person was assaulted, robbed or killed was handled by her squad. When she got the call from the station, she was dressed and out the door in just a few minutes.

She slid her short, trim body into the brown Jeep Wrangler in her driveway and fired it up. The sheriff's radio, in what used to be the glove compartment, squawked to life with the chatter of the other deputies out and about tonight. She knew very little about the call. What should have been a misdemeanor fight had turned into an aggravated battery, a felony assault. The victim and the witness were in the ER with the uniform deputy.

She drove steadily west into the city from her ranch style house off McIntosh Road. Finally, she had been able to buy a decent house on her own after living in apartments and with loser boyfriends long enough. Screwing around with her money after joining the department at twenty-two had seemed like fun times. She took a few years to figure out she needed to slow down her lifestyle and put some money in the bank. Wasn't getting any younger and eight years on the road on shift work was enough.

When she made detective, she started getting decent overtime. A year working property crimes, two years on the narcs and the court hours that came from it built her bank account up quickly. Now she had moved up to the top squad in the detective bureau. More overtime tonight.

The Wrangler rode a bit rough, but she was happy with it. The Sheriff kept the best of the confiscated cars and most of the detectives and narcs drove vehicles that didn't stand out to the bad guys. Christie's light brown hair flecked with hints of auburn was in a neat, thick braid down just over the collar of the jacket covering her .40 Sig. She was starting to sweat so she flipped on the air conditioning. Wind whistled through the Jeep's doors and windows, but the A/C helped. The night was warm but not too humid. The summer heat would be down upon the county soon enough.

~ * ~

Toby and the girl he now remembered was Krystal sat watching videos on the television. She kept asking him if he had any dope, and he kept telling her it was on its way. His trailer sat crooked on cement blocks that had settled when heavy rain came down the gravely side of the hill behind it. The filthy couch was higher on one end than the other, but neither seemed to notice. The text message he found on his phone he had left behind on the kitchen table was from Flathead. Flathead told him to stay home and wait. Toby was a little less sick now, but the booze was wearing off and he was getting snippy with Krystal.

"Stop askin'; shut the fuck up," Toby snarled.

"But sweetie, I, I..." she started to say.

Toby shoved her over and got up to look in his refrigerator again. The same empty shelves were there. Only a moldy orange and half empty mustard and mayonnaise jars. He wasn't hungry anyway, but it was habit.

~ * ~

The road trooper from the Hazleton troop met them at the supermarket parking lot. Sam filled him in and they all dug bullet resistant vests from their trunks and suited up. The address for Tobias Diamond was at the west end of the borough. Sam told Calvin and Johnny to go around back and he and Ozzie would go to the front door with the uniform.

It was a rooming house over an old hotel. A narrow stair led up from the side of the building. Sam followed Ozzie and the patrol trooper up the dark confining stairs. It gave Sam the creeps. No place to go but straight up.

At the top were four doors and a small hall that wrapped around the top of the stairs. Only three had numbers on them and Ozzie pounded on number two, Diamond's last known address.

Nothing. Ozzie waited a few seconds and pounded again. The door to number four creaked open and they all tensed and looked into the face of a middle aged man. He was unshaven and wore a wrinkled, blue checked flannel shirt and boxers.

The man started to speak and then saw the uniform and snapped his mouth shut. Ozzie slid over in front of him. "Know the people in two?" Ozzie asked.

"Nobody there. She's at work," the man's breath smelled like a sewer. Ozzie talked to him and figured out the woman who lived there was probably the fifth or sixth person to have the apartment since "Turd" left over two years ago. "Glad he's gone, real dope head. Gave us a bad name, ya' know?"

"Can't let that happen," Ozzie said. Ozzie got the name and phone number of the landlady and led the rest back down the stairs and outside.

The Labs were very happy to see Ozzie again and wagged their tails in unison, standing on Ozzie's back seat with their noses out of the window. Sam went to the back and signaled Johnny and Calvin it was a no go. Ozzie borrowed Sam's phone and talked to the landlady, but she had no idea where Turd was, and he still owed her two months' rent. The road trooper went back on patrol and they returned to the supermarket lot to unsuit.

"Let's hold off on a photo lineup for now, Ozzie. Calvin, we're in court in Philly tomorrow. You and Johnny talk to the victim again in the morning and see if he remembers anything but the disguise. We don't want him to pass on a good line up. Work the databases and see if Tobias pops up. Do a thorough canvas again now that it has sunk in to the community. We should be back later in the day. Maybe by then intelligence will run down the other AKA." Sam sounded disappointed. He did not like hitting dead ends so soon in an investigation.

The call to the Captain did not go well. She was not happy that Sam had not made more progress. She "suggested" that the crew stand down for the night and pick up in the morning, during regular hours. Sam knew she would have let them run if anything significant was pending, but he was still reluctant to go home.

"Okay, that's it. Go home. Ozzie, run me home and then you get to deal with Marie," Sam nodded at the dogs.

"Ah, she'll love 'em. She's gonna throw me out, but she'll love them dogs." Ozzie thanked Johnny and Calvin and drove Sam west toward home.

~ * ~

Flathead was just starting out the side door to get some crank from his hiding place behind the garage and then to meet with Turd when his phone sounded. The caller was from apartment number three, the one with no number on the door. "Bunch of state cops here looking for Turd," the caller told Flathead.

He stopped and was very still. He stood there for over two minutes listening to the plastic clock on the wall above the sink click over the seconds. He worked his jaw and went out the door and to his truck without getting any dope for Toby. He now had something else in his mind for him.

~ * ~

"Detective O'Shea." Christie showed the redhead the gold star and ID card in the black leather case. "Sit down and let's talk a bit. You need anything? Coffee or some water?" she asked. The redhead shook her head and looked down at her dirty feet.

"I already told the guy everything," the redhead bit the nails on her fingers and kept looking down.

"I know and thank you for helping your friend. You probably saved her life by calling for the rescue unit. You're a hero for her," Christie tried to sound sincere. "I know it's difficult, but could you tell it all to me again?"

It took a while, but eventually the redhead cried it out and told most of it to Christie's digital recorder. She left out the drugs, but Christie had the boys' first names, physical descriptions and the color of their car. The redhead had no clue what make or model it was, only, "maybe a Chevy." The problem was the redhead was supposed to go back to Alabama in three days. Christie told her that her friend would not be out of the hospital by then, but they would work with the hospital social worker to see if there was any help available for her to stay longer.

Christie went in alone to see the blonde, but she was out of it and sleeping but laboriously breathing on her own. She drove the redhead back to the motel and went in to look at the room.

The crime scene people had dusted for prints and probably took DNA and fiber evidence. Christie wasn't sure if the sheriff would pay for the DNA workup unless the girl died.

"Here's my card." Christie wrote her cell number on the back. "Call me if you think of anything else. I'll come to see your friend tomorrow. I'm sure she will be better by then." Christie doubted her own words.

Few of the rooms nearby were occupied. Christie found several people to interview and one thought there was an older grey Mercury in the lot earlier that wasn't there now. She drove north to the sheriff's office and went in to use the computer system. She indexed the first names, but nothing matched. She needed more information. For the next thirty minutes she worked on the supplemental to the offense report then hit the drive thru at Wendy's and went home.

~ * ~

Grace changed planes in Sioux City and ran into some of the crew she knew. They chatted as the passengers filed into the plane and struggled with their overhead bags. The plane was only half full but would pick up more people at Midway before going on to Cleveland and Buffalo. A long night ahead. Tuesday couldn't come soon enough.

~ * ~

Toby heard the truck rev as it pulled into his driveway. He turned to Krystal and said, "Get lost. Go out back and smoke a cigarette. I got some private business to do."

She just sat there and looked at him. He slapped her and pulled her up to her feet. "Okay, okay. I, I'm goin'," she whimpered. She grabbed her purse and saw the big bearded man climb out of the black truck as she waddled out the small back door, disappearing into the darkness.

Toby stood in the door and watched Flathead walk up to the trailer. Toby thought Flathead looked mad. Flathead yanked the door open and hit Toby hard square on the nose. Toby's knees buckled and he couldn't breathe until he opened his mouth and gulped in air and blood from his dripping broken nose. Flathead grabbed Toby's hair and pulled him into the space between the small kitchen and the couch.

"How the fuck did the cops know it was you. You stupid shit. You can't even shoot straight or you ran your mouth," Flathead snarled into Toby's ear. By now the silver .45 was in Flathead's hand and he screwed it into Toby's mouth. "Cops all over your old place. They ain't stupid, they'll track you down."

Toby wrenched his head free of the pistol and tried to get up. "No, Head, no! Can't be, man. You know me, I done what you said!" Tears were streaming down into the blood on Toby's face.

Flathead dropped a knee into Toby's side and ribs crunched. Toby moaned and cried, "I did what you..."

The gunshot hit Toby's left eye socket and exploded out the back of his head. He went instantly limp and his bladder emptied. Flathead stood erect over him and shot him two more times. He stepped into the kitchen and took a dirty dish towel, wiped the .45 clean and dropped it to the floor next to Toby's lifeless right eye. He walked out to his still running truck and carefully backed out onto the road and drove away. He never saw the frightened look on Krystal's face as she hid behind the rusted swing set in the cluttered tiny back yard of the trailer.

~ * ~

"Hey, baby," Johnny said to Annette who was sitting at the small kitchen table smoking a cigarette. He peeled off his coat and sat down beside her. He used her lit end to light his own and blew out a long puff of smoke.

She got up and pulled two bottles of beer from the refrigerator, "Wanna talk about it?" she asked. She set the beer in front of Johnny and pulled off the top of hers, cigarette dangling from her lips.

"Gonna be a loooong day tomorrow," Johnny drawled in his Georgia accent. "Two dead at the garden center down below Fogelsville."

Johnny and Annette were on their second marriage, to each other. It had been better the second time around. She worked shifts at the truck plant in Macungie and Johnny was either working, fixing their cars or riding his Harley. They passed each other often enough to keep it interesting.

"Well, we can use the money," she said. "I wanna get rid of the piece of shit station wagon. Saw a used Mini Cooper at the lot on 100 on the way to work. A yellow one. They're asking $9500. Computer says it's worth $7800. Whatcha think?"

Johnny pulled hard on his beer and looked at her, "The wagon's gotta go, but a Mini?" He scrunched up his face and mimed puking. Johnny had driven fast cars since he was twelve. For a while, before the army, he raced on dirt tracks in Georgia and Alabama.

"They go like stink, and it's cute," Annette offered.

Johnny groaned, "Cute? Oh my, I'll definitely have to look at it. Cute gets me all squiggly."

Annette threw her bottle cap at him. "Asshole." She got up quick and went out onto the porch.

Johnny called after her, "Yeah, but everybody needs at least one!"

~ * ~

Sam stood in the gravel drive and watched Ozzie pull away back through the oaks and the orchard. Molly was not in her barrel, and Sam figured she was in with Ken. Sam just stayed still and listened to the quiet. So far from the main roads there was no traffic sounds. It was still too early in the summer for peepers and no night birds were making a sound. Just quiet. Sam had been thinking about court tomorrow between Ozzie's ramblings and nudges from the Labs trying to get at the front windows with their wet noses. He tried to think positive, but it was of no use. The state police lawyers would barely speak to him, and his personal lawyer was very reluctant to even show up. The check he would receive for his troubles ultimately convinced him.

"Hey, you coming in?" Molly shot between Ken's legs as he called to Sam from the kitchen door. She scrambled down the steps and was at Sam's legs in an instant, jumping up and wanting attention. She suddenly put all four feet on the ground and began sniffing Sam's pants front, back and side. Her tail stopped wagging and she snorted.

"Jealous, girl?" she looked up at him and spun back to the steps. Up and past Ken into the house.

~ * ~

Calvin left his suit jacket and tie in his well-cared for Bonneville and went into the bar. He wore a light workout jacket to cover his weapon and keep off the chill setting in now that it was well after dark. It was crowded for a Sunday night. He needed something for pain. His hip was killing him. He never let on to anybody. The state docs were reluctant to certify him for return to duty. Calvin might have intimidated them a little and they gave in.

He found a table and sat down as the piano player began an old Count Basie number. Calvin liked all kinds of music but had a special feeling for jazz. It made the girls horny. The waitress was not his type. Over thirty and a little chunky. She brought him a double bourbon and soda and he drank half of it on the first swallow. He might have to find a driver tonight. There were several prospects in the lounge.

~ * ~

"No, no, no!" Marie emphatically yelped at Ozzie as he stood at the kitchen door flanked by Salt and Pepper. "No damn dogs in my house! Period!" Her eyes were blazing and her lips had disappeared they were drawn so tight.

Katie shot past her and went right up to Pepper and stuck her face into his. Pepper licked her and both tails started wagging again. "Are they for me, Daddy?" She had both dogs in her face now and was rubbing their muzzles.

"Jeez, Marie they got no place to go. The lady is d-e-a-d and the guy is in the hospital." Ozzie didn't want to upset little Katie.

Junior strolled into the kitchen and went to the fridge. He looked in and then stood up straight and looked at his mom. He wrinkled his brow and then looked over at the door. "Holy...I mean, what the heck, Dad? Where'd they come from?"

"They're not staying," Marie growled and put her hands on her hips.

"Ah, come on, honey. It's just for tonight. I promise. I'll put 'em out in the garage. They ain't gonna be no problem," Ozzie offered.

"They aren't going to be any problem is right. Take them to the pound," she demanded.

"Well, ah, the pound's closed and they're real gentle dogs and nobody's at their place to take care of them. Look, I'll get them outta here and in the garage, no trouble at all. Come on, Junior, help me," Ozzie said.

"They're gone to-mor-row!" Marie snipped and stormed into the living room to watch PBS.

"I'm coming too," Katie chirped. By now Connie and the twins had heard the commotion and followed Ozzie, Katie and Junior to the garage.

The Labs were in dog Shangri La. Gobs of hands and faces to lick, and Ozzie was pouring a little more food into their bowls for them from the huge bag, "Now, kids. Stay back and let them eat. Dogs can be nippy about their food."

Only Junior listened. The girls were hanging on the Labs and pulling their tails while the big dogs devoured their food. Ozzie got one of his plastic buckets and partially filled it with water from the utility sink. The boys quickly finished their food and then went at the bucket. As much spilled out onto the floor as went into the dogs.

"I'm sleeping out here with them," Connie announced.

"Me, too!" the twins said in unison. Katie was too busy trying to get on Salt like a pony to speak.

"School day tomorrow, kids." Ozzie snapped the leashes on the dogs and handed one each to Junior and Connie. Make sure they poop and get plastic bags to pick it up. Your mom's mad enough as it is without dog crap on her sneakers.

"Dad! Ick," Connie protested. Junior led them out to the yard with the twins and Katie following.

Ozzie went into the kitchen to see if any of the chicken was left and was met by Marie carrying a pillow and a blanket. She thrust them into Ozzie's hands. "Ozzie sleeps with the smelly flea bags or with the fishes, you choose," she told him.

Ozzie hung his head as she spun back around and went back to her show. He didn't find the chicken but did manage to find a container of potato salad to take back out to the garage.

He passed by the state car in the driveway. He drove it home because it was farther to the barracks than here from Sam's and he had to be up and out very early in the morning for court in Philly. He looked at the windows and said to himself he would have to clean up the mess tomorrow before they left.

Ozzie made up the old couch in the corner of his workshop in the garage. The kids often camped out here, but this was the first time Marie had bounced him out of the house in all the years they had been married. New ground. The kids kept the dogs busy until Marie called from the house, "Bedtime!"

Junior stayed behind. "What are you going to do with them?" he asked.

Ozzie didn't know. "I've got to go all the way to Philadelphia to court tomorrow. Take them out before you go to school and come right home after. Pray to God your mom stays out of here."

Jimmy couldn't sleep. The couch had sagging cushions and his back hurt. He went into the kitchen and took Mom's last beer from the fridge. He was angry about the smartass girl and Russell's half witted teasing on the way back out to their house. It had started out to be a fun night but turned to shit. The truck wouldn't be ready until Tuesday, and they needed to make some money. He was frustrated. Feeling closed in. He wanted to get out of just scraping by; make some cash. The truck would really help. Make a run to the new homes being built then buy a load of pot from the Miami boys and make more.

It seemed to her like an hour. It was actually only a few minutes. Krystal called out, "Toby?" She had managed to get to the back door but no farther. "Toby?" Tears were running down her cheeks and she was trembling. She knew, but she did not want to know. By now she was sobbing, "T…T…Tooobeee."

Krystal made herself reach up and twist the doorknob. It stuck and then released and she stumbled a bit backward as the door popped open in her hand. Slowly she peered into the trailer. Toby was in a heap on the floor and covered in blood. She never saw the big silver gun on the floor. She tried to scream, but she had no air in her lungs. She just turned and began to walk quickly down the back side of the trailer and around toward the front. She gained speed and by the time she got to the blacktop, she was running as fast as she could, her flip flops snapping as she went.

## Chapter Six

"Sam? You okay? Sam!" Eileen nudged him in the side and shot Grace a look of frustration. "Come back to earth. I think Ken's about to march out." The school band was already on the parade ground and playing something military. They had just entered the stadium as they played each service branch song. Sam had not heard any of it. He was lost in the flashes of memory from the past two days.

"I'm sorry, girls. My head is on vacation. Where is he?" Sam asked. He sat between Grace and Eileen in the crowded bleachers. Down in front of them at field level were uniformed teachers and military guests. He spotted Ken in his full dress uniform marching in from the left end of the field with the Honor Staff. As they took their position directly in front of the Commandant's box, the color guard marched on, followed closely by the first companies from the Corps of Cadets. The seventh graders looked small in their uniforms and the M14 rifles they carried on their shoulders made them look even smaller. Sam remembered when Ken had been in that group. It seemed ages ago.

Grace was squirming in her seat, trying to get a good view of the back of Ken's head. He was on the left of a line of senior cadets with the Cadet Colonel in the middle. Their parade dress hats sported plumes that fluttered in the light breeze. Ken's selection to Honor Staff had freed him from the many hours of rehearsals the Corps had been through the past few days in preparation for these ceremonies. He had been able to spend time with his dad and pick Grace up from the Philly airport yesterday. They had a flight out later today to Sarasota to spend a few days with Grace's mom, and each other.

Sam slipped his hand into Eileen's and held on. His eyes were starting to tear he was so proud of Ken and all he had accomplished. Being a single dad had not been easy, but Sam had plenty of help from both grandmothers and Varnum.

"They look so young," said Grace as the eighth graders took their place on the field.

"Ken was always big for his age, but he seemed to grow out of his uniforms before the end of each year. Some of those boys probably have his old dress grays on now." Sam tried to think about Ken, but he could not get his mind off the events he had just gone through.

His squad was still working the murders at the garden center. They had not found Tobias Diamond and no one in the whole state police had a clue about the nickname of the other shooter. The brass was running out of patience. Calvin had found surveillance camera video of the shooters, but the quality was poor. Knowing Diamond was one of them helped, but the other guy was bigger and older and that was all they knew. Calvin was canvassing up and down route 100 and had stopped at the hamburger place closest to the scene to use the bathroom and spotted a camera covering the parking lot. That video led him to the businesses nearby, and he found the hotel lot video showed the pair switching vehicles and peeling off the disguises. Neither vehicle had been located yet.

Ken and the other staff smartly saluted the passing juniors as they marched by. It was warm and the sun was bright. Sam was carrying his Glock so he had to keep his suit coat on. He and Eileen had a late lunch date with the chief in Radnor Township after they took Ken and Grace to the airport.

The local police there owed a lot to Sam and Eileen. Mostly Eileen. Last November, one of their officers had been attacked during a traffic stop by two Russian mob thugs. Sam and Eileen happened to drive by after dropping Ken off at Varnum and Sam stopped to assist the officer. Sam ended up needing the assistance. Eileen stepped in with one of Ken's baseball bats and evened the odds by putting the Russians in the hospital. It would be a chance for the department to express their gratitude.

~ * ~

Russell parked the truck in the shade at the end of the lot of the strip mall. Jimmy got out and went inside for a six pack and cigarettes. The truck was running well and looked like new with the paint job Popper had given it. They were between Sarasota and Bradenton east of the interstate. There were several new home developments going up in the area, and they were scouting them during the daylight. Jimmy told Russell the smaller development of only thirty five homes was the best bet. None were occupied, and almost half were nearing completion and looked like they had the appliances either installed or in boxes in the garages. They decided to return tonight to see if any security was around.

Jimmy came back to the truck and said, "Gimme your phone, brother." Russell dug the phone from his jeans and handed it to Jimmy.

Jimmy entered a number and then said, "Hey, this is your old friend from up north. We need some t-shirts, green ones like last time. Can we pick 'em up on Friday?" the person on the phone spoke and then Jimmy said, "Okay, Friday at the Waffle House."

Jimmy ended the call and tossed the cell back to Russell. He opened a beer and lit a cigarette. "Now we wait."

Russell fidgeted in his seat and finally took a beer from the six pack and drank it in three swallows. "Well, Jimmy. What if—?"

"No ifs, brother. We gonna do just fine tonight. The dude in Tampa will take all we can load up. We can make two trips and with what we got last night, we got plenty for the boys from Miami. We'll be rich men by Monday.

~ * ~

Ozzie left the hospital after again speaking with Hank. Hank was glad the dogs were being taken care of. The shock of losing his wife had not hit him yet. The pain meds the doctors were pumping into him had dulled the enormity of it all. Ozzie pulled the uniformed troopers from the hallway, and the hospital security chief set up his own guard.

Hank was finally able to tell Ozzie that he knew who Diamond was now. He could remember a skinny kid named Toby who had been one of the probationers sent by the county. He worked at the garden center for only a few weeks and just stopped showing up. He wasn't a good worker, and Hank had almost forgotten about him.

~ * ~

Sam listened to the marching music as the cadets began to fill the parade ground. But he had too much trying to occupy his mind.

*Yesterday another address was found for Tobias Diamond, but when the troops went there they found he had moved from there also. Ozzie was spinning on his own tail. Calvin and Johnny were there to help, but had their own caseloads to manage. Ozzie's stomach churned and he needed another handful of antacids to quiet it.*

*He told Sam he'd slept like crap on Sunday night. His bed in the garage was extra crowded when the two Labs decided they had to sleep snuggled up next to him on the same couch. His alarm went off before daylight, and he had to wrestle his way out from underneath them to go inside and get ready to pick up Sam at the barracks to go to Philly.*

*Sam arrived that morning in the barracks parking lot and found Ozzie scrubbing dog drool from the windows of the unmarked car.*

*"Marie throw you out?" Sam asked Ozzie. Sam handed Ozzie a box of chocolate doughnuts.*

*Ozzie hesitated and then said, "Yeah, sorta. Threw me and the dogs out to the garage. I gotta figure something out for them boys."*

*Sam went inside and was stopped by the desk officer who handed Sam two notes to call the lieutenant. Both from before 5:30 AM. The calls had not gone well. Sam had to listen to him screaming about overtime but cut him off when Sam told him the captain had approved it. Then the lieutenant told Sam they had to drive their personal vehicles to Philadelphia to court. "It's a civil suit, Corporal."*

*Sam had enough. He said, "All due respect, sir. This so called civil suit is because of official police business. We're not driving personal vehicles, and we're charging the state for parking and lunch." Sam listened to him scream a bit more and just hung up. He was not in the mood to fight.*

*Ozzie ate five doughnuts before they got off the turnpike at Mid-County and three more on the expressway. They found a parking garage three blocks from the federal courthouse and walked to the security entrance.*

*The lobby was a marble cavern. High ceilings and indirect lighting gave it a movie set aura. The gray haired security guys were all retired cops standing guard now for the feds. Sam thought he recognized one as a retired sergeant from one of the nearby township departments but just wasn't sure. They had to lock up their weapons and then into the elevator and up to the courtroom. Inside was quiet. A court officer and court reporter were moving around up front, but the judge was not on the bench. The attorney for the family was not there yet, but Sam's personal attorney was huddled with the lawyer for the city and the state police counsel.*

*Sam and Ozzie sat in the front row of spectator seats, both reluctant to move past the gate in the front railing to the defendant's table. The big door at the back of the courtroom opened, and the lawyer for the plaintiffs entered and looked over the room. He spotted Sam and Ozzie and immediately frowned and looked away. As he approached the other lawyers, they parted and as a group walked to him. The lawyer for the city spoke briefly and they all turned and went into the judge's chambers.*

*"Yes, counselor, I'm quite well today, and you?" Sam mumbled sarcastically.*

*After thirty minutes, all the lawyers filed out and shook hands all around. Sam's lawyer and the state police counsel left last and stopped next to them. The state police counsel said, "It's done. Go back to work. Non-disclosure so don't ask." He turned and went down the aisle.*

*Sam started to say something, but his lawyer held up his hand to wait. After the big door closed and the room was again quiet, the lawyer said, "City settled with the family. State and you fellows are out of it, dismissed. The amount is not relevant anyways. You never had anything to worry about; this was in the cards from the beginning." He patted Sam on the shoulder and walked out.*

*Sam and Ozzie stood there watching the doors close. Sam turned to Ozzie, "Breakfast?"*

~ * ~

"Cadet Major Kenneth Deland." They watched Ken stride up the steps and salute the Commandant and receive his diploma. He marched out the other side and resumed his seat with the Honor Staff. Eileen squeezed one of Sam's hands and Grace the other. Sam was unable to speak. He knew if he tried it would come out in babbles.

The rest of the ceremony was again blurred to Sam. His mind was swimming and it hit him that Ken was now on his own. The tow rope had parted. Sam had lost something. He was pulling back the throttle and descending in a left turn and Ken was spiraling up to the right in the lift of the thermal. It felt hollow inside of him.

After a short reception for the seniors and their families put on by the Commandant's wife, Ken returned to his room for the last time. Sam had helped him empty the room last Friday and loaded all his accumulated things into the Pathfinder. He came out to the parking lot in slacks and a golf shirt, carrying his dress uniform in a garment bag over his shoulder.

"Dad, I hope you don't mind, but I gave my saber and parade hat to a junior who is a good guy. His family is scraping by trying to pay for all this…and…well, it seemed like the right thing to do."

Sam said, "Good decision. I don't think it would be very good for chopping firewood anyway."

They piled into the Pathfinder and Grace slid across the rear seat and gave Ken a kiss on the cheek. "There, congratulations. I'm happy for you. Are you ready for a vacation, I sure am." Ken blushed slightly at the kiss and noticed two wrapped presents on the seat between them.

Sam, looking in the rear view mirror, said, "Just a little something extra for your graduation."

Ken unwrapped the smaller package and found a new smart phone. "Thanks, Dad. You read my mind," Ken said as he unwrapped the larger present. That contained a tablet computer. "Oh my, Dad. This is too much to believe!"

"You'll need them both. The tablet is almost required for school. You can probably figure out what to do with the phone," said Sam, grinning.

Sam headed for the airport. They would be early for their flight, but Sam figured the kids would find something to occupy themselves until then.

~ * ~

Ozzie took the call. The crime sergeant from Hazleton was on the phone, "We found a dead body in a trailer on the side of a mountain. Landlord went to collect the overdue rent and collected your fugitive, Diamond."

"Just him?" Ozzie asked.

"And a squadron of blow flies. Been dead a couple of days. A .45 and a .38 were on the floor with him. Thought it might have been a suicide, but he has too many holes in him. Can you come up tomorrow morning and meet with our guys?"

"Yes, sir. First thing," Ozzie said.

Sam's cell phone rang next and Ozzie gave him the news. "Pick me up at the farm, Ozzie. We'll go from there," Sam said as he pulled onto I-95 from the airport.

~ * ~

The methamphetamine came up from Jersey. Flathead maintained his biker contacts there and they ran a tight business. No outsiders. They never wore colors when they did dope business and drove clean, late model sedans instead of Harleys. The scooters were for fun. Low profile. They had learned from their imprisoned brothers' mistakes.

The hotel was just off of I-80 in the Poconos. Not too fancy, but not shabby either. Flathead only used the room for a couple of hours, most of it waiting for the Jersey crew to arrive. Once the deal was done, he left the key card on the TV stand and was gone. He stayed off the interstate so it took a little longer to make his way back to the house with the naked lady picture. The sun was behind the mountain, and it would be dark soon.

"Some mail come for you," the woman said. Flathead used this address and a few others, none of which were actually where he lived. He left most of the dope there and went without saying anything to the woman or the old man. He would be back tomorrow to collect his money. Customers would be arriving soon, and he did not want to see any of them. The girls at the strip club would enjoy a taste and be oh so grateful.

~ * ~

The Chief was not in uniform and bought an expensive bottle of wine for their table. He poured a glass for Sam and Eileen and toasted her for her bravery and "spunk". Eileen was a little embarrassed and Sam even more so. The night that Eileen stepped into Sam and the Radnor officer's roadside battle, Sam had taken a good beating. He still had a small scar over his left eye that itched when it rained.

The officer didn't drink any wine. He was in uniform and had to go back to work after the dinner. "My wife wanted to come, but she's due in a couple of weeks and, well, you know how that is," he said.

"I can only imagine," Eileen said.

The Chief said, "Their case is coming up on the docket next month, but the DA thinks they're going to plead out or try to continue it again. Only one of them is still trying to get a lower bail and is in jail. They have no prior record in the states, but we think they were well connected back in Russia. Money collectors for protection. They had a wad of cash on them that night and probably thought we were going to take it from them, off the books, like they probably do back across the ocean. DA says they'll likely get it back anyway after the case is over. Cheaper for them to hire local talent and plead guilty than to pay a fancy Philly lawyer for a trial."

Ozzie went into the garage to let the Labs out. They were not there. He called them, thinking they were asleep in a corner but nothing. Their bowls were missing too. The now half empty bag of dog food was still under his workbench. Ozzie got nervous.

He quickly walked to the kitchen door and went in. "Junior!" Before he could say anything else, he heard the thump of eight Lab feet rumble across the dining room floor and the dogs burst into the kitchen, all tails, noses and tongues to greet him.

"Junior! Your mother will murder you! Get these dogs outta here," Ozzie bellowed. The Labs sat down and looked as if they had messed on the floor. Ozzie had scared them. He tried to wade through the boys to find Junior, but stopped short when Marie appeared in the doorway.

"Stop yelling, you big ox. You're scaring them," she scolded. The dogs got all happy again and swarmed to Marie. To Ozzie's amazement, she scooped the big heads in her arms and kissed them each on the top of the head. "There, there, babies, big Daddy is just a mean old man to yell at you like that."

Ozzie was confused. His lovely bride just this morning was complaining about dog pee killing the grass and now she was trading spit with them. He'd slept three nights on the lumpy couch in the garage with dogs all over him and here they were in *her house*.

Ozzie started to say something, but Marie jumped in, "I know, I know. We had a come to Jesus moment today. Katie fell off her scooter in the driveway and yelped. Before I could get to her, the dogs had gone through the screen door and were beside her. They knew she needed help and were right there. They wouldn't leave her and forced their way into the kitchen with us. They just looked so sad and worried about her." Then he spotted the food dishes on the floor in front of the refrigerator.

"They're really just big babies, aren't you just big babies?" she cooed to them. The Labs began a fast tail wag in unison and pushed against Marie's legs. "But you have to get the shop vac in here tonight to suck up all the dog hair. My goodness they shed so," Marie told Ozzie.

"Yes, Ma'am." Ozzie saluted as the kitchen began to fill with the Ozliewski tribe and the dogs were torn between kids to play with or follow Ozzie up the stairs to get out of his work clothes. "Never a dull moment," he mumbled as he headed for the steps.

~ * ~

Of course, they got bumped up to first class. The crew knew who Grace was and even the captain shook Ken's hand before they took off and wished him luck at the Academy. He had graduated from there some years before and showed Ken his ring.

"Best advice is, keep your mouth shut as much as possible except at meals. Once the summer is over it's study, study, study. It goes by quick if you pay attention and hit all the marks," the gray haired captain told Ken.

Grace's mom picked them up at the Sarasota airport. Grace had not said a lot about her to Ken. They had many other things to talk about since they met last fall. Ken knew Grace's mom sold real estate and that she lived by herself since Grace's father had been killed in a boating accident a few years ago. Ken didn't expect the slim, blonde, forty one year old beauty hugging Grace at the baggage claim. Grace had jet black hair and dark brown eyes and her mom looked like she could still qualify for the Swedish suntan team.

"Ken, this is my mom," Grace said as they released each other. "Mom, this is Ken."

Her eyes flashed and she smiled, showing perfect white teeth between red lipstick. She grabbed his shoulders. "I am so happy to see you. Finally. My, my you are a big one," she bubbled. Ken was expecting a handshake and was surprised.

After they piled into her white Mercedes and drove to her spacious waterfront home, Katrina Echaverria fed them fried chicken and macaroni salad.

"You have a beautiful home, ma'am," Ken remarked.

"It's a teardown. We bought the place for a song years ago, but now the property is worth more than the house. The thing now is to bulldoze the existing house and build two story marble palaces with columned entrances. The neighbors probably think this is an eyesore. Eventually, I'll sell it, make a bundle and get a condo out on the beach at Siesta Key."

They took their cold drinks out past the caged pool and onto the dock where they sat watching the sun light up the gathering clouds in brilliant red and orange as it set over the bay. Katrina could see the two youngsters catching each other's eyes now and then. She let her native Floridian southern accent slip out for emphasis when she told Ken of her growing up in Arcadia.

"Daddy knew everybody in town. He had a hardware store and would let us kids sneak a penny candy from the glass case if we were good. It was a mixed blessing. Small town, but a lot of big city crap floated in. Mostly it was okay, but I had to get out and got a job hustling drinks in a club on Siesta. Momma and Daddy were beside themselves. Met Grace's dad and wham, bam we flew to Vegas and got married."

Ken sat up and said, "Oh, that reminds me. I have to call the airport. We were supposed to go over there tomorrow to fly, but the weather is going to be better on Friday, and I need to reschedule. Would you ladies excuse me?" Ken stood and went toward the house.

Ken was not to the end of the dock before Katrina scooted her deck chair over next to Grace to get the real scoop.

~ * ~

"Lift; come on, I ain't doin' this all by myself!" Jimmy grunted as he and Russell wrestled a refrigerator onto the bed of the pick-up. They had the back of the truck almost full of the boxed appliances and expensive tools they found the contractors had left behind in the unfinished houses' garages. The deadbolts had not been installed yet and the simple twist knob locks were easy to slip. Jimmy and Russell worked as quick as the beer allowed them. No one was around and the new development was unlighted and unguarded.

The bed was full and Russell started the pick-up. Jimmy lit a cigarette and got in the passenger side. They eased out of the construction and headed south. Russell kept his speed under the limit, but they still would be unloading at the house in about an hour.

"We'll come back for another load tonight. Easy pickins," Jimmy said.

~ * ~

She sunk heavily into her chair. Her desk was covered with papers and case folders. A stack of pink message slips was waiting in her "in" box. Christie was beat. She had been up for over twenty four hours and still had paperwork to file before she could leave the office. She peeled off her ballistic vest and dropped it on the floor. Her black tactical boots came off and she padded in her socks to the coffee pot.

The tip on the location of an armed robber she had an arrest warrant for panned out after a long surveillance. The jerk decided he wasn't going peacefully and earned additional felony charges after he lost the fight with the deputies. His arrest photo was taken with bandages on his nose and forehead.

Now she had to file the arrest report and set up an appointment with the state attorney's office. She would be at least a couple of hours and then have to be back in at 8:30 tomorrow. Then she could go back to work on all her open cases and any new ones the sergeant dropped on her desk. She needed three more of herself to keep up. It didn't make her feel any better that the other detectives in her squad were just as behind as she was. *Job security.*

~ * ~

"Grace's dad? It was love at first sight for him. Me? It took a little while, but he proved he wasn't the big jerk I thought he was at first." Katrina finished her Mojito and stood up. "I'm all tuckered. See you kids in the morning." She walked toward the house and was soon out of sight. Grace wasted no time jumping onto Ken's lap. The deck chair creaked but held.

"Now, you're all for me," she kissed him hard and his arms slipped around her. The world hushed and for the next hour not a word passed between them.

~ * ~

Dutch was in the back yard for the second time since they got back to Eileen's. Sam stood with a beer bottle in his hand on the small back porch watching the big dog make his rounds, peeing on every object that rose above the ground.

"Missed a spot," Sam called to Dutch who just ignored him. Eileen was mixing some homemade salsa for them and had the television in the living room on the old movie channel. They both appreciated the classic movies, and Errol Flynn was going to be flirting with ladies and skewering bad guys with a sword soon. She expected some flirting was going to happen on the couch too.

Dutch bolted into the kitchen through the back door and Sam came in behind him. "Got any diet soda? I have to drive over the mountain later," Sam asked. He tossed the empty beer bottle into her recycle bin and without waiting for her to reply, opened the fridge and pulled out a can of diet orange soda. "Wow, that smells good," he said, looking over at the bowl of chopped peppers, onions, tomatoes and cilantro.

Eileen carried the bowl and another filled with scoop shaped corn chips into the living room. "Do you miss him yet?" she asked.

"Yeah, but at least I get to see him back here before he heads off for basic. Who knows when he will be back again? I think I'll fly out there and visit this fall sometime. Ever seen the Rockies?" Sam asked.

Eileen put the snacks on her coffee table and plopped onto the couch. "Flew over them once coming back from San Diego. Never went back. I was the marine's ex shortly after that."

Sam raised his eyebrows and decided he would leave it there. He sat next to her on the couch and dug into the chips. Dutch took up position next to him at the end of the coffee table and waited for the handout he knew was coming.

"Oh, it's in black and white," Eileen moaned.

Sam said, "Some of the best ones are."

~ * ~

"Detective, ah, she had to have surgery on her throat, ah, I don't know what I'm going to do, where I'm gonna stay. Ah, can you call me here at the hospital?" The voicemail ended and Christie checked the time it had come in on her desk phone. It had been over two hours, but she decided she would try.

The girl answered on the third ring. She was alone in her friend's hospital room. "I had to get out of the motel. I'm out of money. They said I could stay here with Patsy. She's in recovery."

"I'll call the social worker in the morning to see if they have something temporary for you," Christie said. "How is she doing?"

"She had to have an operation to help her breathe. She was injured more than they thought. She's gonna be here for a while." The girl was starting to cry.

Christie talked with her for another ten minutes until there was nothing left to say. After she hung up, she felt like crap. She was tired and called it. Her bed would feel real good tonight. What was left of it.

~ * ~

Jimmy was exhausted and felt sticky and covered with grit and dust.

They had manhandled the last of the appliances into the old house and sat on the porch drinking a cold beer. "They'll be here with the big truck tomorrow at noon. We get to sleep in, if the old lady don't make trouble."

"Fuckin' tired," was all that Russell could manage.

"We ain't gonna blow the cash from the dope this time. Haulin' refrigerators is too much like work," Jimmy said.

The mosquitoes swarmed, but the brothers stuck it out for a while longer and managed to get inside before they both fell asleep and became blood donors.

~ * ~

Flathead pulled the package from behind the truck seat and opened his new cell phone. The last one had been stripped of its battery and thrown in the river. He entered the dark club and found a table off to the right. A pretty young girl, topless and wearing a French maid's apron and hat, came to the table to take his order. She was chewing gum and seemed very bored with the whole thing.

It took him about a half an hour to drink a couple of shots of tequila and chase that with three beers. By then he had the numbers programmed into the phone and sent a text to the important contacts with his new number. With that done he could concentrate on getting drunk and a hand job from one of the girls.

## Chapter Seven

The cloud cover changed their plans. They were supposed to be flying in a sailplane over Arcadia today, but no sun meant few, if any, thermals. Ken rescheduled with Margie at the airport even though the weather wasn't great for Friday, but was going to be better than today.

Ken was up early and went out the side door. He stretched and breathed in the warm humid air. It smelled different here. Wet, earthy plant smells. Very different from the spring in Pennsylvania. He took off at a fast trot and as his muscles warmed, he picked up the pace. Katrina's neighborhood had no sidewalks and the tree lined streets curved and rose slightly from the bay. He worked his way east and crossed Osprey and then Orange Avenue. The homes became smaller and more modest. Soon he was passing apartments and businesses.

At U.S. 41, he turned north and found a sidewalk so he didn't have to run on the busy street. The sun was behind the clouds, but the air was getting warmer and he felt it. Ken was sweat soaked and knew he had missed too many workouts with all the activity of the past few days. He was determined to keep his physical condition ready for the summer ahead. He would need all the advantage he could get in Colorado.

He ran steadily and followed the curve of U.S. 41 around to the bayfront. The view opened up to moored sailboats and a small park next to a busy marina. Through the park and out the front of the marina, he turned back south, eventually running past Katrina's street and continued on kicking in sprints and then slowing to a fast jog. He worked back and forth between 41 and the water until his mental pedometer told him he was beyond five miles.

As he passed the hospital parking lot, he turned back toward the bay and ran as hard as he could back to Katrina's. He found the house, slowed to a walk and went into the back yard. There was a nice breeze slanting off the bay and he went out onto the dock to grind out push ups and sit ups. He didn't see Grace and Katrina watching him intently from the kitchen window.

~ * ~

It was raining hard when Ozzie pulled into the lot at Troop N headquarters in West Hazleton. He dropped Sam at the door and then wheeled the black Crown Vic into a visitor's slot. He grabbed his notebook and hurried through the downpour into the lobby. The desk lady buzzed them through, and they clipped on their state police IDs and went upstairs to the conference room. Sam brought pound cake and the coffee was ready and filled the small room with a rich aroma.

The captain came in through the door and greeted Sam and Ozzie. He had been a few classes ahead of Sam at the Academy, but they had worked together in Bucks County when Sam ran a road patrol squad. He helped himself to the cake and coffee, and they caught up on mutual acquaintances. Ozzie was on his third piece when the sergeant and two crime troopers joined them.

They went over the crime scene and one trooper left to go to the autopsy. Ozzie briefed them on the garden center case and none of the Hazleton guys had a clue as to who this Flathead was. They all agreed that he was a good suspect for both cases. Ballistics had them on the front burner but would not be through testing the guns and comparing them to Ozzie's case until later in the day at the earliest.

Sam said, "We are at a dead end, so we can jump in and help with canvass or interviews if you need any help."

The case trooper said that there were only a few neighbors and all but three had already been interviewed, though they could run over after the meeting and knock them out. "Toby's cell phone was found, and we're getting subscriber information on the numbers he called and that called him. There were only a few text messages saved, and except for the last one he received, they didn't seem to mean anything."

"Any cash on him or in his trailer?" Ozzie asked.

"Only a few coins in his jeans pocket. He was a meth freak. Needles, but no dope. Track marks on his arms and ass. Either he didn't get his cut from the robbery or someone took it. The dropped .45 means the shooter didn't want to get caught with it and didn't care if we found it. Smarter than your average crook," the trooper said.

The meeting broke up and Ozzie and Sam followed the case trooper cross county to Toby's trailer. There was a marked unit on the road in front and tape across the front door. The techs were coming back to search the yard and hillside in full daylight.

The rain had slackened to a misty drizzle. Just enough to be annoying. Sam and Ozzie poked around the trailer a bit, and Sam found a hair brush in the dirty bathroom under the sink. It looked like the crime scene crew had stripped the hair from it for evidence, but a few remained. "Girl's," Sam said, pulling a long strand from the brush. "Tobias, you lover boy."

They split up and Sam and Ozzie knocked on neighbors' doors. The trailer was within sight of only two of the neighbors, and one had been contacted already. Ozzie talked to the other, an older woman stooped over and gray haired. She wouldn't let them in and made them stand on her porch in the mist. Ozzie's pen refused to write in the wet air, so Sam went out to the car and dug out a dull pencil from the trunk.

"He was a dirty boy. Noisy truck, loud muffler. Junk out in the yard. You say he got shot?" she asked.

"Yes, ma'am, several gunshots. Probably two or three days ago," Ozzie said.

"What, didn't hear you," she put up a hand to cup her ear.

Ozzie looked over at Sam who rolled his eyes.

They went up the road to the next house and found that it was abandoned and locked up. The house across the road was a woman home with her two little kids. She didn't know Toby and saw and heard nothing. They met the other trooper back at the trailer and agreed to stay in touch if anything broke on either case.

On the way back to the barracks, Ozzie was hungry, and they stopped in Tamaqua for burgers and fries. "Drop me at the farm and I'll pick up my truck," Sam told Ozzie.

"Wellenhoffer is due to go to the rehab today. I'm gonna talk to him about Toby and see if he remembers any girlfriends or if the meth was an issue back then. Let him know the dogs are okay," Ozzie managed to get out between mouthfuls. "Marie's in love with them dogs now. I got to go back to my own bed. She's a mystery sometimes."

Sam sighed, "Ain't they all, Ozzie."

~ * ~

Christie decided to go straight to the hospital from home. The redhead was asleep in a recliner chair in the corner of Patsy's room. Patsy was awake and had the nurse call button in her hand with a look of suffering on her face. She put her hand to her throat and tried to speak, "...urts," was all she could manage.

Christie could see the call light panel over the bed was lit up for the nurse and went to the door and stuck her head out into the hall. No one was moving. She turned and held up a "wait a minute" finger to Patsy and went down the hall toward the nurse's station. Empty, and Patsy's was not the only call light showing on the board behind the desk. Christie went down the opposite hall looking into the rooms and found a young woman she figured was a nurse in with a patient.

"Sorry to bother you, but the girl in three twelve is in pain and needs someone," Christie said.

The nurse turned from the patient and looked at Christie. "Okay, hon. Someone will be there as soon as we can. There's only two of us on today." She turned back to her patient, ending the conversation.

Patsy was not in the mood or able to talk, so Christie woke the redhead and they left to go to the hospital business office. Christie spent an hour trying to get the girl temporary housing. The social worker was reluctant but finally agreed to set up a place for her by evening. The "relatives only" policy was stretched to include the redhead as Patsy's "sister."

The case wouldn't go away now. The surgery ended the chance the state attorney's office would reduce the charges and only file a misdemeanor. Christie decided she would put it back toward the top of her pile and try a little harder to find these creeps.

She returned to the sheriff's office and wrote up a new and more detailed Be On the Look Out BOLO message for the city and surrounding counties. *Maybe the pot needs a bit of a stir.*

~ * ~

It was still cloudy, but a good breeze was blowing and Grace was in the kitchen putting together a cooler of sandwiches and drinks for them. At the end of the dock, Katrina had a twenty foot day sailor on a lift. The power boat had been sold after Grace's dad was killed in a water skiing accident. Katrina kept the sailboat and took it out a few times in the spring and fall. Grace was excited about teaching Ken to sail and even more excited about a quiet lunch on the beach at South Lido Park.

Ken was put to work carrying life jackets, cushions, paddles and sails out from the garage. He was impressed with the blue BMW Z4 parked next to the Mercedes and was careful not to scratch either as he gathered the sail boat gear.

"Nice little Beemer," Ken said to Grace as she started to unwind the winch and lower the boat into the salt water.

"Mom got it for me after Dad died. Supposed to make me feel better, I guess. I don't get to drive it much, haven't been home. I don't need it in Atlanta. They have a good rail system that takes me right to the airport, the few days I'm there," she said over the noise of the winch's ratchet.

She showed Ken where and how to set the mast and boom and they loaded the gear aboard. Grace rigged the sails and slipped the sheets through the blocks and cam stops. Ken fitted the rudder and centerboard in place and they untied the dock lines. Grace let the boat drift downwind away from the dock and told Ken to drop the centerboard. She started pulling the mainsail halyard and the boat began to move on its own. She worked the rudder and pointed the bow into the wind to take the power from the mainsail and pulled it the rest of the way up.

She said, "Pull that line and raise the jib. Tie it off on that cleat." She shifted to the windward side and pulled the jib sheet tight and dogged it in the cam cleat. Wind filled both sails and the little boat shot forward and they were off across the bay.

"Come over to this side so the weight is on the up rail," she told Ken. The boat settled with his added weight, and Grace adjusted the main and jib to tighten them on the wind. The boat threw out a wake and they plowed through the small waves the wind had formed. A bit of spray came up on them and they felt the coolness of the salty water.

"Wow!" Ken exclaimed. "This can fly!" There were few other boats on the water and they had the bay almost to themselves.

"Grab the jib sheet, that line there," she pointed to it. "See how the trailing edge is flapping just a bit?"

"This one?" Ken asked, lifting the tail of the line.

She nodded, "Yank it out of the cleat and tighten the jib a bit until it stops jumping."

Ken snapped the sheet out of the cleat and pulled back. The jib filled firmly and he re-set the line.

"Let it in and out a few times and you'll see where it maxes out the wind," she said over the noise of the rising wind as they cleared farther into the open water.

Ken experimented with the jib and soon figured it out.

"Now get ready, we're switching places," Grace said. "You take the tiller and the main." She scuttled forward and Ken grabbed the tiller as he switched with her. The bow went into the wind and the sails dumped. Ken was momentarily confused, but then pulled the tiller toward him, put the bow back over and the sails filled. He waggled it a bit and found where the boat responded best.

"Play with it and see what happens," Grace hollered and adjusted the jib sheet. She glanced over her shoulder and then said, "We'll have to come about soon so we can get to the beach over there."

Ken moved the tiller and could feel the power of the sails increase and slacken, "It's almost like flying," he said, "only on a different angle. The sails are like the wings except they're vertical instead." He pulled the bow tight into the wind and the boat stood up on its side. They had to lean out over the water to settle it.

"Push the tiller over through the wind and we'll move to the other rail," Grace said and yanked the jib sheet loose from the cleat and held it tight. "Now."

Ken turned the tiller and the boat eased into the wind, losing power as it crossed. Grace easily moved over to the starboard rail and Ken shifted with her. She let go of the starboard jib sheet and picked up the port sheet and pulled. The main rode across on its yoke and filled as they swung around. Grace tightened and cleated the jib and they were back up and moving on the opposite tack.

"We have to work our way out to the park by tacking back and forth. If the wind holds from this direction, we'll have to come about a couple more times," she said.

Ken was smiling broadly, "This is great!" He worked the boat against the wind and tried to keep it powered as the wind speed dropped and rose. The clouds thinned as the day wore on, and by the time they nosed up onto the beach, the sun was popping through once in a while.

~ * ~

Ozzie was still out and Calvin was on the phone at his desk. Johnny was off today to sign the papers for Annette's new Mini and Sam was wading through paper in his small office. He had been on the phone earlier with the captain and had to deal with the crazy crime lieutenant's ravings again. The captain knew the drill, but she was only able to do so much. The state police were sometimes slow to diagnose and treat their internal problems when commissioned officers were involved. Sam had to tread carefully with his captain; she and Sam had more than just a work relationship. That area had been under strain recently with the entering of Eileen onto the stage. Sam's cell phone rang and Sam looked at the incoming number. *More female issues.*

"Hi, Peggy," Sam answered.

"Got a charter for Saturday in the King Air. All day out to D.C., wait and return. One of our money guys going down to play golf with a senator. Wheels up at 0730. Okay?" Peggy Newell ran the best air charter outfit at the airport. Sam liked her a lot, but not in that way. Peggy wasn't sure she was happy about it.

"Short notice, anyone we know?" Sam asked.

"We flew him and his little friend to Chicago last summer. Remember the cleaning bill for the plane?" asked Peggy.

Sam remembered. The guy owned a bunch of computer repair shops that catered to businesses. Between repair, replacement and IT, he made more than he could easily spend. Liked to take his young girlfriends on trips and used Peggy's planes now and then. Even took his wife on occasion.

"Yeah, I'm available. How's Amy?" Peggy's fifteen year old daughter was also Sam's buddy. Peggy was finishing up her bachelor's degree and Sam tutored her and Amy for a home cooked dinner about once a week.

"Big term paper on the Oregon Trail due soon. She'll need you for editing and your powerful prose," Peggy said.

"Poet that I am," snickered Sam. "Have her e-mail me a draft when she can and I'll look at it. Ken will be home all next week, and he can add his brain to the mix."

"Okee dokeee, handsome. See you early Saturday. I'll send you the weather tomorrow," she said and hung up.

Sam leaned back and looked out the window. Peggy was a pretty girl and smart as anyone; smarter than most. Sam should be all into that, but he just kept his distance. *Work, that's what I need right now. Keep my mind off of the females for a while*. He started into the paperwork pile and tuned out.

Russell was still in bed. Jimmy assumed he was hiding to get out of the work. The truck and crew had arrived from Tampa, and Jimmy really didn't need Russell anyway. The truck had a lift gate, and the two big guys that came with it had a hand truck. They wrestled the refrigerators out of the old rotten house and had the rest of it loaded in just over an hour and a half. Jimmy's pocket bulged with cash, and he went up onto the porch as the truck made its way down their sandy lane to the hardtop. Tomorrow they would convert the cash into dope and probably triple it by Monday. *Ah, free enterprise*, Jimmy thought.

The Hardee County deputy sat in his marked patrol SUV in the dusty parking lot of the phosphate mine office. He sipped on a diet soda and filled out the offense report for the stolen pick-up truck reported by the manager. He was late for his lunch break and would have to drive all the way back to Wauchula to get anything decent to eat. He had to go back to his notes again to try and get the sequence of stolen and switched license plates and truck VINs in the correct order. "Pain in the ass," he muttered. He finally gave up and tossed the whole pile of paper on the passenger seat and headed to town for food. He would deal with the mess on a full stomach.

~ * ~

"Hey, can you give me a ride to work? I gotta be there early today." She was naked and standing in front of the mirror in his bathroom putting on her eye makeup. Up on her tip toes. Made her tight little butt poke out. *Damn nice*.

She turned to look at him and scratched at her shaved crotch, "You want me again tonight? I'll cut it to two fifty, give you a big dick discount."

Flathead thought about it a moment while he followed the lines down her arched back and over that gorgeous ass, but decided he wasn't into commitment. "Not tonight, out of town." He got out of bed and walked into the bathroom past her and took a long piss. She took another look at his package and shook her head.

"You got what it takes, big boy. Look me up anytime," she giggled and left to get dressed.

Flathead figured the three hundred had been well worth it but didn't like to make a habit of spending cash on pussy. Dope usually worked, but this girl didn't use, didn't even drink beer. *Make someone a good second or third wife*. He turned on the shower and lit a cigarette to wait for the water to get hot.

"Be ready in a minute," he hollered from the bathroom. The girl waited for him to step into the shower and then quickly went through his pockets. She took three twenties and a ten from his roll of cash. He wouldn't miss it, but then she was startled when she found a nine millimeter pistol in his boot. She stood straight up and thought for just a second and then returned the seventy bucks back into his pocket.

"I'll be out on the porch," she said and took her shoes out to one of the porch chairs to put them on. She needed to cool down from the hot flash she just had.

~ * ~

Hank finally broke down and cried. He had arrived earlier at the rehab and was sitting in his room talking to Ozzie. The bandage on his head was now off, and the stitches were visible where the docs had shaved the hair away. He had no color and seemed to be shrinking. Ozzie got his permission to call a clean up company to go to the house and get rid of the blood and clean the place.

"It'll be all taken care of. You probably can get reimbursed by your insurance company. You have to keep your mind working. The business needs you to keep going. And the dogs need you too. My wife will miss them, and she'll be after you to take good care of them." Ozzie was trying to think of anything to move Hank along in his grief. "They said I can take you to the funeral tomorrow in a wheel chair. I'll go by your house and bring you a coat and tie in the morning. You got any more food for the dogs? They're about out."

Hank wiped the tears from his eyes and looked up at Ozzie. He thought for a moment and said, "Yeah. In the garage. Are they really ok?"

Ozzie smiled and said, "Oh, they are great. Don't worry, Marie will watch over them like they're her kids."

"Thanks," and Hank started sobbing again.

~ * ~

She hadn't driven a stick shift since high school, but she only stalled it twice in the dealership lot before she caught on to the clutch and gas. Johnny was surprised at how roomy the passenger seat was in the little yellow Mini. Out on the highway, Annette had the seat scrunched up close to the steering wheel and was trying to figure out where fifth gear was. She got frustrated after a couple of miles and pulled into a shopping center and stopped.

"You drive," she said to Johnny and unbuckled herself. "I'm too nervous. I need a smoke." She climbed out and stood behind the car, puffing heavily.

Johnny managed to get the driver's seat slid back and found the lever to move the back of the seat to a much less severe angle, "I hope nobody sees me drivin' this bug."

"It ain't a bug, it's a BMW. BMW makes these in England, I read up on them," Annette said as she flipped her cigarette on to the lot and climbed in beside Johnny. "Show me how to do the shift thing."

"The shift thing? Getting technical, aren't we," Johnny said. He smiled and showed her the shift pattern on the top of the knob. He put her hand on the knob and put his hand over hers. Slowly, he guided her through the gears a couple of times and started the engine. He eased into first and drove back out onto Route 100. Before he was in fourth, he was up to sixty and had the supercharger working hard.

"Little shit'll really go," he said and wound it out. He got north out of Fogelsville and turned west onto one of the county roads. Johnny gave it a good workout into and out of the curves of the country road. The suspension held the corners tight, and Johnny wished some of his old race cars had handled this good. He cut back on another twisting road and a few miles from home he pulled it into an empty parking lot and pronounced it a "real pisser."

"You ready to drive it now?" he asked.

"Now I need a drink," she said as she unbuckled and moved around to the driver's side.

~ * ~

It didn't take a lot of effort for Ken to imagine what was under Grace's skimpy bathing suit. She filled it out just right. The clouds had returned and the sun was mostly missing in action. It was warm and the few spots of sun turned it hot. Ken had to turn over on his stomach when Grace put sun screen on his shoulders. He was embarrassed by his erection and didn't know what to say or do at the moment. Hiding seemed the safest course of action.

The beach was clean and the water a grayish green and a bit cool.

They waded but didn't go all the way in and returned to the blanket spread above the tide line. Only a few other people were out, but Grace said it would be packed on a weekend.

"Most of the snowbirds have gone back north for the summer. The population triples in the winter. Mom sells like crazy over the cold months and takes most of the summer off. She travels and does a computer course for her degree. She's been after me to finish mine too. I just don't know what I want to do when I grow up," she smiled and winked at Ken.

He rolled over to her and wrapped a strong arm around her slim waist, "We can talk about that later," he said as he pulled her to him.

~ * ~

Trooper Camela Townsend stuck her head into the Hazleton crime room to say hi. She knew the Hazleton guys were working a new homicide and wanted to poke a little bit at them. She used to be Camela Cametti before she married an attorney from Stroudsburg. One of her academy buddies was the case trooper on the Diamond murder. She worked crime out of the Pocono Creek barracks and was in Hazleton to interview a witness on one of her cases. She was short and not too slim and she had trouble hiding the Glock she carried. Her black hair was cut short and feathered around her face. The road troopers all lusted after her, but she was mostly business. After only a few minutes of "Hi how are ya?" the Hazleton trooper told her about the suspect and the mystery of his identity.

"I find it hard to believe the nickname file doesn't have it," she stated. The state police index system had been improved greatly in the past few years. Information previously isolated in troop files had been centralized and computerized, but gaps still remained.

She listened some more and the wheels started to turn. "I did a case a couple of years ago with the attorney general's office. An old, unsolved murder. They were working with our headquarters people using the statewide grand jury on a multi-state burglary ring and stumbled across leads on the murder. Guy's doing life now. They have an index system from wiretap cases that has a lot of drug thugs in it. I'll track down the agent and see if they can run this Flathead character through," she said. "I'll let you know if it pans out."

On the way back east to Pocono Creek, she made a cell phone call and passed the request on.

~ * ~

The shower ended cold. He needed that to keep his priorities straight. By the time they sailed back to the dock and washed and raised the boat, Ken was feeling the Florida heat and humidity. They swam in the pool to cool off. It wasn't heated and the water temperature was only in the seventies. Grace excused herself to wash her hair and Ken sat by the pool for a while to warm back up before he realized his skin was getting red. Grace had warned him about the sun. It could burn even through clouds. Lots of tourists ruined their vacations by getting too much sun on the first outing and suffering painful sunburn for the rest of their stay.

He figured she was right and headed for the shower himself. He thought about her on the other side of the house in her shower and it made him a little nuts. The cold shower water brought him back to the real world.

Katrina was out on a showing, so they had the house to themselves. Grace met him in the living room in an oversized terry robe and a towel wrapped around her wet hair. Ken had dressed in shorts and a short sleeved shirt.

"Let's go out to dinner," she said. "I know a good Mexican place. Be ready in a few minutes." And she was.

She drove the blue Z4 down 41 and pulled into a strip mall. The restaurant was poorly lit, but the food was outstanding. They ate and talked for a long time, catching up. After dinner, she drove out over the causeway to Lido Beach and parked. They walked out to the Gulf and watched the sun set, holding hands.

~ * ~

It was a real shit kicker bar, but Jimmy felt at ease there. He listened to the band play their versions of some of the older country songs. He liked them better than the new country stuff that sounded more like light rock than country. Russell had drifted off with a girl somewhere, and Jimmy was getting a good buzz. He had the money in his pocket to buy good whiskey tonight. He left most of the refrigerator money stashed at home, so he could only stay for a while longer. Now that Russell was out of sight, he tried to organize his head around how he was going to get home. He didn't need another drunk driving pinch, so he sat back and had another drink and waited for his older brother to show up. Think it over a bit more...

*Definitely gunshots*, Jimmy concluded through his haze. The bar crowd stirred and the bouncer went out through the door to the parking lot. "Dumb shit," Jimmy mumbled. He slid off the bar stool and made it to the men's room to piss out the booze. He was just finishing when the door blasted open and Russell flew into the dirty room. Russell grabbed Jimmy and dragged him toward the rear window.

"Wait, I ain't finished!" Jimmy protested.

Russell yanked the window crank open and pushed the screen out. The window was just big enough for him to fit through and he yelled to Jimmy as he squeezed his ass to the outside, "Come on, guy's got a gun!"

Jimmy thought a moment and then followed Russell out of the window, dropping down on some scraggly bushes at the back of the bar. Russell helped Jimmy up and shuffled with him to the corner of the building. Russell snuck a look and saw the bouncer packing a kid in jeans and a baseball hat into a red pick-up.

"He's leavin'," Russell panted. "Dude with the gun is leavin'. Thought he had me for a minute." The truck fired up and spun its wheels tearing out of the lot.

"You okay?" Jimmy asked Russell.

"Little girl almost got me kilt," Russell said. "She didn't tell me she had a boyfriend or that he had a gun. Come on, let's get out of here."

After the bouncer went back inside looking for Russell, the brothers slipped into the lot and Russell headed the Mustang west. Just another fun night in Arcadia.

~ * ~

Flathead stayed just long enough to collect his money from the lady in the naked lady picture house. It surprised him that most of the load was sold already. *Stupid buggers*. He lit a cigarette and as he stepped out onto the porch, he said, "Be back Saturday for the rest."

He had the Harley tonight. He finished the cigarette as he roared down the mountain and headed toward Palmerton to deliver a small bag of dope to a very needy and willing lady friend.

~ * ~

Sam left Molly in her barrel. The air had dried and warmed. More rain might hit tomorrow, but it looked like clear weather for his flight down to Virginia on Saturday. He sat on the deck looking out over the field running north from his house. The farmer he leased the field to had planted this week, and the air had the musty smell of disturbed spring soil. He was sure he had seen a doe poking her head out of the brush at the far end of the field, but she had retreated before stepping out. The deer would be fed by the corn left standing out there come fall. The last few rows of corn would be left alone when the field was harvested. Part of the deal Sam had with the farmer.

As it gradually became dark, he glanced over to the woodpile and thought he would have to put in some time on Sunday cutting more firewood for next winter. Ken would be back by then so he would put him to work too. He again thought about calling Ken but would not after all.

Most of the trees were still hiding their spring leaves and only the wild pears and redbuds were showing a bit of color. South of the mountain, spring was almost in full swing, but it hadn't sprung up here yet.

He tried not to think about work, but it crept in here and there. The lieutenant actually had a decent suggestion, and tomorrow the hotel parking lot video of Tobias and the other shooter would be released to the television stations to see if any ID could be generated. The image was not good and Sam wasn't too optimistic, but it was worth a try. Sam finished his beer and made his way inside to make a peanut butter and jelly sandwich. Gourmet fare tonight. He decided he'd make an extra half sandwich for Molly.

## Chapter Eight

The funeral home was packed and Ozzie was a bit surprised. He'd been in to see Hank several times and had not met any other visitors at the hospital or the rehab. Hank was morose and silent in his grief. They had Hank up walking in physical therapy at the rehab facility. He was unsteady and it hurt like crazy, but he was making progress. The docs didn't want to take any chances, though, and told Ozzie Hank should be confined to a wheelchair for the funeral. Ozzie wheeled him into the side room at the funeral home and people lined up to file past and express their feelings to him. Hank decided to keep the casket closed and though Ozzie offered to bring the dogs, Hank said no. It would be hard enough.

Ozzie slipped outside to wait for the services to be over and figured he had just enough time to run over to the Wawa for an apple fritter before he had to take Hank back. Hank was safe here with the crowd around, him so Ozzie's guilt was easily overcome by hunger.

~ * ~

The smell of bacon cooking woke him. He could see it was full daylight outside, and he was surprised he had slept so long. His internal clock had been wrenching him out of bed at 5:30 for the past six years. Ken washed and brushed and dressed quickly, coming into the living room to find Katrina in her robe on the couch reading the newspaper.

"Good morning, ma'am," he said.

"Oh. Please, Ken. Drop the ma'am stuff and call me Katrina. I ain't that old yet. Supergirl is in the kitchen cooking breakfast." She held up her coffee mug without taking her eyes off the paper and said, "Black."

Ken smiled and took the mug into the kitchen. Grace was facing away from him, standing barefoot and flipping bacon on a griddle. She had on a snug pair of lime green shorts and a white top. Ken could make out the important features of her landscape and liked what he saw.

"Refill for your mom," Ken said and filled her mug from the fancy stainless coffee machine next to the refrigerator.

Grace spun and kissed him, "Good morning. You want coffee?"

"Ah, how about juice?" he asked.

Grace got him a glass and pointed to the refrigerator. Ken found orange and cranberry and mixed a little of both. "I don't like a lot of caffeine when I fly. Makes me jittery and have to pee."

She laughed and went back to the bacon. "Go sit with Mom; pancakes will be ready in a little while. Keep her busy and out of this kitchen."

Ken reluctantly went back with Katrina's coffee and sat across from her.

"I put the weather channel on for you, but I can tell it's going to be a nice day for you kids," she said.

It was several minutes before any actual weather was talked about. The on air talent bubbled back and forth about nonsense instead of showing the frontal charts where the clouds stopped and the sun began. Ken waited for the local forecast that reinforced what he already knew from Flight Service. It would be a good day for flying, but not the best. It would have to do. Grace was flying out on Saturday afternoon to Atlanta for work and Ken had a flight on Sunday to Philadelphia.

Grace slipped into the room and sat next to her mom. "It's ready. You two come out by the pool and eat." Grace got up and led them to the small table where she had plates and the food set up.

"Are you going to show Ken the old family homestead in Arcadia today?" Katrina asked.

"Yes and where Grandpa's store used to be." Grace turned to Ken, "They tore it down to build a shopping center. Grandpa would not have been pleased."

"Grandpa was sometimes hard to please about a lot of things. Your father, for instance," Katrina said.

Grace turned back to Katrina, "I thought Grandpa and Daddy got along just fine."

Katrina sighed and rolled her eyes. "My daddy was not pleased that I married a Catholic boy. He was even more shocked when he found out he was a Cuban. By then it was too late, missy; you were cookin' in the oven."

Katrina stuck a piece of bacon in her mouth and chewed deliberately. Grace tried to speak, but nothing came out. Katrina swallowed and said, "Ken, I was your age when I ran off and got married to Grace's dad. Got pregnant on the honeymoon in a rotating, heart shaped bed in Vegas and the rest is history. My daddy did the math over and over in his head, but he finally gave up, and when he saw Grace, he melted."

Ken could relate to that.

~ * ~

Sam was alone in the crime office. Ozzie was at the funeral for the woman victim and Calvin and Johnny were out doing interviews on several residential burglaries. While it was quiet, he checked the weather for his flight to suburban Washington on Saturday morning. Some clouds and wind but it should be fine. He tried to think of how he would burn off the down time while the charter played golf and whatever else after. Quantico was nearby the airport and might be a nice place to tour. He checked the Bing search engine for tour information then for rental cars.

The ballistics lab sent Sam and Ozzie an e-mail heads up that the lab report was finished and would show the murder weapon for the woman and the kid was the same and matched the .45 that killed Toby and was left at his trailer. *No surprise there*, Sam thought.

The .38 shot Hank and there was no record of it; too old. Tobias' fingerprints were on the .38, but the .45 was wiped clean. The .45's serial numbers had been ground off, but the lab was able to raise the number. Stolen out of Morgantown, West Virginia five years ago.

Sam called the crime corporal in Hazleton and went over what they knew. He learned that Toby's last phone call had been to the number of a woman in Weissport who was being interviewed by the case trooper. A text message had come in just before the time of death, but the phone that sent it was a throw away bought for cash and now was not active. They were checking the convenience store where it had been purchased for surveillance footage.

Sam tried to call Ozzie, but his cell phone went direct to voice mail. Ozzie was due back after the funeral, so Sam decided to wait.

~ * ~

Ken helped Katrina with the dishes while Grace finished getting ready. She turned to him and said, "You know, I got a call from Grandma Echaverria after you were there at New Year's. She told me all about it."

Ken thought before he spoke, "She's quite a lady. Lives all by herself."

"She has a whole neighborhood to watch over her. She watches over them too. It's a tight community. We've tried to get her to come here to live; she won't even come for a visit. She'll never leave Miami unless the Castros die and they let her go back to Santiago."

Grace called from the living room that she was ready, and Ken thanked Katrina and went out to the garage. "You drive," she said and tossed him the keys. As he backed the BMW out to the driveway, she lowered the top and put a scarf over her hair.

"Out to 41 south and then turn on Bee Ridge Road," she directed. He wound through the gears and drove through the streets he had run on yesterday. The traffic was not too bad this time of the morning, and they made their way down to Clark Road heading east toward Arcadia in no time.

~ * ~

Christie had to talk herself into going to work. It was a nice day and a Friday and she was worn out. She decided that she would save the vacation day and maybe take a cruise in the fall when the rates were low. St. Martin. No tan lines. She picked up three new cases this morning and kept busy organizing the case folders and checking the initial reports against the evidence logs.

Two of the victims she called were at work and the other was waiting for Christie to come to her home to be interviewed. Christie packed up her travel bag and hustled out to the parking lot. It was going to be a busy day.

She had left the windows of her Jeep rolled down a little so the inside wasn't like an oven. The parking lot had no shade, and as the summer got closer, the sun got higher in the sky and hotter. She peeled off her jacket and turned on the air. Her Sig was exposed with her jacket off, but she had a second badge that she kept clipped to her belt just in front of her pistol. The citizens would just have to get over it. Her cell phone rang before she even got out of the lot. The second victim was calling back and would meet her when she finished interviewing the first one. *No lunch today.*

It was the fastest he had ever had to make another buy. The crank was almost gone and the weekend was coming. Business was good. Flathead set the meet for the late afternoon at the same hotel on I-80. The Jersey boys were happy and even cut the price just a bit for this load. He was glad he had the extra money from the garden center and didn't have to go back to the naked lady picture house before he went to the hotel. *Thanks, Turd.*

Once they went under I-75 there really wasn't much to see except nature. The road to Arcadia curved only a few times. Mostly it was straight east through the state park and then into cattle country, both sides.

"Lot of open space in Florida," said Ken.

Grace said, "It's all ranch land out here. All the development is along the coasts down this far. Beef cattle is big business."

They rode past miles of fencing, spotting groups of beef cattle scattered among the palmettos and oak hammocks.

Ken pointed up, "Look, buzzards circling. That's what we want to find today. That's a thermal and they're riding it up."

"Turbulence in my world," Grace said.

Ken had to watch his speed. The little car had plenty of horsepower and wanted to run eighty. They were almost to Arcadia before they saw any civilization. As they eased into town, Grace pointed out the older homes that had wide porches surrounding them.

"Sleeping porches," she said. "Before air conditioning, people slept out on them in the summer."

She directed Ken to make a couple of turns and they came out behind a strip mall.

"Grandpa's store used to be here. I kind of remember it, but I was just little when he died and then they tore the building down." They drove a few blocks farther and stopped in front of an old home with an overgrown yard. No one lived there and there was a red sign on the front door.

"Mom grew up here. The town has changed a lot in the last few years," Grace said. "People can't afford to keep these old houses fixed up. A lot of new sub divisions have been built." She felt a little sad but remembered what her mom had accomplished and decided it was silly to fret over it. Ken drove on and in a few minutes they pulled into the airport.

~ * ~

Ozzie found Calvin and Johnny and they met for lunch. Calvin limped into the small restaurant and grimaced as he slid into the booth. Ozzie was already finished with his first Pepsi and raised his empty glass for the waitress to refill. Johnny was standing outside smoking.

"I hate to ask, but how's the hip doing?" Ozzie asked.

Calvin frowned and said, "Fine until Johnny racer out there bounced me around. You ride with him and give me your car."

The waitress appeared and Calvin lit up. She was young and blonde. "What would you like to drink?" she asked Calvin and took Ozzie's empty glass.

"Bourbon and soda, but I'll settle for iced tea, unsweetened. You can stick your thumb in it and sweeten it up for me," he showed her his perfect teeth.

She looked puzzled and then it hit her, "Aww get out, you guys."

Calvin added, "The redneck comin' through the door will have coffee, black."

She took off toward the kitchen and Johnny slid in the booth just as

Calvin's cell phone went off.

"Hey, Sam," Calvin said. He listened for a moment and said, "Yeah, I got Ozzie with me. We'll be in right after we eat." Calvin ended the call and said, "Phone's lit up with calls about the video of shooter two on the noon news. Sam wants us to sort the calls and work on the best ones.

Ozzie suddenly looked worried. "After we eat, Oz," Calvin added.

~ * ~

Jimmy was under the oak tree with a beer and a cigarette. It was sunny but not too hot yet. He had just finished checking the oil in the truck and was thinking about food. There was nothing in the house but a box of macaroni and cheese, and he knew Momma would throw a fit if he ate her supper. He would have to send Russell to the grocery store tomorrow after they sold some of the dope. He wasn't going to spend any of the money he had in his pocket on anything but weed. Well, maybe a double burger to hold him over.

"Russell!" Jimmy shouted. He waited and Russell didn't appear. "Hey, shithead, comeer!"

His older brother stood in the doorway looking through the worn out screen door, "What the fuck?"

"Need you to make a food run."

~ * ~

Margie was standing outside the building with a clipboard in her hand. She had a tanned and weathered face and her brown hair was covered by a floppy straw hat. She watched the tow plane rev its engine and pull out onto the grass in front of the fiberglass sailplane at the end of the runway. Her husband, Will, was in the tow plane and a moment later he advanced the throttle of the Supercub and pulled the sailplane into motion. Margie logged the time and looked to her left down the taxiway to where several gliders were tied down with people milling about. She didn't see Ken and Grace walk up behind her.

"You owe me a cold drink," Ken said. Margie turned and smiled.

"Kenny!" she exclaimed, "You made it." She threw the clipboard around him and hugged him firmly. She backed up and glanced at Grace standing behind Ken. Then to Ken she said, "I'm so happy you could come down to see us. We thought we'd miss you next fall up at State College." Margie and Will traveled to Pennsylvania almost every year to run sailplanes in the ridge lift.

"You lost the bet last year, I'm here to collect. Oh, I'm sorry. This is my, er, ah, my friend, Grace. Grace this is Margie, she runs this place."

Margie let loose of Ken and walked to Grace and stuck out her hand. Grace felt a strong firm handshake and said, "I'm happy to meet you. Thanks for squeezing us in today."

Margie said, "Oh, we're so happy to see Ken again. He scorched me last year. Out distanced me by fifty miles. He's a real good pilot." The tow plane cut its throttle and everyone looked up as the sailplane separated and began to circle in a thermal. The white and red trimmed Supercub dove back toward the airport.

"That's Will, my husband. He's got another few tows and then he'll take a break before we get you two up in the 2-33." Ken moved next to Grace and took her hand in his. She was fascinated by the sleek white sailplane tightly circling just upwind of the airport. "Come inside, Ken, and I'll pay up. Coke or Pepsi?" Margie asked. They followed Margie into the small office as the tow plane eased onto the runway.

~ * ~

The second victim solved the case for Christie. Her daughter identified the jerk who stuck a pistol in her mother's face and stole her purse with two hundred twenty dollars, "He used to take me out last year. Momma didn't want to tell the first deputy 'till she talked to me. He did it. He told me he did it this morning and said he was sorry, but he's an addict and needed the money. He's on his way over here now."

*Oh, shit*, Christie thought. She got on her phone and called dispatch to send a patrol car ASAP.

~ * ~

"The ones in Troop N are going to the Hazleton guys. Calvin, you and Johnny take the Allentown calls and Ozzie and I will work north and west," Sam said. The TV exposure had generated a flood of calls. Most callers had left their name, but many had been anonymous. The names attributed to the fuzzy image were being run through the arrest files and BMV by Mrs. Tuttle on the desk. Her printer was spitting out rap sheets, arrest photos and driver's license pictures almost nonstop. Ozzie was scooping them up and sorting them into piles by location. None of the photos closely resembled the big shooter, but it was all they had for now. Some of the callers were only able to give partial identifications and needed to be interviewed again. All of the troops were on the phone calling people back to try and clarify their information. It was mass confusion.

~ * ~

Flathead was on the road back to his house. He needed to shower and put on clean clothes. The girl in Palmerton was a pig and lived like one. But she was a major piece of ass and he kept going back. She drove him nuts all night, though. He was worn out and wanted to sleep, but she got cranked and was bouncing off the walls. At some point in the night she left and went prowling, letting him finally get some sleep.

He took his time winding the big Harley around the twisted mountain roads as he worked north. Assholes didn't look or didn't see scooters, even though most riders ran with the headlight on. Flathead had dumped a bike into the side of a car in the past and didn't want to go through all that again. He watched as cars pulled up to the cross stop signs and if he couldn't see the driver's eyes looking at him, he slowed and got ready to stop himself.

Luckily there wasn't too much traffic on these country roads today. The ride was uneventful and he pulled into his drive and got the garage door open to lock up the bike. He had a few hours before he had to drive down to I-80.

~ * ~

Jimmy fell asleep on the couch after he ate the burger Russell brought back for him. They had a few hours before they had to drive down to Naples.

~ * ~

"You're under arrest for armed robbery, aggravated assault and grand theft," Christie said as she slipped the cuffs on the tall skinny man out on the front porch. The uniformed deputy stood next to him and took control of the cuffs behind the man's back. Christie took a laminated card from her pocket and held it up. She didn't need to read from it, she knew the words on it from memory, "You have the right…"

The victim and her daughter stood in the living room and watched through the open door. The daughter was crying. She still liked the jerk and had convinced him to turn himself in to get off the dope.

"I'll follow you in. Take him to the detective bureau," Christie told the other deputy. To the women she said, "The money's gone, but he won't be sticking guns in anyone's face for a while. I'll take his statement and book him into the jail and log his pistol into evidence. If you want him to dry out, don't post bail for him. He'll have a chance to go into the drug program in the jail. It may be what he needs right now."

She gathered her notebook and digital recorder and put the gun into an evidence bag. She jumped into the Jeep and got on the road behind the marked unit. She still needed to get with the third victim before the end of the day. Maybe no supper either.

~ * ~

Trooper Townsend was writing as fast as she could. The AG's agent was on the phone telling her they found Flathead in their database. She said, "Jersey, yeah that's why the AKA didn't come up in ours. What was the third address?" She had a full page of notes by now and thanked the agent before she hung up and almost ran to the front desk to put Thomas McCall in the system. While she waited for the machine to respond, she used her cell phone to call Hazleton.

~ * ~

Will was happily married but had been in and out of the tow plane a couple of times to hang out with Ken and Grace, mostly Grace. He kept sneaking long glances at her, and the schedule got behind the fact. Margie had penciled Ken and Grace in between her other students who had priority in the two seat trainer, but the afternoon was moving on.

Will was landing again and there were three gliders lined up for tows at the edge of the grass strip. The city paved the cross runway several years ago, but the glider operation still had the use of the grass strip that ran southeast/northwest. There really wasn't too much power traffic to contend with, especially on a weekday, though Fridays could be busier than the first part of the week.

Today there had been students flying a Cessna 150 out and back off the paved strip all morning and into the early afternoon, but they seemed to be finished now. Margie was trying to hustle up the list and get the privately owned sailplanes airborne before the lift crapped out.

She came over to Ken and said, "Sorry, buddy, we're catching up. We'll have the 2-33 loose in a bit."

Ken said, "It's okay, Margie. We are enjoying all the activity. We're ready whenever you are.

"One more student to go and you should be up in less than forty five minutes."

~ * ~

The trooper from Hazleton assigned to the Diamond murder was tracking down the daughter of the woman from Weissport whose name was on the cell phone account Toby had last called. Her daughter actually had the phone; Mom just paid the bill for her. His corporal was in the barracks when Camela called and got on the phone with her. A few minutes later Sam's phone rang.

"Okay, okay, yeah, okay." Sam tore off the sheet of notes and stepped out into the crime room. "Everybody stop. Hang up and come over here."

It took a few minutes for his troopers to get off the phones and pay attention to Sam, "We got an ID on shooter two. Ozzie, any of the tips coming in on a Thomas McCall?"

Ozzie had a master list running on a notepad. He glanced at it and shook his head, "Nope."

"Trooper from Pocono Creek tapped a source in the AG's office and came up with a match on the nickname. Hazleton pulled his arrest photos from Jersey and it looks like he's it. They're e-mailing it down now. They have three addresses on him from the databases. Hazleton wants to kick down doors, but we need to think about that. We shook the trees for Diamond and he ended up toast. I'd like to get this Flathead asshole while he's still breathing. All of the addresses are up in Troop N. They're all old and probably bogus or just mail drops. If we push too hard, he'll smell us and scoot. What do you think, Oz?"

"Well, I'd like to look at his rap sheet first and maybe talk to the last couple of guys who popped him. See what kind of opposition we have. We know he's a shooter and obviously not too stupid, so maybe the slow walk will be the best way. Can you rein in Hazleton?" Ozzie threw it back at Sam.

Sam was silent for a long pause. "The corporal seems okay. The captain's a reasonable guy; at least he used to be when we worked together down in Bucks County. Maybe."

Calvin said, "Sam, the best way to slow everything down is 'Let's have a meeting'."

"Okay. Ozzie, pump the computer for anything you can on McCall. See if any of his recent arresting officers are available. Calvin, Johnny. Pull maps, sat photos, utilities and property records on these addresses, if Hazleton hasn't already done it, we'll have a package ready on each of them. I'll set up the meeting at, ah, how about Lehighton PD. That's about in the middle. Be ready to roll in an hour, or less."

Now Sam needed to massage the egos of his counterparts and see if he could run this the way it should be run. Everyone split in different directions, and Sam went into his office. He took a deep breath and picked up his phone.

~ * ~

The third victim was waiting patiently in the lobby of the sheriff's office. Christie decided she would finish the arrest report on the junkie armed robber later and got him confessed and lodged in the county facilities before she washed up and went out to meet the next in line. A pack of crackers from the vending machine would have to do for now.

~ * ~

Grace followed Ken around the big two seat glider as he did a pre-flight inspection. He took his time even though the plane had been in service without a problem all day. She'd watched the pilots of the commercial jets she worked in do this many times, but always took it for granted.

Ken said as they approached the open cockpit, "It may seem silly, but I don't cut corners when it comes to flying. You can't pull to the side of the road and call for a tow truck if your ride craps out at five thousand feet." He put her to work pulling the glider out to the end of the runway. He kept looking over his shoulder at the landing pattern to be sure no planes had slipped in without calling in on the field frequency. There was no control tower, and the local pilots announced their landing and takeoff intentions on an open channel. The trainer had a radio and it had been quiet after Will dropped the last sailplane upwind and coasted back onto the field.

Ken watched Grace easily climb into the front seat and helped her adjust and buckle the restraints. He pointed out the airspeed indicator, altimeter and variometer on the panel and the big red ball for the tow rope release. He followed her into the glider and buckled himself in the back seat. A young kid brought the tow rope over to the front of the glider and Ken pulled the knob from the backseat so the kid could hook them up. The kid moved out to the left wing and rocked his arm to tell Will to pull the tow plane out onto the runway and take up the slack in the tow rope.

Ken had already checked that the stick and rudder worked the control surfaces properly and found he did not need to adjust the rudder pedals. He closed the canopy and tapped Grace on the shoulder, "Okay, Grace. You handle the takeoff."

She didn't move or say anything. Suddenly, her head whipped around and she found Ken grinning broadly. "Gotcha," he said. "Just relax and gently put your two fingers on the stick and follow my movements. We're ready to go."

The tow rope was taught between the glider and the Supercub. The kid on the wing stopped moving and held his arm steady. Ken checked the landing pattern again and pushed on the rudder pedals, rocking it back and forth several times. It was starting to get real hot in the cockpit under the closed canopy, and as Will goosed the throttle, the prop wash worked back and over the glider, pushing air and bits of runway grass through a vent in front of Grace.

The glider began to move and bumped them a bit as the kid on the wing ran forward with them, holding the tip up. As their speed increased, Ken felt the stick firm up and the kid let loose of the wing. The left wing dropped and Ken fed in right stick to level. More air began to move in the cockpit and the glider lifted off the ground, smoothing the ride. Ken moved the stick forward, bringing the glider back down toward the ground so it didn't lift the tail of Will's plane.

Will then cleared the ground and they were climbing and slowly turning to the right into the wind. Grace could feel Ken moving the stick, keeping the tow plane in front of them. Well above the ground now, Will turned downwind.

"Watch the altimeter, Grace. We release at two thousand feet." They felt the glider rise and Grace saw the needle on the variometer jump up. "Thermal," Ken said.

Will turned upwind again and they passed back over the airport, climbing steadily. The glider bumped up and down several more times, and as they approached two thousand feet, they went up again.

"Here we go," said Ken and Grace heard a sharp bang that startled her. She saw the tow rope fall away and Ken banked the glider to the right. Ken then leveled out for a moment and the glider bumped up again. Grace felt her bottom sink into her seat and Ken put the big glider into a sharp left bank. A dark object flashed across Grace's view in front of the glider and Grace followed it, seeing the shape of a big black bird with wings spread out off the left wing tip.

"Buzzards and the little guy is a hawk. He's the one we want to follow," she heard Ken say over the noise of air rushing past them. She saw what he was talking about. There were actually three buzzards and a smaller bird that had a dark brown, reddish color all flying close by and rising with them. "Four hundred a minute up. A good thermal. Will's a magician."

Grace was amazed at the birds and how they seemed to ignore the big glider and float in the air as if in a ballet. The landscape below was a patchwork of town and fields. She could just make out the cars on the highway. She could feel the glider move in the upward flowing thermal, rocking and bucking but still climbing.

"It's dropping off. There he goes," Ken snapped the plane level and Grace could see the small hawk flying out ahead. "We'll see if he leads us to the next thermal," Ken said. The air rushing in through the vent was noticeably cooler now and Grace looked at the altimeter and saw they were at thirty-seven hundred feet.

"Okay, student pilot. Put your feet on the rudders and hold the stick. Follow the hawk. You have the plane." Ken lifted his hands and put them on Grace's shoulders. The nose dipped and the airspeed began to rise.

"Pull back on the stick and bring us back to sixty," Ken said. Grace pulled back on the control and the nose rose up past the horizon dropping the speed to forty-five. Ken reached down and eased the stick forward. "Follow me now," he said.

She felt it move slowly forward as the nose dropped and then felt him pull back again until the airspeed centered on sixty.

She felt the nose rise again and she pushed forward and pulled back a few times until she was able to keep the speed steady. She had lost sight of the hawk and then Ken said, "He's off to the right. Push the right pedal a bit and follow with the stick. Watch the piece of yarn on the front canopy. Try to keep it centered."

She started the turn and the yarn skewed sideways. She heard the noise of the air rushing past increase. "Too much rudder, back off just a bit," he said. He helped her and the yarn swung back to the middle. The hawk appeared in front of them, and the glider pushed Grace down in her seat again. The hawk split left and Ken said, "Bank left and pull back on the stick a bit."

It was getting confusing to her now, but she tried. The wings groaned and she heard metal ping as she hauled the glider around. Ken was on the controls helping her when she overdid it or didn't move enough. She could feel him through the stick and pedals and they brought the sailplane into another thermal behind and below the little brown hawk.

"I wish you could feel this in our 1-26. This is a beast compared to it. The 1-26 is much more responsive and the fiberglass birds are even better," Ken said as Grace struggled to hold the glider in the lift. This thermal wasn't as strong as the first one, and the hawk punched out and left them.

"Where's the airport?" Ken asked. Grace was stumped. "Roll out to the northeast and fly at fifty-five," Ken said. She did a good job of turning and leveling off. Her speed fluttered a few times, but she was starting to get the feel. "Let's do a ninety degree turn to the right. Keep your speed at fifty-five so watch the nose," he said.

She touched the rudder and drifted the stick to the right. She felt the stick and rudder push back and level the glider before she even got the turn started. Ken said, "Clear for traffic before you turn. Try it again." She cranked her head to the right and looked for other planes.

"Looks clear," she said and started into the turn again. The nose dropped and she fed in back stick to keep the speed down and rolled out after missing ninety degrees but not by much.

"You are going to be a great glider driver, Grace," Ken said and patted her on the shoulder. They did several more turns and approaches to stalls and Grace spotted the airport off the left wing.

"There's a plane down there," she said. She could see the white wings silhouetted over the green of the ground.

"You see the movement first. He's landing on the paved strip. You'll see him turn final in a bit," Ken said. "Turn left about twenty degrees and bump it up to sixty. We'll lose some more altitude then cross over the airport at about eleven hundred feet and enter the left downwind for the grass strip. See the N number on the panel? Pick up the mic and announce that number and entering left downwind for runway one three." They drifted across the airport and Ken followed her on the controls as she turned left parallel to the runway.

"Okay, good job. I have the plane. Follow me through the landing," Ken said as she felt the stick move in her hands.

## Chapter Nine

Sam schmoozed the Hazleton crew into setting up on the addresses and called the lieutenant in Bethlehem. He was gone for the day. The captain was there and cautiously gave them the go for twenty-four hours then re-evaluate. She told Sam to play nice with their northern brothers and said she would call their captain and smooth the waters.

"Get the creep," was her final word.

Calvin helped Ozzie quickly put together folders for each address with McCall's photo and rap sheet. Ozzie briefed them, "Detective down in the Atlantic County prosecutor's office said this Flathead is a biker gang associate. Drug dealer and part time pimp. Actually been through a year of community college interrupted by three years in the state prison. A crook's degree."

Sam said, "Brad's lending us Adams. He's on three to eleven and said he doesn't have any date set up for after, so he's ours. Lehighton PD knows we're coming and the Carbon County DA is sending two of his county detectives over. We'll take Adams' marked unit for a chase car. Any questions?" Sam decided to drive his Pathfinder up to Lehighton PD so he could bug out by midnight if Flathead didn't show and make the flight for Peggy in the morning. Everyone else would keep making the overtime. "Okay, let's head on up there." The barracks became very quiet after they all piled out the back door and met Trooper Adams in the parking lot.

~ * ~

Jimmy was on his third beer by the time they passed through Arcadia and turned south toward Ft. Myers. Russell was driving and had the radio blasting metal music. Jimmy reached over and switched it to classic country, "That's enough of that screamin' shit," Jimmy announced. "My head is pounding. Wish we had some of that weed right now."

Russell scowled but didn't challenge his younger brother. He suddenly slowed and said, "There's a trooper comin' at us."

The black and yellow troop car shot past them at over seventy, heading into town. Florida Highway Patrol had radar and laser units that could clock speeders from a stationary position or in oncoming traffic. Russell hoped somehow he had gotten away with it. He watched the rearview mirror for brake lights on the police car, but none came on. He had been doing seventy-five in a sixty zone. Close call. Now he held it to sixty-five.

~ * ~

Florida Trooper Reginald Goddard, RGod, as his fellow workers and family knew him, was running behind. He actually wasn't technically on duty yet, but he was hungry and didn't cook at home, so the all you can eat place on U.S. 17 in Arcadia was his first stop tonight. He was supposed to sign on in his driveway at home and go from there, but it was an hour before that had to be done, and he wasn't going to drive his personal car just to go get something to eat before work.

Reginald used to be called BigR in high school and college but had trimmed down to 230 on a six three frame. Trooper school was tough, and he caught shit because he was big and very black. Not real bad racist shit, but shit, you know. He stood up for himself and after one violent weekend in town where one of the chickenshit cadets in his class had fucked with him at a bar, the name changed. BigR had taken the chickenshit classmate to the edge of death and then pardoned him, hence the new name, "He ain't Batman, he RGod."

RGod went to Miami after graduation and lost a lot of money paying for expensive housing on meager trooper pay. And a wife and kid. Divorced and struggling to learn functional Spanish, it had taken him six and a half years to get transferred back up near his folks in LaBelle. A lot cheaper to live and pay child support. Plus Grandma could babysit if he had his daughter on a weekend he had to work.

All in all not too bad. He wrote a few tickets, worked a few crashes and got to tear around backing up the deputies in the counties. Nobody fucked with the big trooper anymore.

At a closing speed of one hundred forty-five miles per hour, RGod didn't have much time to notice but he just caught the face of the driver of the dark blue pick-up that barreled past southbound on Route 31.

*Russell Santee. Must have gotten rid of the Mustang.* RGod didn't have his radar on yet and chuckled at the thought of Russell getting away without a speeding ticket and maybe a dope pinch. Russell had so far avoided RGod's full wrath but just happened to be in the passenger seat the night Jimmy got stopped and arrested for drunk driving by Trooper Goddard. RGod remembered Russell because Russell didn't keep out of the way and had made a big nuisance of himself. It had been a close call, but Russell had skated that night. RGod had not forgotten, though.

Trooper Goddard slowed as he came into Arcadia and managed to forget about Russell and Jimmy Santee, at least temporarily, so he could eat his dinner in peace.

~ * ~

Ozzie dropped out of the convoy before they got onto the turnpike. He wasn't going to sit all night watching some dump without supplies. He parked and trudged into the store and grabbed items from the shelves and coolers. It totaled over twenty-three dollars, but some of it could be taken home later for a snack over the weekend.

Trooper Adams led the parade in his marked car and got up to trooper speed on the turnpike northbound. Johnny wasn't satisfied and demonstrated "drafting" to Calvin by closing to within six inches of Adams' rear bumper, "Come on, kid, get movin'!" Johnny hollered through the windshield.

Calvin was pissed, "Stop being a jerk off, Johnny. Leave the kid alone."

Adams didn't do anything at first, but after only a few miles, he put the gas to the floor and pulled away. Johnny whooped and bore down on him once again, coming up just behind. Sam was left in the dust. Sam let them play a bit then called Johnny's cell phone. A brief conversation and Adams had to slow so the rest could catch up.

They blasted through the northbound tunnel and got off at the next exit. Lehighton was only a few miles farther, and the small police building was becoming crowded with uniforms and raid jackets. Ozzie finally arrived and carried a large soda cup in with all the paperwork.

Sam was standing off to the side, talking to the Hazleton corporal and the Carbon County DA who had invited himself to the meeting. Sam knew it wasn't really necessary for the DA to be there, but this was probably good for his image come reelection time to be seen rubbing elbows with the cops. The DA was concerned because there was no way to get an ID from the victim in Ozzie's case.

"The guy just didn't look at him. He only saw the big orange goggles, beard and brown hair. The lab's going back over all the prints again and will run all of them through against McCall, even the partials. Maybe we'll get lucky," Sam said to the DA.

The Hazleton corporal said the case trooper on Diamond's murder would be with them later. He was putting a photo line up together on Flathead to show a young, meth freak girl who maybe saw him with Diamond just before the shots were fired.

Sam and the Hazleton corporal rejoined the group and Sam let him run the meeting. Ozzie was passing out folders and the crews were lining up for each of the three locations. At least two cars with two officers each and a marked unit were to be sent to each location to set up surveillance. The plan was to watch and catch Flathead coming or going. Two Hazleton marked cars and Adams were the chase cars if it came to that.

When the meeting broke up, those that hadn't already suited up in vests and raid jackets did so in the parking lot. Sam left the Pathfinder and got in with Ozzie in the black, unmarked Crown Vic. They drove out of the lot and followed a Hazleton unmarked car east and north onto the back roads. It was almost fully dark by now, and the air was still and cooling fast.

~ * ~

Grace was impressed with how Ken had handled everything. She had to keep reminding herself he was only eighteen. He acted much older and she was drawn to him even more. They sat and visited with Will and Margie after the last of the tows were finished. Will had fueled and parked the Supercub and Ken helped tie down the 2-33 and the rental 1-26. It was a friendly crowd with student glider pilots talking and laughing with veteran sailplane owner/pilots.

Some of the gang was staying overnight to fly a cross country tomorrow, and everyone decided to go out to eat in town. Margie and Will tagged along and they got a big table at the all you can eat place. Ken took a lot of kidding about his upcoming summer at the Academy. One of the older pilots had a brother who went there and he told chilling stories about the hazing the upperclassmen vented upon the new kids. Ken knew all about it. He had been preparing for this for two years. Besides, the upperclassmen at Varnum took no back seat when it came to that.

Grace noticed the time and excused herself to go to the ladies room and call her mom. "We're having a great time. We'll start home right after we finish eating. Probably be home in a couple of hours at the most. We're both worn out. It's been a long day." She rejoined the group and saw Ken's face was red and he was blushing.

Margie leaned over to her and hugged her. "He's a winner. Don't lose track of him," she said. "Comes from a good dad too."

Ken snuck a peek at her, smiled and shrugged his shoulders. These people were a good bunch, and he felt right at home.

~ * ~

RGod was in his car in the parking lot picking food from his teeth with a tooth pick. He'd been off for three days and had a lot to catch up on. Headquarters spit out reams of electronic "paper" for administrative details, and he received the messages on his in-car computer. Training, court, directives, and any number of crapolas the weenies in Tallahassee could think up to justify their existence.

The big trooper was finishing the admin items and started on the actual law enforcement traffic. Recent stolen cars and BOLOs from around the several counties. He took a drink from the water bottle in the center console cup holder and rolled the cursor through the long list. He stopped and read the message on the screen again "...possibly brothers, Jimmy and Russell, last name unknown..." and the physical descriptions matched. "...wanted for aggravated assault, Sarasota County..." *Shitfire*, he thought as he reached for the cell phone clipped to his gun belt.

~ * ~

Jimmy was pissed and Russell was still hungry. The meet with the Miami boys at the Waffle House parking lot at the Naples end of Alligator Alley didn't go as planned. The price of the pot had gone up since their last load. The Miami explanation was, "The governor is running for president and kicked the narcs in the ass to pump up the arrests and seizures. Supply is down and the heat is up."

Jimmy was so mad he wouldn't let Russell go to the Cracker Barrel for biscuits and gravy. They were back on the road toward home with the now, a little lighter than they had expected, load tucked behind the seat next to the Winchester, and Russell had the truck flying.

"We got to figure a way to make more money. Or find a better source for the weed. We ain't gonna make as much as we thought off this load. Gotta be an easier way," Jimmy moaned.

The truck veered onto the scrabble shoulder as Russell tried to light his pot pipe. He dropped the lit pipe in his lap and yanked the truck back into the lane. He fumbled for the pipe as Jimmy yelled at him to slow down and pay attention. Once he got the pipe going and Jimmy took a few hits, Jimmy quieted down. He was still pissed but kept his anger inside. Russell forgot about food for the moment, but his speed picked back up again.

"We take all the risk and do all the heavy lifting and we get shit on," Jimmy came out of his quiet zone. He relit the pipe and sucked in the smoke. "Got to think, man, got to think."

~ * ~

Ozzie drove past the house a few times and settled on a spot up the road where they could back in and not be noticed easily from the house or from the road. One of the Hazleton unmarked cars was downhill and on the other side of the house , and Adams was tucked in behind a grade school about half a mile away. Sam could hear the radio chatter between the other units as they jockeyed into position on the other two addresses. Several of the troopers and the county detectives could only work until midnight, and fresh bodies were coming in to relieve them. Sam's people were staying all night if necessary, and everyone was calling it off if Flathead didn't show by noon tomorrow.

He hoped it would pop tonight so he didn't have to deal with the bosses and fight for more overtime. He wanted to see the base at Quantico tomorrow and didn't want to spend his time on the ground fighting on the cell phone. Then his cell phone rang.

"Hi, Peggy," Sam answered.

"You'll be in the Lear tomorrow. The King Air went down for hydraulics today," she said on the phone.

"Okay. I'm into something at work that might tie me up, so can you line up a 'B' team if I have to crap out on you at the last minute?"

He could barely hear her breathing on the phone, and she didn't say anything for a moment. "You can give a girl gray hair before her time, Sam. Shit," she said. Another long pause and Sam knew to keep quiet. "Okay, I'll set up a backup driver. But you better show up, if you get my drift."

"Yes, ma'am. Understood. I should be okay. See you tomorrow."

Ozzie was stuffing a roast beef sandwich into his mouth and chewed hard so he could say to Sam, "'ou shud mury 'er, 'r Ieen. Un a 'em." A couple of pieces of sandwich fell into Ozzie's lap and he swallowed a big lump.

Sam shot an "I don't think so" look at Ozzie and then turned toward the house and raised binoculars up to his eyes. "Car coming up the hill, pulling in," Sam said in a low voice. Ozzie swallowed again and set the sandwich on the dash. Sam could see a young skinny male get out of the passenger side and walk quickly up on the porch. He didn't fit Flathead's description.

The guy didn't even have to knock. The door opened and a middle aged woman stepped out. She was dressed like a man and was quite overweight. Her hair was a mess and flowed down over her shoulders. It looked gray in the dim porch light. The male handed something to her and she went back inside. In under a minute she came back out and handed something to the young man who looked at it, paused then turned without saying anything and went back down the steps and got back into the car. The vehicle backed out and went back down the hill.

Ozzie had his own binoculars up by now and said, "Driver was a female."

Sam picked up the mic and called the Hazleton car down the hill, "You get the tag on the Chevy?"

The radio answered, "10-4."

Ozzie was back at the sandwich and had opened a big bag of chips. He offered the bag to Sam. "Want some?"

"No, thanks. Drug deal, you think?" Sam asked.

"Yep," Ozzie said between bites.

Sam pulled the folder for the house up front from the back seat and flipped on a small flashlight. He pulled out the sat photo of the house. "Nothing behind it for miles but mountain and woods. I'm gonna slip around and see if I can see in the back side. I'll have my cell phone if anything happens."

"'kay," Ozzie mumbled.

~ * ~

Christie put together a photo lineup with Jimmy Santee's ugly mug, drunk driving arrest photo from Desoto County. It didn't take long. There were plenty of arrest photos of scruffy, unshaved, long haired white guys in their twenties in the files to use for the other pictures in the lineup. Trooper Goddard's call had set off a flurry of activity for Christie. She was finished interviewing the third new case victim and as a result had unfounded the felony assault he had reported the night before and downgraded it to misdemeanor battery. She'd been back at her computer finishing the reports on the junkie armed robber when RGod called.

Jimmy's victim was sitting in her hospital bed sharing her supper with the redhead when Christie showed her Jimmy's picture in among all the others. The girl quickly looked over to the redhead and hesitated. Reluctantly she IDd Jimmy. Christie still wasn't sure if she was going to arrest Russell.

He was technically an accomplice, but it was thin. Jimmy would do for now.

~ * ~

After he got his nose involved in the Jimmy Santee case, RGod figured he'd slip back down 31 a bit and set up. The boys probably would be heading back through from wherever they had gone, and he wouldn't mind grabbing them, and maybe this time Russell would get a little more froggy. His plan fizzled when he got sent to a three car crash in Zolfo Springs.

~ * ~

They stood in the parking lot and talked and laughed with the glider crews for a while. Margie and Will told Ken to tell his dad that they would be up in State College in October or November and wanted Sam to come up. Margie said, "Well, good luck to you, Ken. Study hard and do your very best. You'll be fine."

Will shook Ken's hand and Margie held him in a long hug. She even hugged Grace too. Grace felt as though she had known these people forever. They walked hand in hand to the blue car and Grace said she was worn out and would Ken drive, please. He was beat, too, but didn't complain. He had neglected his run and other workout today, but flying had the same kind of exhausting result. And after a big meal…

Ken eased the Z4 through the town and west out onto Route 70 and then off the split onto 72 toward Sarasota. The top was still down and the air warm but cooling down. Grace slipped an FSU sweatshirt over her head and put the seat back a bit. Ken had to flip the mirror to night driving. A pick-up was behind them and its headlights were just high enough to throw blinding light into the little car.

~ * ~

Sam used the small hand light to pick his way through the bushes until he was almost directly behind the house. The ground rose slowly away from the back yard, but the grade steepened sharply the farther back you went. Sam stayed close in on the flatter part of the hill. He slipped several times and wished he had worn real shoes instead of his tassel loafers. He had the raid jacket yellow "State Police" flaps tucked away in covered compartments so the jacket was all black. It was rocky and muddy and the trees had been cut years ago and replaced by new growth that was thick and brushy.

A game trail crossed down from the top of the mountain and Sam followed it the last few yards to where he could see the light from one of the windows casting a faint glow out into the little yard. He sat and felt the wetness from the muddy ground seep into his good slacks. He didn't need the binoculars; he was close enough to see through the window. There were no shades or curtains and Sam saw the woman walking back and forth from what Sam assumed was the kitchen to the living room. There was another person in the living room, but it looked like an older man, possibly in his seventies or older. No Flathead.

Sam shifted about ten feet farther and got a better angle of the living room. *Just the two of them.* Sam endured his wet ass for the next fifteen minutes while she answered the door and took care of her customers. He noticed the picture on the wall and then brought the binoculars up to see what the picture really was. *Yep, it was.* A full length portrait of a very well-endowed naked lady.

The judge was still in. Christie hustled back to her office and cut and pasted together a brief affidavit on her computer for an arrest warrant for Jimmy Santee. The judge wanted to flirt a little with her, and she didn't feel she could just barge out of his office after he signed the warrant. She finally struck out on the road east and got on the radio for the zone car to meet her just short of the Santee home.

"Pass the rich prick, motherfucker," Jimmy snorted between drags on the glowing pot pipe. Russell was stoned and though he thought he was racing down 72 at high speed in the blue truck, he actually was only going just over the sixty mile per hour speed limit.

Jimmy wanted to get home to piss and leave Momma her beer then go to Sarasota and Bradenton to sell a bunch of the weed. He wasn't as stoned as Russell, but at this point in the evening it didn't seem to make much difference. Now some rich college boy and his whore girlfriend were loping along in a blue BMW, two seat convertible blocking their forward progress.

The girl looked over her shoulder at them and Russell caught a glimpse of her face. S*he's cute!* "She's a babe, Jimmy. Like to have a piece of that." Russell drew in a lungful and held it. "'spensive car," he said and looked over to Jimmy to hand him the pipe.

~ * ~

Flathead pulled his big truck through the gate and into the driveway and shut it down. He was tired and wanted to get to bed. He carried the dope out behind the garage to his stash hiding place and tucked it in for the night. He hoped the naked lady picture house lady had enough to sell for tonight. He would see her tomorrow to collect his cash and drop off this batch. There were no eyes watching this house. It didn't appear on any list anywhere attached to him.

~ * ~

They were passing a swamp on the right shoulder that ran right up to the fencing along the ditch. "Turtle!" Grace shouted at the same instant Ken saw the huge beast in the middle of the westbound lane. Ken forgot about the truck behind him and hit the brakes hard. The low slung car would never clear the hump of the big turtle's shell. Ken started a sharp swerve to the right to try and miss the turtle and bang! They got hit hard from behind.

It knocked Ken and Grace back into the seats and accelerated the car's speed sharply. Ken felt the wind go out of him and his vision went black. Grace bounced forward from the seat and rose just enough to catch her forehead hard on the top of the windshield. Her shoulder had slipped out from under the seat belt and she went out like a light.

Russell never saw the BMW hit the brakes. He struck them at full speed. The BMW had swerved right and the front of the truck hit the right rear corner of the convertible and sent it onto the shoulder and slightly airborne into the barbed wire fence at the side of the road. Neither Santee brother wore seat belts. They were too bothersome and were for sissies. Jimmy almost swallowed the pipe and shot forward into the dash. His right arm took the majority of the impact and he hit his head on the glass in front of him. It didn't give or break and he went even loopier than he already was.

Russell was so relaxed he just flopped back and forth between the steering wheel and the seat. He had no clue what had just happened.

The Beemer hit near the top of the fence just beside a post. The post snapped and the fence didn't stop them and gave way. The car hit the swamp and splashed heavily into the watery muck.

Jimmy was screaming and Russell couldn't react. The truck shot past the still moving turtle, the left front wheel missing it by an inch and rolled to a stop on the right shoulder. It was suddenly quiet except for Jimmy moaning in pain. Russell blinked and wondered what happened to the pipe.

Grace's car floated for a moment and then began to fill with cool water. Ken snapped out of it first and had to sit and think about what was going on around him. He couldn't get his mind to focus. Clipped thoughts and bits of information popped in and out of his head. His vision fluttered a couple more times and then came back.

He was cold. He couldn't understand why. He turned to the right and wondered who the person was next to him with all the blood on their face. Then he realized it was Grace. He panicked. His heart immediately jumped and started beating and he went hollow inside.

Jimmy yelled, "Get going! Get going! Go!"

Russell stared straight ahead and didn't react. Jimmy reached over and slapped Russell. That got his attention and he turned to look at Jimmy and said, "Don't hit me, man, I love you."

"Go, get out of here. We need to go!" Jimmy said again, "Move!"

Russell kind of shook his head and put his foot on the gas. Nothing happened. He pushed harder and still nothing. The dash lights were all lit up in red and orange. The truck had stalled. Russell turned the key in the ignition and got nothing.

"Neutral, asshole; put it in neutral to start it," Jimmy said.

Ken began to move. He tried to go over to Grace, but the seatbelt stopped him. By now the water was coming in over the top of the doors and pieces of vegetation with it. It smelled awful. He fumbled around and found the seat belt release and snapped it free. He pivoted in the seat and tried to lift Grace out of the rising water. She would only move a little and stopped. He had to think a moment and then reached below the water again to locate her belt release. It took some searching, but he found it and the belt went slack. He pulled her to him and pushed with his legs, sliding his butt up and over the driver door with her in his arms.

Russell put the shift lever up into neutral and turned the key again. The starter spun and cranked the engine, but it wouldn't start. Russell tried again and still no engine.

"We got to go, man. We can't be here," Jimmy urged.

"I know, I know," Russell replied, cranking the starter. The truck wouldn't start. They were trapped. Dope, gun and stolen truck.

Jimmy looked up to the long, straight road ahead. No lights. He looked behind, still no lights. They were almost home. He knew this section was lightly travelled, but if they fucked around much longer, someone was going to come along and call the cops.

Ken had her out, but there seemed to be no bottom to this muck. He slipped Grace into a rescue carry and swam through clinging goop toward the lights of a truck parked on the road behind them. When he got to the fence, he held it down and lifted her over. His feet hit solid ground and he moved Grace into the grass and knelt over her. It was dark, but he could see her in the glow of the truck's tail lights. Her eyes were closed and blood was oozing from a gash at her hairline on her forehead and running down the side of her head. He pulled out his shirt and ripped it at the waist tearing off a piece. It was soaked and he folded it over and gently pressed it into the gash to blot the blood away.

"Grace, Grace. You okay?" Ken said to her. She didn't move, but Ken saw a flutter under her eyelids. "Grace, wake up, I'm here with you." Her eyes fluttered again, but she didn't come out of it. He pressed the cloth back against the gash and turned toward the truck.

Jimmy was pounding the dashboard with the one arm that still worked, cursing at the truck to start. Russell continued cranking, but then stopped. "It's flooded. Just gonna kill the battery," he said and cut the lights off.

Jimmy jumped when he heard a knock on his window. He turned to see a young guy standing there with mud on his face. The guy was standing right next to the door and was yelling something. Jimmy opened the door.

Ken was overwhelmed with the smell of marijuana when the passenger door of the truck opened. He knew what it smelled like. Not from smoking it himself, but kids will be kids and Varnum wasn't immune from dope.

"You guys hurt?" Ken asked the unshaven, long haired passenger. He didn't wait for a reply and said, "She's hurt, we need an ambulance."

Jimmy looked at Ken for a moment and started to climb down, "No, we're okay. She's hurt?" he asked, glancing back behind the truck.

Ken then said, "What the hell were you two thinking? You guys are stoned. You could have killed us. She's cut on the head. I'm calling for help." Ken reached for the phone on his belt, but Jimmy saw what he was doing and snatched the phone out of his hand and flipped it onto the floorboard of the pick-up. Ken hadn't expected that reaction and was stunned at what just happened. He took his eyes off the passenger to look into the truck to see where the phone had gone.

Jimmy could see the muscles under Ken's wet shirt and didn't want to be fair. Before Ken could react, Jimmy reached behind the seat and came out with the Winchester, cocking the hammer of the 30-30.

~ * ~

Christie had to stop for gas. She had been so busy she let the tank get too low. It was a long ride out to the eastern end of the county and there were no gas stations out there. There were no bathrooms either. She added that stop to this one.

~ * ~

Sam slipped back into the car with Ozzie. He had walked back around to the road and waited a while so his pants would dry out. They were still damp, but he had brushed most of the mud off. His shoes were ruined, though. Several more cars had come and gone. Each doing basically the same thing. One female had actually gone inside, but she didn't stay long. Ozzie was eating Ding Dongs now. Dessert.

"What happens when I gotta take a dump?" Ozzie asked. Sam groaned and shook his head.

~ * ~

"Back up, rich boy," Jimmy snarled, raising the barrel of the rifle toward Ken's nose. Ken stepped back down the bank and stopped just before the ditch.

Russell hadn't moved, but said, "You gonna shoot him, Jimmy?"

Grace moaned. Ken turned his head to look into the darkness toward her and Jimmy snapped, "Hey, rich boy. Look at me!"

There were no lights out here, but the sky was clear and there was just enough starlight for Ken to see the face of the guy with the rifle. It looked serious. Ken tried to think of what to do. He had to do something. He was off balance and slightly lower than Jimmy, and when he lunged out toward the rifle, Jimmy saw it coming and pulled the barrel back and flipped the stock around to clip Ken on the side of his head. The butt caught Ken on the left ear and tore it open. Ken stumbled at the blow and went to his knees. Jimmy swept the rifle around and slapped the side of Ken's face with the front sight. More blood spit out and over the front of Ken's shirt, mixing with Grace's.

"I'll shoot you in the fuckin' knee and then kill her if you try that again, asshole!" Jimmy shouted over Ken who was down on both knees and slumped over, holding his bloody cheek.

Russell got out and walked around to them. He looked over at the girl in the grass and turned, walking toward her to see her up close. Grace moaned again, "Oh, baby. You got a boo boo," Russell said as he bent over her and lifted up her wet sweatshirt. Her nipples showed through her wet blouse and bra and Russell could just make them out in the dim light. He liked that.

"Russ, comeer!" Jimmy shouted, "Get the fucking truck started. Hurry up."

Russell ran his hand up under the wet blouse and felt Grace's left breast through the bra. His erection was beginning to grow, but Jimmy yelled at him again and he left Grace and went back to the truck. It started on the first try.

Russell turned to the open passenger door and said to Jimmy, "Okay, now what?"

Jimmy said, "We're gonna take rich boy and rich bitch for a little ride. Have a negotiation. I think we just hit the jackpot. Come help me truss 'em up."

~ * ~

The Hazleton corporal called Sam's cell phone and brought him up to date. The meth freak girl IDd McCall as Diamond's shooter. She didn't see the shooting, but heard it and McCall was there. The DA was sitting with the case trooper and fleshing out an arrest warrant. The magistrate was on call and it should be signed soon. Enough to grab McCall on probable cause if he turned up before the warrant was actually punched. The DA said they could get a search warrant for whichever house they could establish as McCall's. Progress.

Ozzie thought about what Sam told him and said, "Should be enough to bag him for the garden center job." He twisted open the top of a bottle of Pepsi and drank a long swallow. "Now I gotta piss too," he announced to Sam. Sam called Calvin and then Adams to let them know about the warrant. Ozzie was squirming in his seat and needed to go to the nearest open store to empty out. *Hold on, Oz.*

~ * ~

They used the ropes and straps in the back of the truck they had to tie down the refrigerators and other appliances. Jimmy was no help. His right arm was getting more painful, and he had to switch the rifle to his left. Russell had to do all the rope work. Russell could barely tie his shoes and he struggled. Jimmy made him retie Ken twice. Jimmy had to prop the rifle against the side of the truck to help Russell lift the tied up boy onto the bed and slide him forward.

Russell took his time with the girl. He had very rude thoughts about this pretty little thing on the ground under him. He flipped her over on her face and her butt jiggled just a bit. He really liked that. Jimmy kept looking up and down the road, but no cars were in sight. He cursed at Russell to hurry. Russ wrapped her small wrists tightly and slipped a couple of loops around her ankles. He didn't have enough rope right there to string her wrists and ankles together, but she was out of it anyway.

Russell was able to lift her up into the back of the truck by himself. He got a shiver when her bare leg rubbed against his cheek while he slid her toward the front. She moaned a few times and seemed to be coming out of the darkness. Russell pulled a plastic tarp over the tied up pair and tied the corners. Jimmy crawled back in the passenger side and grimaced in pain as he slid onto the seat.

Russell got the truck up and moving west. Jimmy told him to pass the turn off to their house and continue on.

Ken heard the passenger tell him through the sliding rear cab window he had the rifle on the girl and if he tried anything stupid she was the first to die.

A car's headlights appeared in the distance behind them coming out of Arcadia. The car lights cast just enough light into the back of the truck for Grace to see Ken's face as she came to. She was shocked at the blood and started to cry. Her mind was still confused, and she couldn't put together her thoughts. She believed this was a very realistic nightmare.

The car lights behind them disappeared and Jimmy said, "They turned off on our road." They were alone again.

Jimmy told him where he wanted to go and Russell remembered the spot. A few miles farther up the road, Russell pulled off on the south side and eased up to a gate in the fence. There was nothing but Florida palmetto prairie on the other side of the gate. No roads or any people for miles in any direction. The rancher who owned this acreage lived in Minnesota. Cowhands were hired now and then to tend to the thousands of beef cattle fenced in this vast property. One of them had been Jimmy Santee. He didn't last long after they caught him stealing gas from a tank on the ranch. Long enough to know some of the combinations at the various gates. He and Russell had been in here many times since to poach deer and hogs.

Ken felt the truck pull off the highway and onto dirt. The bed of the truck was hard and dirty. Covered in grit and trash. Grace's eyes searched for him, but it was now very dark under the tarp. Ken heard one of the truck doors open and then a chain rattle. The truck moved forward and stopped again. The chain rattled and then the truck door opened and closed. They started bouncing along a rough track and it hurt his arms and back. He heard Grace let out a groan and said in a low voice, "How's your head?"

She didn't answer right away but then said, "I'm okay. I have a pounding headache, but I'm okay. What happened?"

"Two guys with a rifle. We're kidnapped. We've got to get away from them, they might kill us," Ken whispered.

She thought about that then said, "Okay, I'm with you."

Ken's hands were tightly tied behind his back and his ankles were tied and looped back to his hands. He wasn't going to break loose quickly. The tarp began to shift with the bouncing truck and fell away from his head. He could see up to the rear window and Jimmy wasn't there. He watched for a few more minutes, but he didn't see the rifle or Jimmy.

Russell was confused and Jimmy wasn't making himself clear. Jimmy pulled his head around from watching the bed to try and get Russell on board, "This is what we've been looking for. It fell into our lap. The little rich boy is worth something to somebody. We don't have to be greedy. He'll bring an easy half million, or more, tax free. Think about what we could do with that. Get away from Ma, get nice trucks and a nice house. No more hauling refrigerators or scrapping copper. Think about it."

Russell tried to miss the bigger holes in the sand track they were following south and west from the road. "But how do we do this? I don't get it. They seen us, they heard our names."

"We get the money and Mommy gets nothing back. No witnesses. Nobody saw us, nobody knows we got 'em," Jimmy explained. Russell pondered that.

Ken heard them talking loudly in the cab. He rolled to Grace and quietly said into her ear, "Back to back." Ken struggled and turned over under the tarp. He felt Grace wiggling next to him and felt his way down to her hands. His fingers ripped at the thin rope around her wrists. His hands were strong, but the poly rope had no give to it. He dug his fingers under the rope next to her skin and felt her shudder in pain. He pulled and twisted with what little movement he could get out of his own tied hands.

"You mean to kill 'em then, Jimmy?" Russell asked.

"Later, after we see how much we can get," Jimmy answered. "We tell Mom and Dad anything they want to hear to get the money. No cops, no FBI. Let him cry and scream on the phone and get Mommy all weepy. Then leave 'em for the gators. No one will ever find the bodies."

"I want me some time with her," Russell said.

Ken heard that and worked harder. Suddenly, he felt a little give in the bindings.

"Head for the chute. We'll tie them up there for now," Jimmy told Russell.

The ropes loosened but not enough to break her wrists free. Ken didn't know how much longer they would be talking in the cab. He rolled his head next to hers and said, "Go for help. Stay out of sight. Go."

She immediately said, "No, I won't leave you."

Ken gritted his teeth and said, "You're gonna get raped and killed if you stay." He spun with his back to the wheel well and tucked his feet under her. He pushed as hard as he could and lifted her up the side of the truck to the top of the bed. She was a small girl, but Ken had to pull something from deep inside to lift and push her over the edge and out onto the sandy ground.

She hit ass first and sharp pain shot up her back and down her legs. It knocked the wind out of her so she couldn't scream. She rolled onto her face and gulped in a mouthful of dirty sand.

Ken rolled back under the tarp and struggled with his own ropes. He tried to flex his wrists apart, but it only seemed to tighten the rope.

~ * ~

Grace worked her hands down the back of her legs and with some effort was able to slide her still-tied wrists under her feet and in front of her.

She glanced up and could still see the lights of the truck as it bounced away through the bushes. She started on her ankles and was able to get them loose, and after only a few minutes had them free.

Now she didn't know which way to go. She got to her feet and looked around. The truck was several hundred yards away, but still close enough to be a threat. She decided to go directly away from the rough trail and struck out at a slow trot, trying to avoid the bushes and palmettos. Surely there had to be a house or a road somewhere out here. The ropes on her wrist fell away with a bit more struggling and she picked up the pace. Her eyes were adjusting to the starlight, but she still managed to stumble over things and fall. Her clothes were wet and she was cold. She stripped off the wet FSU sweatshirt and tied it around her waist. The air quickly started drying the thin white blouse and with the exertion of the running, she warmed up.

She stopped. She looked down at her white blouse and lime green shorts. They seemed to glow against the dark landscape, "Shit." she cursed. Quickly she dropped down and stripped off the shirt and shorts. She rubbed them roughly in the dark sand until they were filthy and dull. She shook them out as best she could and put them back on. Then she did the same for the sweatshirt. The clothing felt gritty and uncomfortable, but that was better than dead. She started jogging again, hoping she was still running away from the truck and the two creeps in it.

Christie had the Jeep hauling ass out Route 72. Once past the state park, there was nothing on either side of the road. She thought she saw lights out in the ranchland to the south of the road, but when she looked again there was nothing. Her sheriff's radio sounded off. The zone car was calling her.

"Sarasota 771, go ahead," she said.

"You better come past the suspect's turnoff and meet me. I think we have a crime scene on the highway," the uniform deputy said. "You'll see my overheads." Now she pushed it up to deputy speed.

~ * ~

The Hazleton corporal was a nice guy and set up a rotation for piss breaks. He was alone in his car and drove to each location to relieve the surveillance troops. Sam was impressed. Ozzie was desperate.

~ * ~

"We get them nice and snug at the loading chute and then we can work on making the call to his mommy. You can entertain the girl while I persuade college boy to cooperate," Jimmy said and glanced back at the tarp covered bed. "Couple of bundles of gold."

~ * ~

Grace had to stop to catch her breath. She still saw no lights in any direction. Her head was pounding. She touched the scalp wound and pulled her hand away to see if it was still bleeding, but it was just too dark to see clearly. It felt dry so she wasn't too worried. She knew she had been unconscious and thought about concussion. Death overruled her concern and she needed to get help for Ken. She started off again and then quickly stopped. She looked up at the stars and tried to remember her high school science.

She said out loud, "North Star, Big Dipper." She was confused, though. The sky was a mass of stars. Out here away from the city lights, every star was visible, not just the brightest ones.

She moved in a slow circle, but could not recognize the dipper. Then she thought to squint her eyes just the slightest bit and circled again. There it was. She followed the front edge of the dipper up and found the North Star. She figured the road they had been on was to the north and that the creeps would think she would head for that. She spun one hundred eighty degrees away from the star and moved off. She just knew she would hit the next road pretty soon and flag someone down.

~ * ~

The chute was a metal structure at the west end of the big ranch. Not much to the west of it but the lower lake of the state park. The lake was closed to vehicles and anyone coming in to it had to walk. It was usually a very lonely place filled with bass, snakes and gators. When it came time to round up the beef cattle and ship them off to market, trucks would haul cattle trailers in and back up to the chute. The cowhands would search the prairie for the scattered herds with horses and ATVs and drive them into the metal corral and then up the chute to the waiting trailers. Hamburger on the hoof.

Russell pulled into the clearing and the headlights illuminated the rusting metal. Jimmy piled out of the truck with the rifle and walked to the tailgate. He dropped it down and pulled back the tarp.

~ * ~

Christie could see the flashing lights of the marked unit from a long way off. He was about a mile east of the road Jimmy and Russell lived on and she glanced to her left as she passed it. She approached and saw the deputy's vehicle pointed west behind two other cars on the shoulder. She went past, did a U-turn and pulled around in front of the first vehicle. As she got out of the Jeep and started back, she noticed the tail lights of a small car submerged in the swamp on the north side of the road. Her first thought was *fatal accident*, which normally didn't involve a detective. As she walked up to the uniform deputy, he flipped his flashlight on and illuminated a bloody piece of cloth on the grass.

~ * ~

Ken passed out from the beating he took when Jimmy dragged him by the feet out of the bed and thumped him onto the ground behind the truck. He dreamed of dragons and snakes. It wasn't a pleasant dream.

~ * ~

She had to stop again. She'd slowed to a foot dragging walk and her legs felt like heavy logs. The hammer pounding inside her head was too much. She couldn't think and she was exhausted. And thirsty. She plopped down on the sand next to a palmetto thicket and tried to control her breathing. In only a few minutes she went blank and fell into the darkness.

~ * ~

"You're going to kill him too soon. You better stop," Russell told Jimmy, who was kicking the unconscious Ken. Jimmy was enraged at the loss of the girl. Russell was confused again but sorted it out. It wasn't a good thing the girl had gotten away. She knew way too much. Their quickly assembled plan was leaking badly.

Jimmy stormed around the truck in big circles walking off his rage. Finally, he said to Russell, "Tie him up good to the chute and wait for me. I'm going to find her and get rid of her. I'll be back."

He went around and got into the truck. As Jimmy roared out of the clearing, Russell dragged Ken over to the chute and tied him there. That done, Russell sat next to Ken, dug the pot pipe from his back pocket and lit it up. *Might as well relax until Jimmy comes back.*

~ * ~

"It'll be a good while before we can get a tow out here," the patrol deputy said. Christie had pieced together what had happened. Chunks of the BMW and the vehicle that hit it were evident on the road and in the grass on the shoulder. More blood was found and the other deputy was ready to string yellow tape. The civilians who stopped had been interviewed and sent home.

Christie said, "Well, unless the striking vehicle bundled everyone off to a hospital, we have a felony hit and run and kidnapping, or worse." She already had dispatch start calling emergency rooms in Sarasota and Arcadia to put them on alert.

Christie didn't want to wait that long to ID the owner or driver of the little submerged car. She pulled out her digital camera and photo'd everything she could see and then pulled her Jeep around to use the winch on the front bumper to pull the car out. She decided she would also volunteer to wade in to hook it up. *Yuk!*

As she was jockeying her Jeep into position, a set of headlights came into view from the east. The car was flying toward them and Christie was starting to get concerned when blue lights came on up on the roof over the headlights. RGod had arrived.

~ * ~

Time moved slowly for them, but at least they had the dope buyers coming and going to keep them busy getting descriptions and tag numbers to pass along to the narcotics troopers. Sam wanted to stick with it, but it didn't look like McCall was going to show. He set up a switch at midnight when he was going to get the Hazleton corporal to drive him back to Lehighton PD to get his truck. Calvin and Johnny would switch with the Hazleton car and set up below Ozzie. Sam felt better about that; having his own men together. The troops didn't seem to mind; it broke up the boredom.

~ * ~

He found the ropes at the side of the trail. *What are the chances?* Jimmy felt the enormity of it all as he'd earlier pulled out of the chute clearing and started back on the sandy, rutted trail. He didn't know where to start to look for her. He decided he would backtrack to the road; she would probably head back there. He half expected to find her tied up next to the trail but found the discarded ropes instead. He cut the truck lights and the engine. He got out and grabbed the rifle as he went around the other side. He needed a flashlight, but they hadn't thought of that. He bent over and looked at the ground. It was too dark to make much sense of it, and he got back in the truck started and backed it up. He angled the lights to play over the spot where the ropes were and got back out.

He now could clearly see her struggle in the sand and her tracks leading south into the wilderness. Jimmy grinned. *She'll never survive on foot. Warm night like tonight, rattlers will be all over the place*, he said to himself. He sat for a few more minutes and tried to decide what to do. He couldn't just let her go. He got back in the truck and engaged the four wheel drive. He slowly pulled off the track and into the scrub. He picked out her footprints when she hit the softer sand and tried to follow them with the headlights. If he got stuck, he could always walk out.

~ * ~

His stomach rumbled. He hadn't eaten and the pot was making him even hungrier, but it was making him sleepy too. He smoked the pipe down to ashes and wished he'd grabbed another handful of weed before Jimmy took off.

Russell looked over at Ken who was breathing but was still out. He tried not to think about food, but he wasn't strong enough. Thinking about food drifted into dreaming about it as Russell fell asleep.

~ * ~

RGod opened the trunk of his patrol car and dug around for a minute. He came out with a chest high set of waders. "No need for you getting your nice clothes all wet, miss," he said to Christie. "My fishin' pole's in there, too, if we stir up any largemouth lunkers."

Christie played out the cable from the winch and RGod slipped off his shirt, gun belt and shiny black boots and slithered himself into the waders. He grabbed the hook and worked his way over the bent fencing to the back of the car. "Hope there isn't a body under this thing," he said over his shoulder.

He snapped the hook to something solid under the rear of the car. "Haul it out," he shouted to Christie.

She engaged the winch and slowly the car started back toward the road. RGod stepped on the fence and his weight held it down so the car could back over it. The right rear was mangled, but both taillights and the headlights were still on.

Water poured out of every opening, and the uniform deputy opened the passenger door as it rolled past him. He popped the glove box and fished out the registration. A woman's purse was on the seat and he brought it all back and spread it out on his warm car hood to dry out.

RGod unhooked the winch cable, and Christie rolled it back onto the spool. By the time she finished and RGod had reassembled himself, the other deputy was on his phone. He said to Christie as she came over, "Cell phone in the purse is dead. Car's registered out of Sarasota city. No phone numbers so I'm having the city PD go by the residence. Give me your cell number for them to call."

~ * ~

She heard something rustle the palmettos near her. She didn't know how long she had been asleep, but it was still dark and her head pounded. She thought her stomach was rumbling, but it wasn't. *What was that sound?* A low rumble and a hissing. She stood up and the bushes near her exploded in sound and movement. She watched the panther leap away, its tail flailing as it went. Her heart almost stopped. The dim starlight was not enough to see beyond the next bushes. She had to force herself to breathe. It had been that close to her, watching her, stalking her. Her hands were shaking, and just a trickle of urine slipped out into her panties.

She calmed herself and found the North Star again. She was looking up at it, but there was something below it. Headlights. *Oh, God, they're coming.* She spun and ran as fast as she could. *How the hell did they track me?* She tried to think, but her head hurt so bad. She had to slow down. She knew if she couldn't separate herself from them, come daylight she was dead.

~ * ~

Katrina was startled by the heavy knock on her front door. The doorbell rang almost at the same time. She went to the door and she could hear a big car engine running in front of the house. Cautiously, she looked through the peephole and saw the cutest young policeman she had ever seen. He had close cropped blonde hair and big broad shoulders. *Maybe he's here to ask me to the policeman's ball*, she said to herself.

She opened the door with her big perfect smile and noticed his dark uniform was crisp and had creases in the short sleeves. His big gold badge glittered in the porch light. Her heart felt like it was going to drop out of her ass when he asked, "Do you know a Grace Echaverria?"

~ * ~

Jimmy was getting worried. The tracks started out clear enough but faded when she went through places where grasses actually grew up through the sand. He knew she would see him coming, but if he could keep her ahead of him until it got light…

~ * ~

Katrina pulled herself together and tried to wipe the runny makeup from under her eyes. The Sarasota cop was in the kitchen making coffee, and she was on the phone to Detective O'Shea. "She was supposed to be home by now. She and Ken, that's Ken Deland, he's from Pennsylvania. D-e-l-a-n-d. Oh God no, he's a good kid. His dad's a cop up north. He wouldn't do anything like that at all. No, I don't have his father's number, but wait, I have a number for his, ah, his friend, or girlfriend I guess." She started misting again and got more tissues to blow her nose. She plopped down on a chair and took a deep breath, "I'll call her and have his dad call you back. Where are they, what could have happened to them? Give me your name and number again." She found a pen and a slip of paper and scribbled Christie's information down.

~ * ~

"They were going back to Sarasota from the airport in Arcadia. Glider flying. Should have been home by now. That puts it about one to two hours ago give or take. Right before we got here," Christie said to Trooper Goddard.

"Humor me. Can you have the deputy check to see if there are any vehicles at Jimmy Santee's house? Just a drive by for now," RGod asked. He was working on a measured drawing sketch, running a wheeled device over the ground.

Christie sent the marked unit to Jimmy's and then looked at the photo on the driver's license she found in the purse, *Where are you, young lady?* she said to herself. Christie hoped she was sitting in an emergency room somewhere, but as time moved on, the chances of that grew slimmer.

RGod was walking over the scene again using a hand held light and a metal clipboard. He stopped several times to bend down and touch the bits of damaged vehicle or the road surface. He'd picked several pieces out of the rear of the BMW and from the ground and had them laid out on the hood of his car. He would work the crash part of what this all turned out to be. He was a qualified accident reconstructionist and really knew what he was doing.

"Miss Christie, come on over here for a minute," he said. She went to him at his car and he began, "What we have here is a big coincidence, and I don't really believe in coincidence, do you?" he asked. Before she could say anything, he continued, "This here is a piece of a Ford truck. It's been painted a nice dark blue. Used to be white. You don't see too many dark blue Ford pick-up trucks here in the Sunshine State. Most are white or black. Some light blues, greens or reds, but fewer dark blue." She was following him so far.

"Now you're the detective here, but it seems to me that we stand not a mile or so from the home of wanted felon, Jimmy Santee and his faithful sidekick, Russell. The same miscreants observed by yours truly, a surely magnificent specimen of law enforcement expertise and raw talent that is mostly ignored by the dickheads in charge of the Patrol, driving a dark blue Ford pick-up earlier today. Your deputy, at this very moment, is cruising past the Santee mansion and will report to us if the blue Ford is there and if it has front end damage and if there are one or two otherwise harmless people dead, injured or tied up awaiting rescue."

Christie had to take a step back to take it in. RGod pulled a huge cigar out of his shirt pocket and calmly lit it. "Ya think?" he finished.

~ * ~

The phone ringing woke her up. She glanced at the clock and realized she must have just gone to sleep. Dutch was sitting up on his pad under the window watching her struggle from under the covers and try to find the darn phone in the dark. Eileen managed to catch it after the fourth ring and before it rolled over to voice mail. "Yeah?" she answered and closed her eyes again.

"Hello? Hello?" a female voice asked.

"Who is this?" said Eileen grumpily. Dutch was up and now was standing next to the bed between Eileen and the bedroom door.

"Katrina Echaverria, Grace's mom?" Eileen had to think about that. The wheels cranking inside her brain were spooling up to speed and then it clicked into place. "Yeah, Grace. Why are you calling me?"

Eileen sat up and swung her legs out of the bed. "Ma'am, ma'am, what's wrong, what's going on?" She could hear the woman sobbing.

It took a few minutes more before Eileen could get Katrina to make sense. Eileen tried to put together the fractured pieces of information Katrina gave her between more crying. She got up and started moving with the portable phone. She got a robe on and went downstairs to the kitchen door to let Dutch out.

"Okay, Katrina. I'll find Ken's dad and have him call the police down there. I'm sure it's going to be okay." She wasn't, though. A feeling of dread began to overwhelm her. "Let me find something to write with."

~ * ~

He couldn't feel his hands. They were numb. His head was pounding and he had trouble breathing. He saw double when he opened his eyes. The metal bars next to his head wiggled in mid-air for a few seconds in his vision but then steadied and took shape. He tried to sit up, but sharp pain in his side stopped him. He could see his feet in the starlight and had to pee. He kept blinking, but his eyes felt crusted over and he was spitting sand.

*Snoring?* He could hear snoring close by. The initial confusion was clearing away and he remembered he had been roughed up and he was still tied hands and feet. He scooted his butt under him and puffed through the pain, trying to roll onto his back. He realized he was also loosely tied from his hands to the metal bars so he was having trouble rolling over to sit up. The snoring was coming from behind him, but he wasn't able to turn that way. He hoped Grace didn't snore.

~ * ~

The pot had worn off. His arm was swelling to twice its size and hurt like crazy. He was trying to go as fast as he could, but he kept having to stop, get out and try to find her tracks again. He thought she would be down by now. Twice he had seen big rattlesnakes in the headlights, warming and hunting on the sand. He didn't want to wander around too much in the dark and *damn this arm really fuckin' hurt.*

~ * ~

The sandals were wearing a blister on her right heel. At least they had straps. She would have been barefoot by now if she had worn the backless ones she at first picked out this morning. Or was it yesterday morning by now. She had lost track of time. Her legs and arms were scratched and several trails of blood ran down to her ankles. She stopped again and could not see the lights of the truck. She needed to rest and needed a drink of water. She had nothing with her. Only her determination to get help for Ken.

~ * ~

Sam had just gotten the Pathfinder started in the parking lot of the police department. He needed to get home and get some sleep so he could stay awake tomorrow. It was before midnight, but he didn't feel guilty leaving the surveillance early. His people knew what to do. The relief crews were trickling in, but it would still be a long night for Ozzie, Johnny and Calvin. Adams was glad to have the overtime.

As he pulled out on the street, his cell vibrated and he saw the call was from Eileen. *Why is she calling so late?* "Hi, what's up?" Sam said as he pulled to the curb.

~ * ~

"Mustang sitting in front of the house, no truck," the uniform deputy told Christie over the radio. By now a Desoto County sergeant had come to the scene and offered the fire station just over the Desoto line as a temporary command post if they needed one. There was nothing to the west. No place with a roof at all. Christie was unsure how she wanted to handle this. She didn't want to go overboard, but this was now more than a hit and run.

She called her sergeant and woke him up to brief him on the case. He called her back a few minutes later and said he was coming and bringing a couple more detectives. A K-9 car and another marked unit were already en route. The helicopter was out of service, but the sergeant had sent a message out to the whole state to find the blue truck.

"Don't wait for me. As soon as the next marked unit gets there, hit the house," he told her.

Another Desoto deputy and RGod's corporal also rolled up. It was starting to look like a convention.

Christie excused herself to answer her cell phone. "Detective? This is Ken's dad, Sam Deland."

~ * ~

It really hurt to move even a little and Ken was moving a lot. He worked his way to a sitting position without waking Russell. Ken knew he was hurt, but didn't think he was going to die from it. He was worried about his hands and fingers. Seemed silly, but there was no rifle pointed at his head at the moment so he allowed himself.

The man was leaning back against the metal bars sleeping soundly. Even if Ken could reach him with his feet, there was nothing he could do until he could get loose from this metal thing. And he really did have to pee.

~ * ~

Jimmy was out in front of the truck trying to see the footprints. He didn't hear the cell phone in the waterproof and shatterproof case, vibrating under the truck seat.

~ * ~

No answer. Just Ken's new voice mail message and a beep. "Call me ASAP," was all that Sam said. He called the phone again, but it went to voicemail. The quiet deserted streets of Lehighton stared back at Sam through his windshield.

~ * ~

They left the Highway Patrol corporal with the BMW and the rest all went to the Santee house. The Sarasota deputy that had just arrived went to the rear with a Desoto deputy and Christie led the rest up onto the front porch. She felt it sag under her as the weight of the men came up and spread on either side of the door. The front door was open, and Christie could see through the ripped screen that the TV was on in the house. No other lights were on. She'd checked the Mustang hood on the way to the porch and it was cold.

"Sheriff's department!" she hollered and pounded on the paint flaking door frame. A few bits of graying paint floated down to the worn flooring. No response. "Sheriff's department with a warrant!" she pounded again. When she stopped pounding, she heard the floor inside groan and then footsteps coming toward her. Her Sig was in her hand and she waited for the form of the person to appear. She looked across at RGod who also had his handgun out and pointed at chest level through the front door.

A heavy, short woman in a man's dirty and torn T shirt and nothing else came to within two feet of the door and stared at RGod.

"You're a big one," the woman said.

Christie spoke, "Is Jimmy here?"

The woman sniffled and rubbed her nose. Christie knew she was about to lie. "Jimmy, who? Ain't no Jimmys here," the woman said.

RGod stepped over, flung open the screen door and marched past the woman, "Well, ma'am, we'll just see about that."

~ * ~

Eileen had given Sam Katrina's number, and as he drove quickly out of Lehighton west toward home, he called her. She had no idea where the kids were. She told Sam they had switched days to go to Arcadia, and Grace had called earlier and said they were stopping to eat and then coming home. It didn't make sense. Sam told her to call him right away if she learned anything new.

Alarm bells were clanging between his ears. He had to force himself to focus on the roadway as he pushed the Nissan just as hard as he could toward home. He slowed and cruised to the side of the road and picked up his cell from the seat where he had thrown it in frustration. He stared at it, but couldn't think of who to call. Who could give him answers.

~ * ~

Grace was moving much slower now. She needed water and her vision was blurring if she ran too fast. She held it to a walk, a fast walk. It was all she could do. Now she wished she had eaten more, she needed the energy.

She could see the looming shadows of trees ahead. Several big oaks were clustered together, and she came up to the edge of the starlight shadow and stepped in. At the base of one of the oaks was a clear spot and she sat down to rest. She was determined not to fall asleep again and actually slapped herself twice to keep alert.

There was a fallen piece of thin oak branch close to her legs, and she reached over and flipped it away into a palmetto cluster. The sound she heard puzzled her. Then all the TV shows and movies she had seen in the past told her what the buzzing sound was. She couldn't see the snake, but it was there. The buzzing got louder and she was afraid to move.

~ * ~

Christie told the woman to sit on the couch. The house was emptying out. The cops wanted to get outside as soon as they could to escape the smelly dump. Of course, several items with Jimmy's and Russell's names on them were found in the house. Also found was an empty box of 30-30 ammunition. Christie shuddered and sat next to her on the dirty couch with RGod looming at the end of it.

"I ain't tellin you nothing," the woman said.

"Look, we need to see Jimmy and straighten this out. Some girl is just probably mad at him and wanted to scare him by claiming he did something to her." Christie lowered her voice and leaned in to the woman, "We know how women can be, don't we."

The woman's eyes flickered and she took a deep breath. Then she sniffled and rubbed her nose again. "He don't live here no more," she said and shut up. Christie worked on her for another twenty minutes and she wobbled some more, but wouldn't say much about Jimmy and Russell.

RGod had enough. He stepped closer to the unkempt woman, the now unlit half cigar clamped in his teeth and shoved papers he had hidden behind his back under the woman's sniffling nose. "Death and taxes, ma'am. 'Cept you ain't dead, but you ain't paid your taxes in quite a while." The papers were from the county real estate tax offices. "Owe quite a bit. Says here you gonna be put out on the street."

The woman looked at RGod with a nasty sneer, "They been screwin' with us for a while now. Ain't no big thing."

"Yeah the tax folks puff and dally, but sooner or later you gotta pay." RGod pulled the cigar from his mouth, turned and spit on the floor. "What'll get you out on the street tonight is the Health Department. Have you sitting in a blanket at the homeless shelter before daylight, I call 'em and tell 'em what I see here." He was bluffing, but she didn't know it.

Christie had read this kind of script before and sat up. "Trooper, don't you bully her! This poor woman has lost her man and has two boys to take care of. She's got a lot to worry about. You don't need to push her around." The woman didn't see Christie roll her eyes at RGod.

~ * ~

Margie couldn't get to sleep. Too much food and old friends. Her tummy and her head wouldn't slow down. She popped three antacids and got a can of beer from the fridge. She went through the sliding glass doors out to the lanai and sucked in a lung full of night Florida air. She sat on a lounger for a while trying to settle down, but it was no use. Too much in her mind and she needed to zone out.

It was too quiet so she flipped on the scanner on the end table to keep her company and provide a distraction. She had several aircraft frequencies programmed into it, including the Unicom from the airport down the road.

She liked to imagine where all the planes and people were going and what they would see and do once they got there. The local ambulance was on the scanner and a couple of sheriff's department channels, too.

She heard pilots from Miami and Fort Lauderdale checking in and out with the south Florida center and on some nights she could get planes talking to the tower at Sarasota. There seemed to be something going on with the sheriff's deputies. A lot of back and forth about something out at the county line on 72. She almost shut it off because they were blocking the air traffic when she heard a familiar name, "Kenneth Deland, white male eighteen years old, six foot tall, medium build possibly being held by James Santee who is wanted for felony assault out of Sarasota County."

"Will!"

~ * ~

The young cop left when a sheriff's detective showed up. The detective looked tired and his shirt was wrinkled. "Is there a house phone?" he asked.

Katrina shook her head no and said, "I live on my cell. I haven't had a land line for two years. My cell is over here. I have the charger plugged in."

He picked it up and scrolled through the recent calls then checked her text messages. "No calls from either of the kids since earlier this evening?" he asked.

"No and I hope the next one tells me they're safe," she said. He just raised his eyebrows and sat down on the couch.

~ * ~

Ozzie was fighting sleep. He got out of the car and walked around behind to piss. He then did about fifteen laps, but had to jump back in when another drug buyer pulled into the driveway.

"You chasing your tail around up there?" Johnny asked over the car to car frequency.

Ozzie stuck his head out of the open window and shouted as loud as he could, "Fuck you!" The young guy on the porch turned to look, but didn't see anyone around and thought he was hearing things in his head again.

~ * ~

It stopped. Grace was straining her eyes hard to try and see the shape of the blasted thing in the palmettos, but it was getting darker and she couldn't see anything past her toes. She shifted her weight to ease the cramp in her upper thigh and the rattler buzzed again.

She froze and a tear started down her left cheek. She had never been so scared in her life. She sat very still and in a few minutes the rattler stopped again. She tried to breathe normally, but it was coming in gulps. Then she heard the door of a vehicle slam out in the distance.

~ * ~

They actually had a website. McCall scrolled down and looked at the pictures. Baskets of flowers and bedding plants, fruits and vegetables. The roadside stand was at the front of a big Mennonite farm out near Kutztown. Long, plastic covered greenhouses spread out around the farm buildings. They sold the baskets for ten dollars apiece. Lower than the box stores or the garden centers. Mostly cash out there, not very many credit card sales; Amish country.

Sunday was Mother's Day. The little whore the other night babbled about getting hanging baskets for her mom and how she had been going to this place since she was in college at Kutztown U. Flathead wasn't sure if they sold on Sundays, so he decided he would hit them on Saturday night. Ride the Harley out there in the morning and check it out. Stash the bike and come back later in a stolen car. Plus there was a great wing place up on the hill behind the college.

~ * ~

Will found Sam's cell phone number on a piece of Christmas card from last year. He had torn it off and thrown it in his junk drawer. Never got around to entering into his own cell phone. "Hi, Sam. It's Will down in

Arcadia."

Sam was standing with no pants or underwear on in the laundry room of his converted barn house. The wet and muddy dress slacks were in the washer.

"Have you heard about Ken and Grace?" Will was hoping for a good answer.

"Not much, do you know what's happened?" Sam asked.

Will was confused, "We just heard the police on the scanner and wanted to call to see if they had called you."

"Grace's mom put me in touch with a detective down there. Just that they were in a hit and run accident and they can't be located. She, the detective, said maybe they had been driven to an emergency room."

Will hesitated, then said, "I think it's more serious than that, Sam. The broadcast said they were possibly kidnapped by a wanted felon."

Sam's knees buckled and he had to reach out and hold onto the dryer. His stomach went hollow, and he felt like his veins were popping out of his forehead.

"She, she didn't tell me that. Kidnapped? What the hell is going on?"

Will told Sam about the day and that they all went out to dinner and the kids left for Sarasota. "The road back to Sarasota is where the deputies are. There's nothing out there but swamp and pasture. Thousands of acres."

"Will, call me on my cell if you find out anything, please," Sam said.

"Sure, Sam. Is there anything I can do?" Will asked.

Sam breathed into the phone for a moment then asked, "You have jet fuel at Arcadia?"

~ * ~

Ken worked hard on his hands. He twisted and pulled. It was exhausting trying to free himself and breathe with cracked ribs. He was sure at least one or two were pushing the wrong way. His head was banged up pretty bad too. He pushed that all aside and concentrated on the bindings.

~ * ~

Mrs. Santee broke after forty minutes. She told them about the blue truck and that the boys were due back tonight with beer for her. They should have been here long ago. She needed that beer.

Christie pushed her about the accident and the people in the car. She wouldn't budge on that. Hadn't seen the boys since before dark. She had no phone so they felt confident she wouldn't rat them out to Jimmy.

Christie and RGod were in her front yard splitting up the troops to cover the approaches to the house in case the boys ignored the hordes of police out on 72 and decided to come up the dirt lane.

She heard her phone ring. "O'Shea." The phone seemed to explode in her ear. The boy's dad was wanting to know what was going on and why she hadn't been straight with him.

"Settle down, mister. We're working on it. No, we haven't yet. No, we're not positive, but pretty darn sure." She could hear the roar of a vehicle engine in the background. "Why do you need to know where the scene is?" Christie asked. He'd hung up on her. She shook her head and looked over to Goddard.

"He's pissed. A state trooper from PA. I guess I can understand, but what a pain in the ass. Hope he has enough sense about what to do if he gets a ransom call from Jimmy." They drove back to where the BMW was being hauled up on a tow truck. Her sergeant was there and agreed with the Desoto County sergeant to take the car to the fire station for forensic work. At least temporarily. It was actually closer to Arcadia from here than to Sarasota.

~ * ~

Jimmy was struggling to drive the truck over the sandy brush and palmettos. He could just make out a big oak hammock out in front. The light was going. High clouds were skidding in from the southwest blocking the starlight and the wind had picked up from that direction too. The air warmed, but the humidity was climbing also.

His right arm had been crunched in the crash. He could hardly use it. The truck had power steering, but it was still hard to control in the sandy soil. Several times he'd bogged down and had to goose it back and forth to get out. He had to reach over the steering wheel with his left hand to shift from drive to reverse and back again. He hit an ATV trail the cowhands used and made a bit of progress but then had to backtrack to find her trail again.

He stopped and got out to look at the ground and bumped his sore arm on the doorframe. He yelped and slammed the door hard.

Grace needed to move. If she stayed here the truck would find her. She very slowly untied the FSU sweatshirt and pulled it around in front of her. Holding the arms out, she tried to use it as a shield between her and the snake. She scooted her feet under her and started to get up. The snake sensed her movement and began to rattle louder than ever. She was shaking now. She had to just do it.

She held the sweatshirt out in front of her and stood up. She sidestepped to her right and she felt the sweatshirt buck and it was pulled from her hands. She didn't stop or even slow down. She ran out of the hammock and went over one hundred yards in record time for a scared girl in sandals. She stopped to catch her breath and looked up to find the North Star again. She was just able to get a brief picture of it as the high clouds drifted across, covering it from view. What she could see, though, were those damn truck lights again.

~ * ~

"Peggy, believe me I have to do this. I have to do this for Ken. It's important." Sam really didn't know why, but he had to go. He had the means if Peggy went along with it. He dressed, grabbed what he needed and rushed out of the house. He forgot the alarm but didn't even think about it. Molly peeked out of her barrel as the truck spun dirt through the oaks. She yawned and went back to sleep.

His drive out onto the highway and then over the mountain seemed to take forever, even though there was almost no traffic. Bad things kept dancing into his head, and he put off the next phone call, trying to figure out just the right words to say. He had his 12 gauge and a box of magnum double ought in a black nylon case lying on the front seat and was flying low, trying to stay on the road and talk on the phone at the same time.

Peggy yawned and tried to clear her head. "What am I going to do with the golfer?" she asked. "He's going to be mad as hell."

"Tell him the Lear was stolen. It's almost the truth. Send him down in the Baron. It's still a good plane. He was expecting a twin engine anyway. He won't know the difference. I'll pay half, give him a big discount. Okay?"

"Oh, okay Sam. You really think Kenny is in serious trouble down there?" she asked.

"Sounds bad. Bad enough. My gut tells me to do this. Wish me good luck?" he was coming out onto route 22 and would be at the side gate to the airport in thirty five minutes at this speed.

"It's only got enough fuel for Manassas and return. You won't get any at ABE without waiting for the fuel guys to wake up," she said.

"I'll stop on the way. Don't worry, Peg. It'll be alright. Probably be bringing him back with me tomorrow," he hoped.

~ * ~

Ken saw the clouds blocking the light and couldn't see past the clearing now. He didn't know where Grace was or the other guy, Jimmy. The prick who needed a good beating. Russell had stirred once or twice and had opened his eyes to check on Ken, but was snoring again. Ken's hands were still mostly numb, but he felt something wet and warm on them. He was bleeding from the ropes cutting his wrists.

~ * ~

There really wasn't a lot more to do. No houses on the highway to canvass or witnesses to interview. Christie's sergeant sent the other detectives up the road to interview Mrs. Santee's neighbors to see if they heard or saw anything. Wake up a bunch of extra eyeballs.

A Desoto deputy drove up and pulled two fold out canopy tents from his trunk to set up in a small field at the intersection of the highway and the Santee's hard road. Courtesy of the farmer's market in town. When the sun came up they would need the tents. The firehouse was about nine miles back toward Arcadia, and the troops shuttled back and forth to get something to eat and drink. The K-9 sniffed the car before it left and started west but pulled up only a few yards down the road and quit.

Shortly after the canopies were set up, the sheriff showed up.

~ * ~

"One five Quebec, goodnight sir," Sam was accelerating through fifteen thousand feet heading south. He figured his arrival at Arcadia would be around dawn. No commercial flight could have gotten him there sooner. They probably would have had something to say about the Glock on his hip and the 12 gauge shotgun in the case strapped into the co-pilot's seat.

~ * ~

Katrina couldn't sleep. The detective was flipping through her TV channels and playing with his computer tablet. The clock didn't seem to move. The thought of losing Grace overwhelmed her. She still wasn't over losing her husband. So sudden and shocking she hadn't had a chance to anticipate it. Now her baby. She felt the nausea come on quickly and just made it to the powder room off the kitchen.

~ * ~

Grace tried to move faster, but it was really dark now. She kept stumbling into scrub and falling down. She was very thirsty and needed water. She thought about what Ken had said to her earlier, *Spring was the best time to fly sailplanes in Florida. It was the dry season.* Great.

She kept pushing, trying to miss the bushes. Finally, she had to stop and sit. Her head would not stop pounding and she was feeling dizzy. After she caught her breath, she stood up and looked for what she hoped wasn't behind her. *No headlights*. As she sat back down, she heard an unusual noise. What sounded like a jackhammer off in the direction she was trying to go. She had trouble placing it.

She listened for a while longer and then heard what sounded like a tractor trailer. *Traffic*. That meant a road. She was heading for a road. She got back up and moved on.

~ * ~

Jimmy heard the jake brake from the truck on I-75 south of him. He tried to picture where it was and how far, but had done poorly in geography and couldn't read a map if he had to. He was sitting in the truck with the engine and headlights off. He had lost her trail. He needed to do a wide circle and try to pick it up but wasn't about to wander out into the prairie in the dark. He was starting to worry she might get away. *Then what?* He didn't want to think about it. He had the rifle and a load of pot, but he didn't want to have to go on the run. He had to get rid of her and then they could work on college boy.

## Chapter Ten

The sheriff said the Auxiliary would be out in the morning with horses. He didn't think it was very likely the Santee boys and the kids from the BMW were in the woods on either side of the highway, but he wanted to make the effort. He was sorry the chopper was stuck on the ground, but the Auxiliary was always anxious to get in the game. The crime scene crew was split up. Part went to the fire station to work on the car and the rest got the pleasure of wading into the swamp where the car had been.

Christie and her sergeant spent a while with the sheriff, briefing him on what they had so far. He had to do a phone press conference at six AM with the local TV that would be taped and sent to New York for the network if they wanted to run the story. The sheriff said, "Frankly, I don't think it'll go national unless we come up with a body."

Coolers of water and soft drinks had appeared in the canopies. A portable generator was running and light bars had it lit up. The sheriff cracked a Diet Coke and said, "Damn nice little substation we got here."

His smile faded when the sergeant came over with a cell phone outstretched and said, "It's the FBI, sheriff."

~ * ~

The ground fell away from under her and she fell through space. She didn't fall for long and hit the muddy bottom of the canal hard. She couldn't move for several minutes, and when she could, it hurt. Her ankle was twisted around and she knew it was sprained. She hoped it wasn't broken. She flopped over onto her butt and tried to pull herself backwards out of the ooze.

She struggled for nearly half an hour and managed to get to the edge of the bottom of the canal, but couldn't get back up the side. She figured the mud on her legs and feet was probably the best poultice for a sprain for now. Then the mosquitoes found her.

~ * ~

Sam had picked Orangeburg, South Carolina for his fuel stop. The books told him they had twenty four hour service and clean bathrooms. Sam worked his way down following the center's instructions and then made contact with the tower. There was no traffic about this time of the night, and the tower guy sounded like Sam had awoken him up from a nap.

He brought the slippery little Lear jet onto the runway and followed ground control instructions to the ramp for fuel. He hoped they took his Visa card.

~ * ~

When the news truck showed up, the sheriff made them turn around and drive back to the state park entrance. He went with them to give them an on camera interview and told Christie and her sergeant to stop traffic on this section of the highway. Deputies set up road blocks at the park on the west end and at the fire station on the east end. They were ready for daylight.

~ * ~

Pennsylvania is farther east than Florida and the first streaks of daylight were a welcome sight to Ozzie. He'd struggled to stay awake since the last doper had come to the house at three thirty. He stepped out of the car and poured water from a bottle into his hands and splashed his face. He rubbed it pink with napkins and stretched. The house was dark. Nothing moving. Ozzie doubted they would stay until noon, but he wasn't complaining. The Commonwealth was paying him very well for sitting on his considerable ass.

Down the hill, Calvin was hurting. Johnny was asleep while Calvin watched so he didn't see the look on Calvin's face. Grimace was more like it. His hip was killing him. He popped four ibuprofen an hour ago, but it wasn't doing much. He needed a stiff drink.

The birds were chirping and singing merrily in the trees all around him. Calvin wanted to shoot them. He was grumpy with pain and wanted to go home and soak in a hot bathtub with a bottle of Old Grandad.

~ * ~

The southerly headwinds had thrown off his original estimate. The computer told him he would be in sight of Arcadia Municipal forty five minutes after sunup. He pulled up the airport and studied the layout. He had never been here before. He'd flown into Orlando and Miami several times on charters, but this was very different. The runway wasn't that long, but he wasn't heavy on fuel and was confident he could get the Lear on the ground safely. The wind was almost on the nose. He would have to crab it a bit, but this was nothing compared to landing an EA-6B on the deck of a moving carrier at night.

~ * ~

Christie came out of the ladies locker room at the fire station after a much needed wash up. She had the whole locker room to herself. There weren't any women assigned to this station. She went to the Jeep and spent a few minutes putting a light paint job on her face. She was going into Arcadia to interview the people at the airport. They were supposed to be there early in the morning.

The horse trailers began arriving even before daylight. The special deputies of the Sheriff's Auxiliary were really just civilians with the willingness to contribute their time and money to support the department. It got them a badge and an ID card but no arrest powers unless they were directly assisting a sworn deputy. They rode their horses in parades and once in a while volunteered for searches. Today they would fan out on both sides of 72 and work west from the scene. They parked along the road leading to the Santee house and milled around their trucks greeting each other and looking anxious.

The sheriff didn't need their help, but there wasn't much he could do about it. Two guys in FBI raid jackets hovered together under the canopies talking on cell phones and looking serious. He got blank looks from them when he met them at their car as they drove in earlier and asked them where their horses were. As long as he included them in any press face time, they would be happy and stay out of his way.

RGod was back. He had gone home to change into a clean uniform and feed the dog. His corporal had to leave and tend to the other troopers in the area. Deputies from the night shift had been relieved by the day shift and most were sitting in their cars or standing around waiting for someone to tell them what to do.

A folding table and chairs had been set up under the canopies, and a uniform captain was standing over the shoulder of a uniform lieutenant seated at the table looking at a topo map of the area. It was about to start.

~ * ~

The ropes gave way. Ken could feel the first loop slide loose and then that was followed by the next. His hands felt the rush of blood past the now loosening ropes and into his fingers where it sent zaps of pain to the tips. The blood from his wrists earlier had helped lubricate the rope, and he was almost finished. He still had a rope running to his ankles and something lashing him to the metal bars.

He slowly turned his head and looked over at Russell. *Man could that guy sleep.* Russell had lain down in the sand and was in a fetal position, breathing through his mouth. Ken got one hand loose and started on his ankle ties.

~ * ~

At the first hint of daylight, Grace crawled and waded through the muck to the other side of the canal. She struggled up the bank and fell exhausted on the top. At least she could see now. That was the good news. The bad news was that there was nothing to see but more scrub and palmettos. She was covered in mud. That was the only protection she had from the bites of the bugs at the bottom of the canal. An oak hammock was off to the left, but she wasn't going near it after what happened at the last one. She got to her feet and started south. Her ankle hurt, but she was moving. She looked behind her but did not see the truck. Then she heard a tractor trailer pass on the far highway and that gave her some hope. Grace heard the jet and spun around to watch it fly low over the prairie and pull up. The plane turned north and then west and appeared to be making another run.

~ * ~

Jimmy had fallen asleep in the cab of the truck. Daylight didn't wake him. He was sweating in the closed cab because he had rolled up the windows to keep the bugs out. He woke suddenly as the jet roared overhead. It startled him and he sat up and tried to remember where he was.

~ * ~

Ken heard the plane and was able to catch a glance at it as it flew low west to east just north of him. "Damn," he muttered. "Dad."

He threw all his strength into the ropes. Russell stirred, but only rolled to the other side and went back into the fetal position. Ken got his other hand free and put both to work on his ankles. He was surprised that the rope holding him to the metal bars fell away when the rope from his ankles to his wrists was off. Ken tried to stand, but his legs wouldn't hold him and he fell forward onto his face. His ribs hurt, too, and he had to work hard just to breathe.

He turned his head to look at Russell, but he hadn't moved. Slowly and as quietly as he could, he worked his way up to his feet and took a few short, cautious steps. He turned back to the sleeping Russell and debated with himself what to do. Kill him or sneak off. The jet went by again and Ken was now sure it was Peggy's Lear. It had to be his dad flying it.

The gunshot answered his dilemma about Russell. He heard a second shot and zeroed in on a direction. It came from the southeast. *Grace. He's shooting at Grace*. Ken felt the rage swell within him. Something he had never felt before. Russell could wait; he had to get that maniac stopped before she was...

Ken took two of the deepest breaths he could and began to walk then jog toward the sound of the gun.

~ * ~

Grace was moving steadily and heard a sharp buzz pass by her left ear. She thought it was some kind of bee and then she heard the boom of the rifle from behind her. She stumbled as she turned to look. Another buzz that she now knew was a bullet passing close by her and she heard the boom follow. She could just see the truck at the edge of the canal and a figure standing next to it shooting at her. She cut left then right trying to make herself a smaller target.

Jimmy thought he had her now. She was dodging and was too far away for accurate fire. He jumped back in the truck and started down the bank of the canal. He was pretty sure there was a crossing just down that way.

~ * ~

The horses acted up but none broke loose. The cops all looked up to see the white jet fly low over the crossroads turn around and make another pass at a higher altitude. The plane then accelerated and flew east toward Arcadia.

~ * ~

Sam was tired but got his adrenaline pumping as he approached the GPS coordinates he had punched in earlier. He descended and slowed the Lear down with flaps. He could see a large open area of pasture land with a river and two lakes at the far west end. The road was straight and wide. He thought it was plenty wide enough to land but didn't want to risk it. Police cars were gathered at a crossroads ahead and he could make out horse trailers lined up on the side road. He overflew them then turned a wide 180 and came back around. He wanted to get down there and find out what was going on.

Sam pushed the throttles forward and dumped the flaps. He was only a few miles from the field and switched to the Unicom frequency to call in. No answer came back at first then he heard Will's voice, from what sounded like a portable, call back to him.

"Lear landing, no traffic to report. Winds one two from the southwest. Recommend runway two three."

Sam replied, "Lear one five Quebec, roger. Entering downwind two three." Sam reduced his airspeed and dropped the flaps and gear.

Will turned to Detective O'Shea and said, "That's the boy's dad, Sam Deland."

~ * ~

Ozzie needed more than Pepsi, he needed a big steaming cup of coffee. He hoped the Hazleton corporal would swing by to relieve him so he could run down the hill to a store. He'd taken off his vest and raid jacket earlier, and it felt much better with them off. The weather forecast was for a nice day, and he would have liked to take Junior trout fishing. *Maybe if this thing craps out.* He busied himself by going back through the folders and picking up the trash in the car. He could just make out Johnny and Calvin down the hill and the house looked quiet.

~ * ~

"What was that? Turn that radio down!" the detective sergeant yelled. He was exhausted and a bit grumpy trying to keep all the brass happy and off his butt. He turned to face the prairie. Then he heard it again. *Gunshots.*

~ * ~

Grace ignored her ankle and ran, lopsided. She seemed to get really motivated when Jimmy started shooting at her. She only knew that if she didn't get to that road soon, she was going to give out. Then die. And be of no help to Ken. The tractor trailer noises were getting louder, and she thought she heard cars too. It still was a ways off, but she had to keep going in that direction.

Ken was up to a steady run by now. He was in good physical condition and he pushed through the pain of his ribs and charged through the brush heading toward where he last heard the shots. He was almost frantic with worry about what it meant. *Is Grace okay?* What was he going to do when he got there? He would have to figure that out when the time came.

Russell woke up and stretched. Man he was thirsty and hungry. *Why the hell am I out in a field? And what is that pile of rope doing over there?*

Jimmy had the truck stuck. He had been moving as fast as he could down the side of the canal thinking the crossing was just up ahead when he put the truck in a bull hole. It stopped hard there when the nose piled into the wallow. He was once again bashed into the dash. This time he ran his sore, swelling arm into the steering wheel. It brought tears to his eyes it hurt so bad. He had to sit back in the seat and let the pain subside for a while.

~ * ~

"They must pay real well up north," Christie said to Will as they watched the Lear taxi up to the ramp.

"Sam works for a charter service on his days off. Ex-navy fighter jock," Will told her. Margie had joined them and they'd given Christie as much as they knew about what the kids did before the crash.

Christie remembered the terse conversation she had with this Deland character. She wasn't looking forward to this.

~ * ~

Grace stumbled every few yards, but she just willed herself to keep going. She could see some thicker trees ahead of her and was angling for a small opening between them. She hobbled through into the shade and felt the cooler air. She stopped to catch her breath and heard a dog bark. What a glorious sound. She pushed into the trees and then broke out at the edge of a wide canal filled with clear water and a road on the other side. There was even a house about a quarter of a mile down the road to the left.

She didn't hesitate. She jumped into the water and did her best breast stroke to the other side. There was actual grass on the bank of the canal and a wide road. She limped down toward the house and turned into the dirt driveway. The house sat well back from the road and was big. Wide covered porches surrounded the first floor and there was a row of windows all the way across the second. As she got nearer, she could see a woman in a green robe sitting and rocking in a chair on the front porch with a huge mug of coffee in her hand.

"Good morning, can I call the police?" Grace said and slumped onto the first step up to the porch.

~ * ~

Calvin punched Johnny's shoulder as the Harley rolled by with the big bearded guy on it. Calvin said, "Shit, Johnny. I think that's him."

Johnny worked himself up in the seat and yawned, "Him, who?"

"The fuckin' guy who, asshole," Calvin grabbed the microphone. "Oz, I think that's him on the bike."

Ozzie had the binoculars up to his eyes with his left hand and hit the mic button two clicks with his right. The rider had on a helmet, and as he pulled into the driveway, he stopped the bike and put down the kickstand. He left it running and took off the helmet and set it down on the seat then pulled a small backpack from the left rear saddle bag.

Ozzie could see his face. It was McCall. He dropped the glasses and started the car. Without picking it up, Ozzie mashed the microphone button and hollered, "That's him!"

McCall hesitated, cocking his head but then turned and walked toward the steps.

Calvin was screaming at Johnny to get the car going. For once in their partnership Johnny was moving too slow to suit Calvin. "Hold yer water, beefcake. We're movin'," Johnny said as he dropped the burgundy Crown Vic into gear and spun the tires out onto the pavement.

Ozzie heard Adams on the radio, "Where do you want me?"

Ozzie just pushed the button again and yelled, "Charge!"

~ * ~

Sam and Christie O'Shea were circling each other verbally. It was tense in the little office at the glider side of the airport. They'd started in on each other as they walked over from the power plane, side and now they were getting further in to it as Christie tried to sum up the case for Sam. He was stopping her and asking sharp, pointed questions. She was trying to answer and was having a hard time treating him like a victim's father.

Finally, she'd had enough. "Look, pal. Back off with the Mr. know it all routine. You may be a big shot where you...," she stopped to take a breath and answer her cell phone.

"Where? When? How bad? It'll take me almost an hour to get there. No, have the rescue unit go there right now. I'll get there eventually. Where's the boy?"

By now Sam was almost at her ear trying to hear what she was listening to.

She spun away from him. "Can we get in there? How long until the horses can? Do we have any ATVs? Gunfire? Shit. Sorry, Sarge," she looked over at Sam who was about to explode. She pulled the cell phone from her face and said to Sam, "They found Grace. Or she found us. She's in North Port. Walked out from the cattle ranch. Ken's still in there."

Sam sunk down with mixed joy and despair.

Christie said into the phone, "Okay, let me think about it. I'll call you back," and ended the call.

"Is Grace okay? What cattle ranch?" Sam asked, looking her square in the eyes.

"Yes, she is, the biggest one. Runs from Route 72 all the way down to North Port. They must have taken them in there. Grace says it's two guys in a blue pick-up. Our Santee brothers, Jimmy and Russell. They have a rifle. Took a couple of shots at her," Christie paused.

"And Ken's still in there?" Sam growled.

"Yeah, but it isn't that easy to get in, let alone find them in those thousands of acres," Christie said.

"What about H-1?" Sam asked.

Christie looked puzzled, "Oh, you mean Air-1, the helicopter. It's out of service. All we have is a couple of four wheel drives and horses."

Sam spotted a sat map taped to a cardboard mat leaning against the wall behind one of the chairs. He went over to it, picked it up and dropped it on a table. "Will, can you show me where this ranch is?"

Will stepped over to him. "All of this," he said and ran his hand over a quarter of the map. "If she came out in North Port, that would probably be over here. These streets back up against the ranch. Used to be drug planes flying into those streets at night before the houses got built. Street along the canal is real wide and no utility poles. Ken could be anywhere in this stuff. It would take forever to cover it all."

Sam picked up the sat map, pulled it free from the cardboard and ripped it down the middle. He ripped it again, pulling away the part with the cattle ranch on it.

"Cover it a lot faster from the air. Can I borrow your Supercub?" Sam asked.

Will stared at him. "I...I...I don't know what to say. I've got students coming," he paused, "Oh, hell, why not. It's full. Go find him."

Sam spun and went for the door. Christie ran after him, "Stop. What are you going to do?"

"Got a shotgun in the jet. Might need it. I'm going to get my son. The fastest and most effective way we have." Sam started to run back to the ramp where the Lear was parked.

Christie shouted again, "Wait! Come back. I got a sheriff's portable in my Jeep and something better than a shotgun, I'm going with you," and ran to her vehicle to unlock the door. She reached into the back and came out with a Panther .308 semi auto rifle and several spare mags. Also, she grabbed the portable radio from between the front seats and ran back to Sam.

He looked at the rifle and said, "Yep, that's a winner. I'll try to put you on the shitheads that you can use that on. Let's go."

~ * ~

Ken didn't hear any more gunshots. He'd run until he thought he was going to pass out. He just kept going into the scrub but finally had to stop to breathe. His ribs were screaming, but he just gutted through it. He had found a stout piece of oak branch as he ran through a hammock and stuck it in his belt behind his back. He hoped he could get close enough to this Jimmy to use it.

~ * ~

As the cars converged on the driveway, Flathead heard them coming. He stopped and turned to see the shiny unmarked police cars on the road heading toward him. He dropped the backpack on the ground and ran back to the still chugging Harley. He was not going back down the drive, the two police cars were sliding into it from the road. The helmet went flying off the seat as he mounted the bike and hit the throttle. He spun dirt, whipping the big hog around the left side of the house into the small back yard.

Johnny beat Ozzie to the drive and threw the car into park as the motorcycle cleared the side of the house. He opened the door and flew across the yard after it. Johnny knew the mountain behind the house rose sharply and hoped he could catch the guy when he fell off the bike.

Ozzie hauled himself out of the car and tried to follow Johnny. The bike disappeared behind the house through a gap too narrow for a car to follow. Calvin just couldn't make it. He tried to run after Ozzie, but he came up lame before he got to the side of the house. He hobbled back to the car and got on the radio to let everyone know their guy was here.

Adams drove to the end of the now full driveway and left his car on the road and ran up the drive past Calvin who was pointing to the side of the house. The big mean dog under the porch just watched the frenzy pass by, then laid his muzzle back between his front paws and tried to get back to sleep.

Flathead went through the back yard and ran up the game trail, the back end of the Harley spraying rocks and dirt and swaying from side to side. Flathead's rear tire wasn't made for hill climbing, but the bike had enough horsepower to make up for it. He continued up and hit a switchback where a spring storm had washed out a path through the scrub. He gassed the bike and disappeared up into the trees.

~ * ~

"Clear!" Sam hollered and hit the starter. Christie was in the back seat. She had her jacket off and tucked the .308 down beside the seat where she could get at it. There was a stick in front of her between her legs and she could see it move as Sam checked the controls. The engine wound up, and she felt the wind whip through Sam's open window. As he taxied out to the end of the grass strip, she saw him looking up and to each side. She had been in the helicopter several times but had only flown in commercial jets. This was her first tail dragger.

Sam motioned for her to put on the headset. She found them hanging on a hook to the left of her seat. They looked like shooter hearing protectors with a microphone attached. She slipped them on and heard Sam say, "Hear me okay?"

She answered, "Yes, okay. When we get up higher, I'll call us in on the sheriff's radio. Let them know what we're doing."

Sam shrugged his shoulders, "Okay by me. I don't know how much help they'll be."

The plane accelerated down the bumpy grass strip and crabbed into the air. Sam brought the nose around to the west and climbed into the wind.

~ * ~

Things were scrambling back at the crossroads. With the information Grace had relayed, the focus shifted west and south. The horses were loaded back into the trailers and driven back toward the state park. A deputy went to each gate along the road and broke open the chains with bolt cutters so the horse trailers could get in. The captain ordered the marked units to stay out of the pasture for fear they would get stuck. He had two four wheeled drive SUVs on scene and had called back to headquarters for more. Desoto County was sending a couple of ATVs, but they were over half an hour out.

~ * ~

Russell didn't hear any of the vehicles out on the road. He finally remembered why he was at the chute, but when he woke up he found Ken gone and the ropes lying in a pile. He thought maybe Jimmy had come back and taken the kid. B*ut why would he leave me behind. Curious.*

Russell sat for a while, but the sun was up and even through the clouds it was getting warm and muggy. He started jogging out to the road. It took him a while, but he made the fence and climbed over. He walked east toward home and figured he'd thumb a ride. He was walking with his back to the traffic. Just exactly the opposite way he should and even grade school kids know better. He heard the hum of tires on the road and the sound of a car approaching. He turned to stick out his thumb and saw the black and yellow Highway Patrol car pull up to him. The car stopped.

Russell was surprised when the door opened and RGod stepped out with a big fat cigar in his mouth, "Why hello there, Russell. It's so good to see you again. And oh, stop resisting, you heard me, stop resisting."

~ * ~

Ozzie was sure the guy was going to dump the bike at any moment. Johnny was out in front of him and scrambled up the game trail and turned up the washed out switchback. They could hear the Harley revving and it backfired a couple of times. The mountain was steepening the farther up they went, and then they heard the Harley engine stop. Johnny was a smoker, but he was also an ex-army ranger. He bounded up the hill using small trees and branches to help him climb. Ozzie was having a much harder time of it. Soon even Adams passed Ozzie. His uniform was spattered with mud, but Adams kept going right up toward Johnny.

~ * ~

Katrina's cell phone rang. The detective was asleep on the couch with his jacket and shoes off. Katrina was up pacing between the kitchen and living room. The detective jerked upright and hit the start button on the digital recorder attached to her phone and stuck a small earphone in his ear. Katrina bolted over to him and he nodded to her to answer the call.

She didn't recognize the number and her stomach turned a flip, "Hello?"

"Hi, Mom. I'm okay," she heard Grace say. The detective gave her a signal to keep going waving his arm in a circle.

"Grace," was all Katrina could get out.

"I'm okay, but Ken is still in there. I'm in North Port. The police are here. Happy Mother's Day."

~ * ~

Sam kept the Supercub low, but the throttle was pushed all the way forward. They covered the distance to the ranch in just a few minutes. Sam banked left and flew toward North Port.

"Where are you going?" Christie asked over the intercom.

"Grace, intel," Sam replied.

Christie started to object then thought better of it. She put the portable up close to her mouth and called her sergeant. No response. Nothing but static. She tossed the radio under the seat and held on.

~ * ~

RGod pulled up to the intersection and rolled down the driver side window. The uniform lieutenant stepped from the canopy over to him.

"Hey, Lou. Got Russell Santee back on the highway. It was a hell of a fight. Takin' him into the hospital. You fellas'll have to get old Jimmy without me."

The lieutenant looked past RGod into the back seat and saw a slumped over figure lying down and handcuffed.

"Great. I'll tell the dicks and they'll send someone over to meet with you."

RGod snapped off a salute and roared away to the east.

~ * ~

Johnny had to stop and breathe. He thought it odd that he wanted a cigarette right now. He started up the hill again and came to the smoking Harley dumped over on its side and clicking as the heat drained off the exhaust. He reached down and yanked the plug wires off and stuffed them into his jacket pocket. Adams joined him.

Johnny looked back behind Adams and asked, "Where's Calvin and Ozzie, kid?"

Adams took a gulp of air and shook his head no, "Livingston is back at the house. Ozliewski is coming." He didn't feel right saying their first names yet.

Johnny turned and looked up the hill. He heard a branch snap and something hit a rock. "He's up there," Johnny panted to Adams. Ozzie struggled up to them and looked down at the bike.

In the distance they heard the first police siren coming to them. "Here comes the cavalry," Johnny said as he started up after Flathead again.

~ * ~

The Supercub flew over the two North Port police cars and the rescue unit parked in the driveway and in front of the house. The North Port sergeant looked up from where he had been watching the paramedics tending to Grace in the back of the ambulance.

The plane turned and flew east then banked left and lined up on the wide road.

"He's going to land. Who the hell is this guy?" the sergeant said to the other officer.

Sam chopped the throttle and dropped the wing, side slipping down onto the paved road. His wings had plenty of clearance on both sides, and it looked better than a lot of runways he had seen.

The sergeant saw the plane twist sideways and said, "He's gonna' dump it!"

By now the woman who had helped Grace, her husband and all three kids were piling out on the porch to see what all the noise was.

Christie could only get out, "Oh, God."

Sam said, "No, but damn close," as he pulled the plane straight and the wheels touched pavement.

~ * ~

Jimmy thought he heard a plane, but it was off to the south. He was gunning the engine and rocking between drive and reverse, trying to pull or push the truck out of the deep sand in the bull hole. He wasn't going to give up. He was determined to kill the girl. Even though his arm felt like it was going to fall off. But first he had to find her.

~ * ~

Ken was slowing down. His busted ribs were too much. He was stopping every hundred yards and trying to breathe. He thought he heard brush moving to his left. He dropped low and looked that way. More noise, but he couldn't see anything. It was beginning to dawn on him he might want to be a little more careful about coming up on Jimmy, the guy with the rifle.

Ken kept very still. His shirt was a medium blue color, but had been stained with blood and dirt. It didn't stand out too badly. Now he heard noise behind him. *Surrounded?* He twisted slowly around and looked into the face of a brown and white cow. Another appeared to his left and soon he was actually surrounded by about ten of them and a couple of calves. *Well, at least I won't starve.*

~ * ~

Calvin had the woman and the old man out on the porch and handcuffed to porch chairs. The small backpack McCall dropped in the yard was in his car's trunk. They both wanted a lawyer so Calvin got on the cell phone to call Sam and tell him what was going on.

"Are you in Virginia yet?" Calvin asked.

Sam had walked away from the ambulance where Christie was talking to Grace and rapidly writing in her notebook.

"Not quite. Florida. Kind of on a little side trip. It's a long story and getting longer," Sam said.

Calvin gave Sam the scoop. Sam said, "Try not to get shot again, you're enough of a pain in the ass, to Johnny that is." Sam smiled for the first time since last night.

Sam spent a few more minutes telling Calvin about Ken and Grace and then cut it off.

Christie was out of the rescue unit by then and fast walked with Sam back to the plane, talking to him as they went.

The sergeant turned to the officer and said, "I didn't know the sheriff gave them Glocks and I sure never knew they had a plane."

~ * ~

Cars were converging on the naked lady picture house. Calvin directed people where to go and called the Hazleton corporal on the radio to try to get H-1 in the air. The corporal was still on his way to Calvin and got as busy as he could on the radio and cell phone and not crash the car.

Shotguns and ARs were popping out of trunks and several troopers were sitting sideways in their cars changing into boots. Calvin pulled the map case from his car and went back up to the porch. He wanted a bigger picture of the area than the sat photo of the house.

Nothing. There was nothing for miles until the mountain went down the other side to a state road.

Calvin called the corporal again, but it went to voicemail. He hollered down to one of Hazleton troopers in the road, "Send a couple of cars around to the state road on the other side of the mountain."

The Hazleton trooper wasn't sure who the black guy in the white shirt and tie on the porch was, but he sounded like he knew what he was doing, so he grabbed his partner and motioned for one of the marked cars to follow him and took off down the hill.

~ * ~

Flathead was still shaken from the moment he saw the unmarked cars swooping in on him. Now he was nearly exhausted as he pulled and scrambled his way up the steep hillside through the bare trees. Only the thorns had greened up and the rest was still just budding out. The forest floor was open from the winter. He was dressed in black leathers, which blended with the dark tree trunks and had sturdy boots, but there was just no cover. A few rhododendron patches were on the hill, but he didn't dare to stop and hide. He could hear the troopers talking loudly below him and climbing the hill after him. He slipped the 9mm out of his boot. He was not going back to prison today.

~ * ~

Sam spun the plane around and taxied back down the road to the east. The side window was still open so Christie could bring the Panther to bear if need be. A carload of teenagers pulled up to a stop sign on a side street as the Supercub rumbled past. The pilot held up his hand in a 'stay there' motion. The seventeen year old driver decided maybe he better listen. A few minutes later the plane roared past in the other direction and vaulted almost straight up into the sky.

~ * ~

Ken heard the truck engine grinding loud then soft. He trotted toward it. The truck would rev then quiet down. Ken started to think it might be stuck. An oak hammock was between him and the truck, and Ken made for it to use the cover to get closer.

~ * ~

Jimmy heard the plane off to his right. He couldn't see it because it was so low. He stepped out of the truck and tried to kick some of the sand from in front of the front wheels. It looked like he was digging himself deeper. His right arm was now so swollen the skin was stretched tight over it. Every heartbeat sent shooting pain up into his elbow and shoulder. He thought maybe he should smoke some of the dope to ease the pain. After he got the girl.

~ * ~

Sam climbed and leveled off at five hundred feet. He circled to the north and they could see the riders and horses fanned out and moving southwest into the pasture. Some had light colored hats that stood out. A white sheriff's truck was moving slowly down a sandy trail, but another looked stuck. Police cars lined the highway in both directions.

Sam turned back toward North Port and said to Christie, "We'll fly a grid north to south and back. Watch for color or movement."

Ken saw the plane fly over, but he was just coming out of the hammock and was partially blocked by the trees. He recognized it as Will's tow plane and was wondering why Will would be out here.

~ * ~

The Hazleton corporal arrived and got the troopers spread out on both sides at the back of the house and told them to keep the next man in sight and move up the mountain. He went back around and talked to Calvin and the case trooper who was now up on the porch. They decided to get a search warrant for the house and Calvin got the old man separated from the woman.

It only took Calvin half an hour to sweet talk the old meth junkie into telling him where Flathead really lived. Calvin knew he couldn't use the statement against the old man, but it didn't matter at this point. He doubted they would arrest the old man anyway.

H-1 was on the way but would be a while. Ozzie was back in front and they picked their way up the mountain finding spots where McCall had slipped or scraped the leaves away. Ozzie was pissed now because his vest and black raid jacket were on the back seat of car sixteen. He stood out in his blue dress shirt, but he kept going.

Flathead was leaving a clear trail and Adams informed them he had been an Eagle Scout and had a tracking merit badge.

"Regular fucking bloodhound, eh, kid?" Johnny teased.

Adams' uniform was a mess by now and he was not happy. Normally he was fastidious, but there wasn't much he could do about it now. He even got down on his hands and knees a couple times to sort out marks on the forest floor.

"He turned north here. Cutting across to the ridge over there," Adams said then stood up and pointed. Something struck a tree branch next to his head and pieces of bark flew. They heard the sound of the shot follow and hit the wet ground.

~ * ~

Jimmy was beside the truck and looked up to watch the plane fly north over the prairie. He didn't connect the plane to anything but tried to remember if there was an airport down there. He moved to the rear and worked on the sand built up at the wheels. He heard the plane engine change sound and looked up again. He was surprised to see the college boy running at him at full speed.

Jimmy backpedaled to the driver's door and reached in with his bad arm to grab the rifle. He kept thinking, *That fucking Russell, fucking Russell.*

His right arm couldn't pick up the rifle and he switched to his left. He brought it out and cocked the hammer while holding it between his legs. By the time he could raise it up, the college boy was closing to within a hundred yards. Jimmy propped the rifle up on the side of the truck, put the front sight on the boy's belly and yanked the trigger.

Ken could actually see fire coming from the rifle and dove. The bullet had already hit the ground ten feet in front of him before he made contact with the sand.

~ * ~

"There!" Christie shouted in the intercom.

Sam swiveled his head, but didn't see anything. "There where?" Sam shouted.

"Left, out the left window. The truck!" Christie said loudly.

The special deputies and the stuck deputies in the SUV all heard the gunshot south of them. Some of the horsemen stopped, unsure if they should go on. All were armed with some kind of handgun and some had rifles and shotguns in scabbards on their saddles. But this was a lot different than riding down Ringling Boulevard in the Fourth of July parade.

Sam banked left and put the truck under his nose to close the distance. As he got nearer, he banked left then right again to fly parallel to the truck.

"Gun!" Christie shouted.

Sam looked down and saw a figure standing next to the truck holding a rifle and pointing back behind the truck at something, or someone.

~ * ~

Jimmy pulled the rifle down between his legs and worked the lever to chamber another round. The boy had vanished, but Jimmy remembered where he had dropped and fired again.

Ken heard the splat as the bullet ripped through the palmettos and sunk into the ground two feet to his right. He thought just a second and rolled left several feet. Another round found the spot where he had just been.

~ * ~

Christie was struggling to get the .308 out from under the seat where it had slipped when Sam did the near vertical takeoff from the street. They couldn't hear the gunfire but saw Jimmy shoot two more times. Sam was furious. He knew Jimmy could only be shooting at Ken. He was almost as mad at Ken as Jimmy. Ken should have gone the other way. He would be safe by now.

~ * ~

They all pulled their pistols out. They'd left them holstered up until now so they could use both hands to climb. That seemed secondary to self-defense at the moment.

The troopers advancing up the hill from the house had different reactions. Some dropped to the ground, others crouched and others tried to pick out where it came from.

Adams' portable radio blurted, "Shots fired."

Johnny looked over at Adams and said, "No shit." Johnny then turned to face back up the hill and yelled, "Hey, McCall, you asshole! Knock that shit off. There's a hundred guns all around you. Come down here and do your time and stop being a jerkoff."

Nothing happened for a minute and Ozzie said to Johnny, "That sure did the trick."

Adams, who had played the target, started back up the hill pulling himself up one tree at a time, "Motherfucker."

Ozzie was surprised. He had never heard Adams even say darn it.

~ * ~

Ken heard the plane roar overhead. Sam pushed the throttle full forward and put the Supercub on its right wing and dropped right at Jimmy.

Jimmy pulled the trigger again and heard a click. He was out of ammunition and needed to reload. Just as he stuck his head back in the cab to pull the box of shells from behind the seat, the right wheel of the plane skimmed across the roof of the pick-up. It shook the truck violently and sounded like a bomb exploding. He nearly pissed himself. His head would have been right there moments ago. The crazy guy in the plane was trying to kill him.

Christie thought her stomach was going to squeeze out through her ears. She had a hand on the rifle, but couldn't pull it free and the dive to the truck didn't help.

The plane soared back up into the air and topped out, going level flight again. Christie felt a moment of weightlessness and the rifle broke free and came up into her lap. If she didn't throw up, she might actually get the thing up and on target.

Jimmy struggled to get the 30-30 shells into the feed ramp on the side of the rifle. He laid it out on the truck seat and got five shells in the rifle and stuck one in his pocket. The rest had fallen on the floor when the plane's wheel had tried to decapitate him. He didn't take the time to look for them; he heard the plane coming back.

Ken was up on his knees and snuck a look over the palmettos. After that dive at the truck, Ken knew it was his dad flying. He could see the Supercub pull up and do a wing over, coming back down on the truck again, He saw Jimmy come back out of the truck cab and point the rifle up at the plane.

The sheriff stopped his car in the middle of 72 and stood next to it watching the white plane dive and climb over the ranch. "Who the hell is that?" he said to several deputies standing near the fence. None of them had an answer.

~ * ~

Johnny and Ozzie fell in behind Adams and worked their way up. It was slow going. They made a real effort to keep a tree between them and McCall's gun.

Calvin heard the gunshot from the mountain and his hip twinged. Someone keyed a portable and called out the "Shots fired." Calvin couldn't tell if it was one of the state issued pistols. It was too far up and from behind the house.

Adams stopped and was looking intently at a spot up ahead. He suddenly raised his pistol up and yelled, "Drop the gun! Let me see your hands!" Ozzie didn't see anything and Johnny was blocked by Ozzie. They all froze in place watching the woods above them and watching Adams. Nothing happened. Adams' arms started to tire and he put his gun down to his side. He moved to the other side of the tree and looked again. Then he started up the hill. The mystery of what he saw remained.

~ * ~

Sam rolled the plane out and flew to the other side of the truck so Christie could point the .308 out the open window. Sam slowed and banked to the right, pointing the wing at the figure next to the truck.

Jimmy swung the Winchester with his left arm up toward the plane and fired. He dropped the rifle back between his legs and worked the lever. The plane banked hard left and then swung back to the north, flew level and turned back toward him again. Jimmy held the rifle out at full arm's length and followed the path of the plane. He pulled the front sight in front of the prop and fired.

The bullet passed through the open window and thunked against the roof and went through. Christie yelled, "We're hit!"

Sam jinked left and climbed a hundred feet. He jinked back right and leveled off. "Lucky shot. Can you put some fire on him? Ken's down there somewhere. We need to keep him off Ken until the troops get here."

"Okay," she said and brought the rifle up and stuck it out the window.

Some of the horse deputies stopped and dismounted. They weren't real sure they wanted to be up high when someone was shooting.

The ATVs were starting to unload now and the four wheel SUVs were filled with deputies and going slowly over the soft sand toward the truck.

The sheriff found the uniform captain and asked, "Who the hell is that?"

Ken crawled closer using the scrub growth for cover. He wanted to stop this madman from shooting at his dad and he was still not sure where Grace was.

Sam dove down to two hundred feet and cut his speed to eighty. "Get ready," he told Christie.

Jimmy saw the plane coming nose on and then bank left, drop down and bank back to the right. He raised the Winchester and fired again. As the plane passed, he levered in another round and fired at the tail as it flew by.

"What happened?" Sam said over the intercom. Christie had not fired on the shooter.

"Ah, forgot the safety was on," she said somewhat quietly.

Sam cranked the Supercub back around and passed over the truck. Jimmy fired again, but Christie opened up with the .308 and pumped out ten quick rounds.

Jimmy hit the ground as pieces of truck began to fly everywhere. Bullets slammed into the windshield and the bed. Heavy rounds that sliced right through the steel body. Jimmy crawled under the truck and squeezed around where he could support the rifle on the rear tire. "Come on, you prick, come on!" Jimmy yelled. As the plane flew past, Jimmy managed to slide one loose round into the Winchester and crank the lever.

Sam wasn't sure if any of Jimmy's last rounds hit the plane. The instruments and gauges were all okay. He yanked it around again, looking for Ken as he turned. Christie was changing mags behind him and leaned back out the window with the rifle.

Jimmy had one round left in the rifle and would have to expose himself to get more from the cab. Whoever was shooting from the plane had a big rifle and he was afraid. The plane was coming around again low and slow and he waited until he could see the pilot and pulled the trigger just as the truck began to fall apart around him.

~ * ~

Flathead reached the top of a ridge and had a few yards of flat ground in front of him. He needed to put distance between him and the troopers so he could slip out somewhere and find a car to steal. He didn't know these woods at all and was surprised he hadn't come across a road or a cabin. There was nothing but mountain and woods.

He moved to the far end of the ridge and found several big boulders that he could squeeze behind. He had an extra magazine with ten rounds and ten still in the pistol. He slid down behind the rocks and waited for them.

Two troopers came in from their right and joined Ozzie's group. One had a twelve gauge and the other an AR-15. Ozzie filled them in and they spread out and started up.

~ * ~

At first Christie didn't see Jimmy, but she saw the rifle sticking out from underneath the bed. Sam had the plane up on its side again as they passed by and she opened up.

Jimmy heard the heavy rounds slamming into the truck and as soon as he fired, he tried to move under the truck again.

Christie was sure she was hitting right where Jimmy was hiding, but suddenly the plane rolled left and the nose came up. She thought she heard Sam say something, but the noise of her rifle firing drowned it out. She flipped the safety on and looked at Sam. His head was tilted forward and the plane was losing speed as it gained altitude. "Sam, you okay?" she said into the intercom. "Sam?"

She saw Sam's head come back up and his left hand reach across to his right side. He pulled his hand away and it was covered in blood.

"Sam, you're bleeding!" she shouted. The plane's nose came down and the speed picked up.

"Sam!" Christie shouted again.

"It's nothing, Christie, but I gotta get us on the ground now," Sam said weakly. He put the plane in a slow left turn and came around, flying southwest into the wind. He aimed for a relatively clear patch of pasture and cut the power. They dropped rapidly toward the ground.

Jimmy couldn't feel his legs. The bullet had cut through the bed and struck him in the middle of his back. His right arm hurt even worse now and he looked at it. His hand and wrist were lying two feet to his right and blood was pouring out of the stump of the rest of his arm just below the elbow.

Ken saw the motion of the Supercub and thought it odd. The plane had been whipping back and forth smartly and now it wobbled and was coming down into the scrub. He stood up and saw no movement at the truck. He jogged toward it trying to keep behind cover as he went.

Sam picked a good spot. ATVs had run a rough path through here and he dropped the gear into it and stood on the brakes. It really wasn't necessary; the sand slowed them to a stop. Christie was too scared to do anything but hang on. As soon as their forward motion stopped, she unbuckled and crawled out with the rifle. She looked over at the truck, but saw no sign of Jimmy. She caught movement in the bushes and started to raise the .308. She stopped when she saw it was a young male.

"That's Ken," she said out loud.

"Yeah, it is," Sam said behind her. The engine was off and it was quiet. She turned back to Sam and gasped. His right side was soaked in blood. She tossed the rifle into the back seat and pulled Sam's shirt up to see where he was hit. A neat bullet hole was in his side just in front of the grip of his Glock. The shirt over the hole had absorbed a lot of blood. She leaned him forward and saw that the bullet went out his back and through the seat.

"Come on, get down and I'll put pressure on it." Sam unbuckled and slid out with her help. She sat him next to the wheel.

Ken ran up and was shocked to see his dad bleeding and looking very pale. She looked at Ken and thought he looked terrible. His face was cut and covered in dried blood and his clothes were ripped and filthy.

Christie turned to him and said, "You know how to use a rifle?"

Ken looked at his dad and back to Christie, "Yes, ma'am."

"Grab the one on the back seat and see if that piece of shit at the truck is still wanting a fight. And Grace is safe."

"Yes, ma'am," Ken said, stepped around her and reached into the back seat, took the .308 and left.

Christie was having trouble stopping the blood flow. She ripped Sam's shirt and held the cloth over the wounds, but it kept bleeding. She was very worried he was in danger of going into shock or bleeding to death. She stood and leaned into the back of the plane. Her nice cream jacket was in the bin behind the seat. She snatched it out, rolled it up and pressed it around Sam's middle. She pulled the sleeves around him and tied it tight.

Ken covered the short distance to the truck quickly. He flipped the safety off and moved carefully to where he could see Jimmy under the rear of the truck. The Winchester was on the ground next to his severed right hand and Jimmy wasn't moving. Ken kept the .308 pointed at him and walked over. "You give up?" Ken asked.

Jimmy only groaned. Ken grabbed Jimmy's left arm and dragged him out from under the truck. Ken saw the spreading blood stain on Jimmy's back and figured it was a serious wound. "Well, asshole. You got what you deserved," Ken said and looked back toward the plane. He could see the woman working on his dad. Her back was turned. Ken moved around to Jimmy's side and kicked him hard in the ribs three times. "Payback's a bitch, Jimmy."

Ken rolled Jimmy over and unbuckled Jimmy's belt. He slipped the belt out of the loops and then rolled Jimmy back over onto his belly. Ken looped the belt over Jimmy's left hand and then back through the rear belt loop and tied it off tight. Ken picked up the Winchester and jogged back to the plane.

~ * ~

McCall waited until he could see three heads moving up onto the top of the ridge. He opened fire and saw the heads drop down. He waited and caught movement to the right of where the heads had disappeared. He fired five more rounds and ejected the magazine and reloaded. He crawled away from the rocks to a clump of birch and then got up and started back up the mountain.

Adams was shot at for the second time in his career. Both times today. He dropped as the rounds zipped over him, Ozzie and the trooper with the shotgun. They hugged the ground and Johnny moved from behind them to the left and tried to get behind cover and see where McCall was. More shots came at Johnny, but no one was hit. They decided to stay down for the time being.

~ * ~

"We have to get him to a hospital very quickly," Christie told Ken. "I don't know how long until they can get to us from the road and then get him back," Christie said.

"Jimmy's dying or already dead, so the heck with him. Let's get Dad in the back seat. I'll fly him over to the airport. It's the fastest way. We can put him an ambulance there," Ken said and reached down and lifted his dad to his feet and guided him into the back of the Supercub. Ken ignored the sharp pain in his ribs and concentrated on what he had to do. He strapped his dad in and turned to Christie.

"Help me lift the tail around the other way," Ken said to her. They picked up the rear of the Supercub together and slowly spun it in the sand so it faced back to the east. Ken climbed in the front of the plane and strapped himself in.

"You really know how to fly this thing?" she asked Ken.

"Clear!" Ken shouted and started the engine. He yelled to Christie over the noise, "It's okay, I'll figure it out." Ken pushed the throttle forward and got the plane moving over the soft sand. It was downwind, but Ken knew the Supercub had more than enough power to make up for it. He kept his hand on the throttle and pushed hard.

Christie watched the plane rumble down the ATV tract and held her breath until it bounced a couple of times and lifted off. She picked up the .308 and the Winchester and walked over to the truck. Jimmy was dead. She found a clear spot and sat down to try and call out on her phone. It didn't seem to be working at the moment.

The sound of the plane faded toward Arcadia, but was replaced by the noise of ATV engines grinding through the scrub toward her. Two minutes later, two camo painted ATVs rode up to her, and the sheriff himself got off the lead four wheeler. He walked over to her and asked, "Who the hell was that guy?"

~ * ~

Sam was slipping in and out of consciousness. Ken got on the Unicom to Arcadia and told them to have an ambulance at the field for a gunshot wound. Will answered and said he would call it in. Ken had the throttle at full speed, and it didn't take long to cover the distance and for him to slow and enter the downwind for the grass strip. He suddenly thought of Grace, and for just a moment the dread he felt for the guy in the backseat was pushed aside and he was glad she was safe. Now he had to help his dad.

~ * ~

Johnny figured Flathead was behind the rocks at the other end of the flat spot on top of the ridge. He stepped left and fired three rounds into the rocks and advanced to a double trunked maple tree. He looked to his right to see where the others were and only saw Adams duck walking from one tree to the next.

Johnny motioned for him to fire at the rocks and Adams braced against a tree and fired five rounds. As soon as Adams fired, Johnny went around the tree and moved up about ten yards. He found another thick trunk and stopped. He switched his Glock to his left hand and fired from that side of the tree. Adams figured it out by then and ran forward as Johnny fired and opened up on the rocks, emptying his magazine as he ran to where McCall had been.

Johnny appeared beside him and they both were breathing heavily. McCall was gone, but several 9mm shell casings and an empty ten round magazine were on the ground. He turned to Adams and said, "Where'd you learn to do that?"

Adams was already reloaded and was stuffing his empty magazine in his side pocket, looking up the mountain. "Paintball," he answered.

~ * ~

The ambulance was coming down the taxiway and met Ken at the intersection of the paved runway and the grass landing strip. Following the ambulance was a red pick-up driven by Margie with Will in the passenger seat. An Arcadia city police car was also coming at them with his overhead lights flashing.

Ken shut down the engine and the prop slowed to a stop. He quickly unbuckled and climbed down as the EMTs came up carrying their medic boxes. Ken started to reach in to pop Sam's restraints when the first EMT said, "Are you the one who's been shot?"

Ken finished moving the seat straps away from his dad and turned to look at the EMT. Margie was right behind the EMT, and when she saw Ken she let out a yelp and covered her mouth in horror. She swallowed and said, "My God, Ken, what happened to your face?"

He didn't realize he had bled all over himself, but it didn't concern him right now. He turned back and lifted his now unconscious dad from the seat and carefully laid him down under the wing. The EMTs knelt beside him and one rushed back to the ambulance to get the gurney. The other checked the wound and then checked Sam's vital signs. He looked up at Ken and said, "You need to go with us, too, you look pretty banged up."

Ken shook his head and said, "I'll ride with my dad, but I'm okay."

The stretcher rolled up to them and they got Sam strapped on and into the ambulance. Both EMTs worked on him in the back for a while and then one got out and Ken slipped in beside Sam. They had an oxygen mask over Sam's face and an IV drip going. Christie's blood soaked jacket was on the ambulance floor and fresh bandages covered Sam's wounds. The driver got them moving and drove them out toward the highway, lights and siren going with the Arcadia cop following.

~ * ~

The first of the horses beat the SUVs to Christie. A Desoto deputy had driven up with the sheriff on the other ATV and was on his radio telling everyone the bad guy was dead and Christie and the hostage were okay.

The sheriff said, "Detective, you did just fine. Now there's going to be a lot of fuss about this and how we did it. Everybody will tell us how we did this or that wrong. You worry about putting the evidence together and taking care of your victims and witnesses. I'm going to take the shit from your back. That's what I get paid to do. Anybody gets on your ass, you tell them to come see me."

Christie was so tired she could just nod. The horse deputy handed her a bottle of water, and it was the best tasting thing she had ever had. She heard another vehicle coming. She stood up and stretched and saw a black GMC with huge tires bouncing over the palmettos and stop behind the horses. The passenger door opened and RGod stepped out with the big cigar in his mouth and his metal clip board in his hand. He walked over to her and said, "You okay, Miss Christie?"

She nodded and drank some more water.

Trooper Goddard said, "Just got to get the plate and VIN off the truck and take a few pictures for the accident report. Gonna write young Russell a couple of tickets. You folks can lay all the felonies on him." A Desoto deputy followed RGod out of the black truck and spit tobacco juice out onto the ground, "Fella brought his own vehicle in and was kind enough to bring me across the prairie."

Christie asked, "We got Russell?"

RGod took a bow, "Yours truly, ma'am. I see Jimmy lost the great 'Battle of Big Slough'."

RGod went to work at the truck and was finished in about ten minutes. More troops were arriving, and the sheriff made one of the deputies keep everyone back until the crime scene crew could get out to them.

RGod asked Christie if she wanted him to do anything for her. She thought a moment and then said, "Take me to the hospital to see Sam."

RGod looked puzzled, "I thought the boy's name was Ken."

"Sam flew the plane. He's Ken's father, a trooper from Pennsylvania. But I need to talk to Ken too."

RGod still was in the dark. "You can explain it to me on the way."

Christie handed the Winchester and the Panther to the sheriff and walked to the black 4x4 and got in on the passenger side. She needed ten hours of sleep.

~ * ~

The others filtered in next to Johnny and Adams at the rocks. As they milled there, they heard branches snapping below them and another trooper climbed up the hill.

Johnny said to Ozzie, "Someone's gonna get shot. Most likely one of us by one of us. Me and young Adams here are going to go after him. You set up a CP here and wait for us to call in what we need. Adams has a portable and a cell and I have my cell. No use risking everybody and having people wandering all around. McCall is leaving a trail a blind moron could follow. We'll pressure him and try to get him cornered or make him give up. We'll bring the rest of you up as we move along. Post guys out on your wings in case he doubles back, but keep the extra troops here for now."

Ozzie said, "Okay. The chopper should be on the way. I'll let them know the plan. We have cars on the other side of the mountain, but it's a long ways out to the road. Let's get this guy before dark."

Johnny turned to Adams, "Did you qualify with the AR at the Academy?"

"Yeah, expert," Adams said. Johnny reached over and just took one out of the hands of a trooper standing there and gave it to Adams. "Give him your spare mags," Johnny said to the trooper. "And those with long guns, each of you give me a spare .45 magazine."

Johnny collected the hardware and stuffed his pockets. He flipped the yellow State Police flaps inside the covers on his and Adams' black jackets and then found the blackest mud he could in the small flat area. He rubbed his hands and face with the mud to dull the skin color and Adams did the same. The whole process only took minutes and they moved off toward the birch cluster to pick up McCall's track.

On the other side of the birches, they found leaves flipped over and muddy water swirling in footprints. He went this way.

~ * ~

The hospital room was empty now. They had fussed over her and drawn blood twice. She had an IV stuck in the back of her hand and there was a Styrofoam cup on the tray next to the bed filled with ginger ale. Her mom was on her way, but she could only think of Ken. No one would tell her what was going on. A uniform deputy had been in briefly but had gone out in the hall somewhere.

She was tired but not sleepy yet. Still too wound up and scared. She had been furious when Ken lifted her and pushed her out of the truck. She didn't want to leave him alone. Now, after she thought about it, what he did saved her life.

Her head hurt a little less. They'd cleaned and bandaged the gash, and one of the young doctors had said a plastic surgeon would be in to see her later. Her legs and arms were a mess. Scratched and torn and now stinging from the disinfectants.

She heard voices in the hall and her mom flashed around the corner and burst into the room. She took two steps and stopped in her tracks. A tall man in a coat and tie came in behind her and bumped smack into her back. Katrina stumbled forward and then came up beside Grace.

She put her hand to her mouth and said through her fingers, "Oh God, honey." Tears formed and began to stream down her face. She sobbed and put her head down on the bed. Grace didn't know yet, but this was the first time since late last night Katrina was able to cry. She made up for the lost time. The guy in the suit looked embarrassed and just stood back.

They had to almost force Ken into a separate stall in the emergency room. He didn't want to leave his father, but there were lots of people hovering over Sam, and there wasn't anything Ken could do but move back out of the way. He could hear the voices from where Sam was, but couldn't make out what was being said. A girl in green scrubs came in, pushing a blood pressure cart. She looked at the chart in her hand and said, "Ken, what's your date of birth." Several more people followed her, and he was stripped and his ear and cheek gently washed with various potions. After a while, they wheeled him off to X-ray and took shots of his head and ribs. They stuck him with an IV and then left him in a hallway all alone.

~ * ~

It was a terribly bumpy ride across the pasture out to the road. They passed more ATVs going the other way and the portable radio in her lap was now working and told her the helicopter was back in service. Thanks.

She switched to RGod's cruiser out on the hard road and rode with him at much too high a speed into Arcadia and the hospital ER parking lot. He went in with her and they stood around for a while until someone finally told her Sam was in surgery and critical, but Ken was stable and down that hall somewhere.

Ken thought he recognized the lady detective as she walked toward him, followed by a huge Florida trooper. "High ma'am, do you know if my dad is okay?" Ken asked and tried to sit up. RGod moved next to him and cranked the bed up so Ken could see them without having to look straight up.

"Did a tour in a nursing home in college," RGod said.

Christie introduced herself and Trooper Goddard and thanked Ken for his help. "I'm just sorry we couldn't get to you and Grace sooner. If it hadn't been for your dad, it would have taken a lot longer. He's a hell of a pilot."

Ken asked, "How's Grace?"

Christie took a deep breath and told Ken some of it. Enough to get the point across that she was in the hospital in Sarasota and was okay.

Christie took a note pad from her pocket and said, "Give me the short version. We can talk more later, after I've had a bath and a stiff drink."

~ * ~

Adams was a quick learner. Johnny would cover while Adams moved up along McCall's trail and then they'd switch. Johnny thought he saw McCall's black jacket flash between trees once, but didn't have time to get off an accurate shot. They moved up to another lip in the hillside. Wide enough to hold Ozzie's troops. Adams called them to move up and he and Johnny went back to hunting.

~ * ~

McCall had grown up in Atlantic City. This mountain climbing shit was not pleasant. He was sweating and wet. Every time he stopped to catch his breath, he started to get cold. His black jeans were even blacker with dirt and wet mud. He didn't think he was ever going to reach the top of this fucking mountain. *And then what? Slip and fall down the other side? Fuck!*

~ * ~

They put stitches in his ear and when he finally got them to let him look in a mirror, he was really pissed about the scar that would be left on his face from the gash Jimmy put there with the rifle sight. But the worst was the binding they put around him for his three broken ribs. He kept thinking the Air Force was going to bag him from the Academy class because of the injury. Even if he still made it, he figured the upperclassmen would have really funny names to call him like The Pirate Plebe or Scarforce. *Whoopie.*

Sam was in recovery minus a spleen and part of his liver, but still alive and kicking. They forced him awake and then pumped more pain killers into him. He didn't know where he was, but the dope made him not give a shit.

He came out of it again after an hour and saw Christie sitting in a chair next to him slumped over sleeping. His throat was scratchy, but he managed to croak, "You get him? Where's Ken?"

She didn't budge. There was a clear plastic breathing thing on his tray. He slowly reached out and got his non IV hand on it and threw it at her. It plopped in her lap and she jumped awake.

"How's Ken?" he asked again.

She rubbed her eyes and looked at the plastic breathing thing then at Sam. He's here, just beat up, but he'll be okay," she said. "How do you feel?"

"Just fuckin' ducky," Sam said. "Am I gonna be able to piss standing up?"

"Maybe in a few days," she answered. "They cut you open and rearranged you a little bit. Should be a neat scar to show your grandkids."

Sam looked at the ceiling and tried to focus through the haze. "Let me ask you. You always bring that big gun out on every first date?"

~ * ~

Johnny saw what he thought was McCall's ass move past a tree near the top of the mountain. He got off four rounds, but didn't see him go down.

Adams moved quickly to the next big tree and tried to see what Johnny had just shot at. He covered as Johnny moved forward and then Adams moved up again. They had leapfrogged up the hill and could hear McCall busting through the branches ahead of them. In the distance, Adams thought he heard the helicopter approaching. About time.

~ * ~

McCall felt the .45 rounds buzz past to his right. The pricks were getting too close. He finally hit the crest and started down the other side. He hoped there was a house or cabin somewhere down there where he could get a car and vanish.

~ * ~

The gobbler stopped making noise after the last shots echoed down the slope. He had worked it up the hill and across from way upwind. It had been a long morning and he was running out of time before he had to quit for the day and drive to work at the machine shop. His fingers were stained with the grit and lubricants he handled every weekday and sometimes on Saturdays on the three to eleven shift. Damn, more shooting. He was pissed at all the racket. He had hunted this mountain for the last five years and didn't remember ever seeing a cabin or camp up in that part of the woods. Sounded like someone was out behind their camp blasting away with handguns. He concentrated on the slope in front of him and struck the slate call with the striker held in his rough hands again.

~ * ~

Adams saw McCall slip out from behind a tree way out there and lit him up with the AR. He tried to count the shots, but paid more attention to the front sight. Johnny followed with eight rounds of his own.

~ * ~

*That was a rifle*, thought Eivan Bucholtz. He turned to look up the hill behind him. The gunfire was coming closer and he gave up on the gobbler. Asshole out here with a rifle in spring gobbler season was downright dangerous. Eivan pulled the cammo face mask off and stood up, putting the big oak between him and the gunshots. He looked around the tree, but couldn't see any movement or color in the drab woods. He propped the Remington 870 pump against the tree and stood there wondering what to do. He had a blaze orange hat tucked into his camouflage game vest he used for walking in and out but wasn't sure he should put it on right now.

Johnny told Adams to call Ozzie and move the men up to the crest. The helicopter flew over and continued east. Adams finally got H-1 on the radio and directed him back to them.

McCall heard the helicopter fly over, but keep going. He thought maybe it was just a civilian, but didn't have time to ponder the issue. He pulled up into a patch of thick hemlocks and got prone. He would give these cops something to think about.

~ * ~

Ken walked in wheeling an IV stand beside him. "I checked out. I came to see you then I'm going to Sarasota to see Grace. RGod is going to give me a ride." He moved next to Sam and touched Sam's hand. "You did a heck of a thing out there. Thanks and thanks for Grace, too."

Sam saw the bandages on Ken's face and his ear. He couldn't see the ones under the clean borrowed shirt. Sam said, "You get hurt?"

Ken answered, "It's nothing. Be healed up in no time. I'm just waiting for them to take this IV out and I'm gonna go if you don't need me. I'll be back as soon as I make sure Grace is okay."

"I'm going to be in here a while, I think," the groggy Sam said. "I bled all over Will's plane." Sam teared up and tried to keep talking, but the words wouldn't come out.

"Dad, don't worry about it. I'll make everything right with Margie and Will. I owe them a lot of thanks. I'll take care of it. Please don't worry or even think about it. Just get better. You've got to help me practice for baseball tryouts."

To Christie he said, "Thanks again, detective. I'll either be here or at Grace's tomorrow if you want to talk some more."

Christie stood up and reached out to shake Ken's hand. He moved past her arm and enveloped her in a big hug. She was surprised but then hugged him back. He coughed as she squeezed his busted ribs but held on to her.

~ * ~

The helicopter circled and called Adams, telling him they could not see McCall. Adams nodded at Johnny who then stepped out and began to move down between the trees. They only made about thirty yards when Johnny felt the 9mm round enter his left shoulder just above the top of his vest.

"MAN!" Johnny yelled. Adams couldn't see where the shot came from, but the only cover to their front was a bunch of pine trees. He emptied a magazine into them and stepped over to Johnny while he reloaded.

Johnny was leaning against a tree and swearing like a sailor with his nuts in a vice. "Motherfucker shot me," he said as Adams pulled Johnny's jacket back.

Johnny put his .45 between his knees and reached into his back pocket. He pulled out a big red bandana and stuffed it up against the wound, flinching in pain as he worked it tight.

"Okay, that's it. Let's get him," Johnny said.

Adams didn't look too sure about that.

Johnny leaned out around the tree and yelled, "McCall! State police! Give up now or you'll never make it off this fucking mountain upright!"

McCall pissed his pants when twenty .223 rounds shredded the hemlocks all around him. One round went through the sleeve of his leather coat. He scrambled out the downhill side of the pines and hid behind a beech.

~ * ~

Eivan Bucholtz ducked when he heard the pistol followed by the barrage from the rifle just up the hill from where he was. Then he heard someone yelling something about the police. This was not good. Eivan didn't know if he should run or try to dig a hole to hide in. He peeked around the tree and looked up hill. Way up, he saw a figure all in black standing behind the light colored bark of a big beech tree. The figure reached around the tree and shot a pistol back up the mountain. Eivan jumped when a louder pistol and the rifle returned fire. Bullets whipped through the tree branches overhead and pieces fell all around him. The black clothed figure slipped backward and crabbed down the slope in his direction. He didn't even realize he did it, but he picked up the shotgun and held it at port arms. He didn't know what he was going to do. He had three high brass #6s in the 12 gauge, but that was no match for real bullets. His pretty little daughter's face suddenly flashed in his mind; not a good omen.

~ * ~

Ken followed RGod out to the parking lot and got in the passenger side of the patrol car. "Buckle up, Ken. We're gonna get you to see your little girlfriend directly." RGod took it easy through the light traffic in town, but when he hit the highway, it was all a blur until they passed under I-75 coming into Sarasota.

~ * ~

Christie knew she should be doing something else, but didn't leave Sam's room. She looked up at him and felt her eyes tear. Wow, what was this all about? She watched the blanket over his chest and waited for it to rise with his breathing. She really had a lot to do. Lots of people were depending on her. Why did she just have to stay here? But she did. There was no doubt in her tired mind, she was staying right here. Sam fell back to sleep so she did, too.

~ * ~

Ozzie heard Adams call back that Johnny had been shot, but they were right on McCall and were continuing. Ozzie hollered at Adams to hold up and wait for relief, but Adams didn't answer.

Ozzie said to the rest of the troopers, "Spread out and watch the front, we're moving out!" They quickly stepped off toward Johnny and Adams.

Johnny didn't slow down. He stepped around the tree and moved. Adams covered him and when Johnny stopped, Adams moved. McCall shot in their direction but missed. They both returned fire and the woods vibrated. Adams saw McCall run from behind a light colored tree trunk down the hill, stumbling as he went. Adams charged after him with the AR up and ready to shoot. But the target had disappeared down the hill. He didn't see Johnny slump to the ground and pull out his cigarettes.

McCall heard the bullets fly past and knew the cops were right up there on his ass. He tried to keep his feet under him as he slipped on wet leaves. There was still nothing but woods in front of him, but down he went.

Eivan snuck a peek and the guy in black was trying not to fall face first as he hustled down toward Eivan. Bucholtz needed to make a decision and quick. The guy in black was almost to him. Was he a cop? Eivan tried to put it all in order, but he was good at micro measurements and what machine did what to metal, but this was real life. He peeked again and now he could clearly see the bearded guy in black had a pistol in his hand. He didn't look like a cop. He kinda looked like a guy at work who smoked dope and rode a big motorcycle.

McCall didn't even look around. He was covering the ground at a pretty good clip, and if he didn't fall, maybe he could put some distance—

Eivan called it. He looked around the tree and as the guy in black came past, Eivan grabbed the barrel, swung the butt end of the 870 out at chest height and hit a homer.

The wooden stock hit McCall just under the chin and though his momentum pulled the shotgun from Eivan's hands, McCall was knocked out before he crumpled into a heap on the ground.

Eivan felt the sting in his hands and it hurt like crazy. The shotgun flew down the hill and the guy in black dropped his pistol and fell on it ass first. Eivan just looked at him and then heard branches crashing just up the hill. He looked around the tree and threw up his hands. A young guy in a mud stained black jacket and black stripes down his gray pants was pointing a black rifle at him. The young guy looked very serious beneath his mud covered face and Eivan didn't want to make him mad.

~ * ~

She was sleeping when he came in the room. Katrina was startled seeing the bandages on Ken's face and ear. She got up from the chair and went to him. She put her arms around him and held him to her. He could smell her perfume and realized he really stunk and needed a shower.

~ * ~

Ozzie stopped next to Johnny and waved the rest of them on. Johnny grinned and blew his cigarette smoke out past Ozzie's head.

"Looks like me and Annette get to go to the shore after all. She'll have to drive her new Mini. I can't shift or steer for a while. Little unscheduled vacation. Heal up in the salt air." Johnny looked down the hill and heard Ozzie's radio cough out the capture of McCall.

"Kid did a good job. Someone needs to make sure the colonel does him a solid." Johnny puffed on his smoke some more.

Ozzie said, "We'll make sure, Johnny. Let's get you fixed up now."

The chopper pilot suggested they move Johnny about three hundred yards back along the crest to a fire tower. There was enough space to put it down there. Have him to the trauma center in Bethlehem in no time.

Adams had handcuffed McCall and enlisted Eivan's help to drag him down to Eivan's truck. The other troopers split. Some followed Adams and a few worked their way back up the hill to help carry Johnny to the fire tower.

Calvin was already working up material to use on Johnny once the worst was over.

~ * ~

Ken borrowed Katrina's phone and tried to call Ozzie. His cell went to voicemail and he didn't want to upset Marie. He decided to call Eileen.

She saw the call was from Grace's mom again. "Hello?"

"Hi, Eileen, it's Ken. Now don't get upset, but Dad's been in a little scrape down here, but he's going to be okay."

Ken talked to her for half an hour and finished by asking her to run up to the farm and feed Molly. Might need to feed her for a few days.

Eileen said, "That's silly. I'll bring her down here. Dutch will have someone to show off in front of."

Ken was happy as he could be under the circumstances and glad that his dad, Grace and Molly would be well taken care of.

~ * ~

Later that afternoon, Eileen took Dutch with her and loaded him into her SUV for the ride up to Sam's. She backed out and turned to go to the state road that ran north over the mountain.

As she passed, the big man in the passenger seat of the black Suburban parked on a side street, turned to the driver and said in Russian, "There goes the woman. Should we visit with her now?"

The driver flipped a black cigarette out of the open window and replied, "No, wait until she is with the cop. We will visit them both."

## About the Author

After writing professional documents for many years, Mike has finally devoted time to his true passion, writing fiction where the story and characters come alive in the reader's mind. While his days were filled with authoring hundreds of detailed crime reports, arrest affidavits, search warrants and grand jury presentments, he took some of his own time and devoured books by the dozens. Reading not only was a rewarding diversion, it provided him with the added education he needed to function at a high level in his profession.

This has led to the creation of Mike's crime/suspense/detective novels SINK RATE and the follow up, ROPE BREAK, the first two in the Sam Deland Crime Novel series. Both are expected to be published in 2015 by: http://www.roguephoenixpress.com/ More recently, CAPTAIN'S CROSS, a historical land and sea adventure novel set in colonial America has also been accepted for publication.

Mike writes with the real life experience that many years of law enforcement shaped and influenced. The stories may be fiction but are based on how things happen in the real world. His books are honest and captivating novels written with a unique voice that will both chill and charm.

Mike is a veteran police detective. He did it all from rookie patrolman to Senior Special Agent. His life has been enriched by a wonderful marriage, parenting, work, flying, sailing and good books. Mike is a lifelong outdoorsman, an experienced tactical firearms instructor, champion sailplane pilot and the captain of his own sailboat. All of these skills have made his novels vivid, exciting and real. Now retired after a career with three law enforcement agencies, Mike enjoys winters writing in Naples, Florida and summers sailing, writing and researching the next novel at his rural Pennsylvania home.

Web/Blog: http://mikefullerauthor.com
On facebook: http://www.facebook.com/mikefullerauthor
On Twitter: @mikefullerwrite

## Also by Mike Fuller
at
Rogue Phoenix Press

### *Sink Rate*
Sam Deland Crime Novel Book One

Corporal Sam Deland has a lot on his plate. He's a dog lover, single dad, jet pilot, likes girls and his tight knit state police squad is buried under the weight of an unsolved brutal double murder that has stunned his quiet upstate community. The pressure mounts as Sam's team tracks the bad guys into Philadelphia's tough, gritty streets. The characters are the real story though, and with humor, hard work and luck, Sam's team draws the reader's mind to unexpected and surprising places. Realistic police work with a rich descriptive character and scene portrayal is carefully crafted into a story that you will not want to put down.

www.ingramcontent.com/pod-product-compliance
Lightning Source LLC
Chambersburg PA
CBHW051428170626
46809CB00006B/2367
*9781624201998*